KU-440-138

Elizabeth Taylor

A VIEW OF
THE HARBOUR

Introduced by
Sarah Waters

VIRAGO

This edition published by Virago Press in 2018

Published in paperback by Virago Press in 1987
Published by Virago Press in 2006
First published in Great Britain by Peter Davies Ltd in 1947

3 5 7 9 10 8 6 4 2

Copyright © The Estate of Elizabeth Taylor 1947
Introduction copyright © Sarah Waters 2006

The moral right of the author has been asserted.

*All characters and events in this publication, other than those
clearly in the public domain, are fictitious and any resemblance
to real persons, living or dead, is purely coincidental.*

All rights reserved.
No part of this publication may be reproduced, stored in a
retrieval system, or transmitted in any form or by any means, without
the prior permission in writing of the publisher, nor be otherwise circulated
in any form of binding or cover other than that in which it is published
and without a similar condition including this condition being
imposed on the subsequent purchaser.

A CIP catalogue record for this book
is available from the British Library.

ISBN 978-0-349-01030-4

Typeset in Goudy by M Rules
Printed and bound in Great Britain by
Clays Ltd, Elcograf S.p.A.

Papers used by Virago are from well-managed forests
and other responsible sources.

MIX
Paper from
responsible sources
FSC
www.fsc.org   FSC® C104740

Virago Press
An imprint of
Little, Brown Book Group
Carmelite House
50 Victoria Embankment
London EC4Y 0DZ

An Hachette Company
www.hachette.co.uk

www.virago.co.uk

INTRODUCTION

A *View of the Harbour* was Elizabeth Taylor's third novel, published in 1947 when Taylor was thirty-five. She would go on to publish fourteen more novels and short-story collections before her death in 1975; she would write articles for magazines, give occasional broadcasts for the BBC, and regularly have her fiction adapted for radio; she would forge friendships with writers such as Robert Liddell, Elizabeth Bowen, and Elizabeth Jane Howard, all of whom were passionate admirers of her work. And yet, she remains one of the great under-read and underappreciated British writers of the twentieth century.

This is due partly, I think – and it's a daft reason, but by no means a trivial one – to the eclipsing of her reputation by the *other* Liz Taylor; for even booksellers confuse the two, as I discovered when I asked for 'anything by Elizabeth Taylor' in a second-hand bookshop recently, and was promptly offered a book on the making of *Cleopatra*. The high-glitter style of the actress, and the gentle comedy and sadness of the Taylor oeuvre, could not be further apart; indeed, it's perhaps the very quietness of Taylor's novels, with their careful dissection of the subtleties of English domestic life, that has helped secure their relative obscurity. Taylor has always had her champions, but she has had her critics, too: reviewers, for example, who complained – as Robert Liddell puts it in his book *Elizabeth and Ivy* – that 'her people did not act, but merely behaved'.

There is certainly little melodrama in Taylor's novels; there are no heroes, and no improbable villains, only flawed, likeable characters negotiating the ordinary small crises of marriage, family and friendship. With the exception of her seventh novel *Angel*, which presents an entire life in one extraordinary sweep, her novels typically offer us small communities, captured for a brief but crucial period of time. Like Jane Austen (a writer she greatly admired, and with whom she's often compared), her fascination is with the collision of personalities and the deceptions and self-deceptions practised between them.

This evocation of community is particularly vivid in *A View of the Harbour*, structured as it is around the group of people occupying the sea-front row of 'buildings, shops, café, pub' described in the book's painterly opening. One of the things I've always admired about Taylor's work is its wonderful economy, the very precise and nimble movements of its prose. The effect of such sureness of touch, of course, is artlessness (or 'bonelessness', as Jonathan Keates has memorably put it), but Taylor's novels are more tightly constructed than they appear. Here the narrative moves from one viewpoint to another, so that, within a mere twenty pages, all of the novel's protagonists are established: Bertram, the elderly incomer and would-be artist; Robert and Beth, the doctor and his novelist wife, and their daughter Prudence; Tory, Beth's friend and next-door neighbour; Lily Wilson, widowed proprietress of the decrepit Newby Waxworks; and the domineering Mrs Bracey and her daughters, Iris and Maisie. Like the view of the harbour itself, its jumble of houses shifting and regrouping depending on the stance of its observer, these characters will connect and withdraw, form rivalries and poignant alliances, as the novel unfolds.

For, above all, Taylor's fascination here is with the perils and the pleasures of perspective. This is a novel in which people *watch* each other – from doorsteps, from bar-stools or, most typically, from windows. Windows allow characters to frame and contain and impose meaning on the scenes before them; to experience them, precisely, *as* scenes, sometimes ones of great beauty. Here, for example, is Prudence's particular 'view of the harbour', as she leans on the sill of her bedroom window at night:

> Out on the quay two old men stood under a lamp talking about a boat. The lamplight painted the folds of their dark jerseys with silver. A piece of newspaper was taken up by the wind and went dancing idly forward, to be impaled upon a coil of wire and hang there quivering. When the pub door was opened a river of yellow ran out across the cobblestones. In it Bertram stood for a moment before he shut the door.

Throughout her life, Taylor was interested in painting; many of her novels feature artists; and certainly her own artist's instincts are evident in a passage like this. But fiction, I think, gave her opportunities to explore the roundness of personality, the nuances of human exchange, in a way that painting could never have. The protagonists of *A View of the Harbour* are not fixed in a single tableau; crucially, the windows and doorways at which they linger allow them, in their turn, to be framed and observed by others, so that a page or two after the moment captured above, for example, we learn that 'Bertram had seen Prudence at the window and had been startled by her white face, wondering why she sat at the window of a dark room.' To be an observer, here, is to be isolated; this is a community of glances half-caught, of opportunities missed, of desires baffled – a community, in other words, of loneliness.

'I think loneliness is a theme running through many of my novels and short stories,' Taylor once wrote; and certainly in this novel she excels at creating images of frustration and yearning. Lily Wilson lies to one side of her bed, 'as if at any moment Bob [her dead husband] would come and lie down beside her'. Iris Bracey mentally plays out a scene of Laurence Olivier arriving at the pub at which she works, but has to replay it endlessly, unable to complete the fantasy; unable to imagine what a man like Laurence Olivier would actually say to her if he was ever to reach the bar. Beyond them both, ominously, is a sound so familiar to them, and to all the harbour-dwellers, they've ceased to notice it: the sound of the sea, 'slapping unevenly against stone, swaying up drunkenly, baulked, broken, retreating'.

The sadness that saturates the novel at moments like this is in part generated by, and in part reflects on, *A View of the Harbour*'s very specific 1940s setting. 'There had been a war on,' we are told, casually, as Bertram watches soldiers gathering up the rusty barbed wire from the beach; and the aftershocks of war course quietly but significantly throughout the book. They are there, for example, in Lily Wilson's lingering fear of spies, and in the morale-boosting notice, 'We Do Not Recognise The Possibility of Defeat', hanging crookedly in the pub; they are there, too – in a detail of great subtlety, poignancy and weight –

in the open sea, where the fishermen's nets draw up 'bits of wreckage, parts of aircraft' along with the fish. But the repercussions of a six-year war are evident most of all, perhaps, in the overwhelming *shabbiness* of everything, in the drab, exhausted feel of surfaces and materials: the worn stockings, the dreadful meals, the rationed milk, the mice-dirts, the faded wallpapers and dribbling plaster beneath.

Taylor's obvious perverse delight in such details strikes me as somehow peculiarly British; it's an enjoyment that can be found, I think, in the work of other key British writers – in Philip Larkin, say, in Alan Bennett and John Betjeman. ('I put my final shilling in the meter / And only make my loneliness completer', Betjeman writes in 'Felixstowe, or The Last of Her Order'.) Taylor's triumph, I think, is that she manages to temper this drabness with such perception, such compassion, and such humour. For, to linger over the drab fabric of *A View of the Harbour* is to do the book a disservice; it's also a wonderfully funny novel, and the comedy ultimately wins out over the dirt and the darkness, just as the beam of the harbour lighthouse briefly but reliably thrusts back the blackness of the Newby night. Whenever I read this novel, in fact, its vein of bleakness takes me by surprise; what I always take away with me from Taylor's work is a sense of warmth and wit. The moment, for example, when Tory reads Beth her son's letter from boarding school, I like so much I can remember it almost by heart.

'Dear Mummy,' Tory read, 'I hope you are well I am. Please send envelopes. It is not very nice here. And stamps. I have a bad throat. Other boys have pots of honey. I am having a lovely time. Regards. Yours truly Edward.'

'Oh, dear,' said Beth. 'They just don't think what they're saying. They write what they can spell. I remember when Prudence went away once. She wrote: "I am in agony. I cannot say what." When I telephoned I discovered that she couldn't spell diarrhoea – indeed, who can? – and was better anyway long before the letter arrived. I shouldn't worry.'

'At least I can send some honey.'

'Yes, they measure affection by what comes in the post.'

Conversations like these generate many of the novel's best lines. There's a great celebration of female friendship in *A View of the Harbour*, even as the novel recognises that female friendship can be betrayed and undermined by women's relationships with men.

There is also in this novel, as elsewhere in Tayor's work, an interested, sympathetic depiction of working-class people. This was an effect, I'm sure, of Taylor's politics (for she was committedly left wing all her life, and briefly a member of the Communist Party), and an aspect of her writing that makes it stand out, for me, in an often snobbish British literary scene. In *A View of the Harbour* we might sense that her primary interest is with the genteel domestic dramas of Beth and Robert, Tory and Bertram; and certainly, the novel's own narrative voice is very firmly middle class. But the narrative is a genuinely shared one, and Taylor devotes much time and imaginative energy to the working-class characters of Maisie and Iris – and, most strikingly, to their mother, Mrs Bracey.

Mrs Bracey, in fact, emerges as one of the most complex and perceptive characters in the book. She picks up on the revealing nuances of behaviour, for example, between Tory and

Robert (realising that 'the very fact of [them] not smiling at one another when they met was a plain endorsement of their guilt: for friendly smiles between lovers are so laboriously devised that when they imagine themselves to be alone they seldom make the effort'). And consider this dialogue with Bertram, as she lies dangerously ill:

'Christmas,' she began, 'that's a wonderful time for children . . .'

He half-glanced at the hot day outside, but quickly said: 'It's part of the magic we lose as we grow older. I remember it as if it were yesterday, the excitement of it all . . . undoing the presents, pudding ablaze, Christmas carols . . . nuts,' he added lamely.

But Mrs Bracey closed her eyes. His recollections were of such banality that she could not lay hers alongside them. She did not know what she had experienced, could not describe it, nor impart its magic to another, and: 'in the things that really matter to us,' she thought, 'we are entirely alone. Especially alone dying!'

This dark epiphany coincides with Taylor's own firmly atheistical sense of human solitude. Her treatment of Mrs Bracey is very different to the depiction of working-class characters by other post-war writers – by Angela Thirkell, say, whose comedies of manners might superficially be seen to resemble Taylor's, but who remained content to pursue a conservative literary tradition in which the lower orders were unimaginatively represented as comical housekeepers and cosy Mrs Mops.

Taylor's friends complained that, within her lifetime, she did not receive the attention she deserved; and certainly, her work has at times suffered the fate of that of other twentieth-century women writers – Sylvia Townsend Warner, Barbara Comyns, Barbara Pym, Ivy Compton-Burnett, to name but a few – and been allowed to slip out of mainstream literary memory while supposedly less 'domestic' male writing has remained inside it. But Taylor is finally, I think, being recognised as an important British author: an author of great subtlety, great compassion and great depth. As a reader, I have found huge pleasure in returning to Taylor's novels and short stories many times over. As a writer I've returned to her, too – in awe of her achievements, and trying to work out how she does it.

Sarah Waters, 2005

1

No gulls escorted the trawlers going out of the harbour, at tea-time, as they would on the return journey; they sat upon the rocking waters without excitement, perching along the sides of little boats, slapped up and down by one wake after another. When they rose and stretched their wings they were brilliantly white against the green sea, as white as the lighthouse.

To the men on the boats the harbour was at first dingy and familiar, a row of buildings, shops, café, pub, with peeling plaster of apricot and sky-blue; then as the boats steered purposefully from the harbour-mouth to sea, houses rose up in tiers, the church tower extricated itself from the roofs, the lettering on the shops faded and the sordid became picturesque.

The view remained the same, however, to Bertram, who leant on a wall by the lighthouse. He seemed stationed between sea and land; water rocked queasily on both sides of the arm of the harbour wall where he was. He looked over the boats and seagulls to the public-house on the harbour front.

When he got up in the mornings and went to one of the front windows of that pub to do his breathing exercises, the view was reversed. The lighthouse was the pivot and the harbour buildings, the wall, the sea were continually shifting about it; re-grouping, so that it was seldom seen against the same background. In the same way the harbour wall would lengthen or diminish to almost nothing. 'Ideal for an artist,' thought Bertram, taking out his sketch-book and running a line across the middle of a page. He drew in the buildings in squares and oblongs – the largest stone house at one end of the row, the pub, the Mimosa Fish Café, the second-hand clothes shop, the Fun Fair, the Seamen's Mission, the Waxworks, the lifeboat house. Above he sketched in more roofs and the church tower.

Then he noticed that in the narrow house wedged between the big house and the pub a door opened and a woman came out with a black scarf on her head and a white jug in her hand. She went quickly towards the next house, the doctor's house, her head bowed over the jug. Often at tea-time he had noticed her going that way with a white jug; at other times she went in the opposite direction to the pub, then carrying a pink jug.

Bertram slipped the sketch-book back into his pocket and took out his pipe. He was not much of an artist, in spite of having found a very good way of painting waves with tops folding over whitely, realistically. As soon as he had mapped out his little scene, curiosity waylaid him, the woman or a man in an apron writing something white upon the window of the Fish Café, having wiped off the 'Egg and Chips and Tea 1/3' which Bertram had noticed passing on his way to the lighthouse. 'Nice Fried Fillets,' Bertram murmured, 'not, I hope, Beans on Toast or misspelt Rissoles.'

The inscription, whatever it was, completed, the man went inside. The scene was empty again, except for men gathering up coils of rusty barbed wire (there had been a war on) from the foreshore.

'The light's going,' Bertram said to himself.

All his life at sea he had thought of retiring thus, of taking rooms at some harbour pub, of painting those aspects of the sea which for thirty or more years he had felt awaited his recognition. 'Make a fine picture,' he had said, at every sunset, every moonrise, every storm, every jewelled coast-line, seeing not the scene itself but the crystallisation or essence of it, his picture of it, completed in his imagination. 'Bertram Hemingway, that delightful painter of marine and *plage* subjects.' But on paper, with water-colours, the greens became mud, the birds suggested no possibility of movement, stuck motionless above the waves, the crests of the waves themselves would never spill. 'Perhaps oils,' he thought. 'Always trouble with medium. Media, rather. When you go into a harbour café you don't expect to get tinned salmon.'

The Waxworks Exhibition looked sealed, windows covered with grey lace; next door, the second-hand clothes shop was having a lick of paint; the first coat, salmon-pink, framed the display of dejected, hanging frocks; shutters covered the Fun Fair; one of the men had separated himself from the loops of barbed wire and had entered the café; he came to the door now with a cup in his hand, shouted something to his mates, his palm curved like a shell at his mouth. The sound came faintly across the harbour.

Yes, the light was going. Turning, Bertram saw the trawlers spread out widely upon the horizon. Loneliness came down over him. He knocked his pipe against the stone wall and began to go back down the curving mole. 'Bertram Hemingway, R.N., Retd., the well-known ...' 'Other famous men began late in

3

life,' he interposed quickly to himself. 'Look at . . .' But even if he could have found an example he did not bother, for there was that woman again, tripping along the other way, dodging into her house, her head held up this time, a hand white upon the dark scarf at her throat. No jug. She seemed never to bring them back. Except from the pub. Then she walked slowly, carefully, like a little girl.

A car drew up at the house she had left, the doctor's house. Out he stepped, slammed the door, paused for a moment to look at the fishing-fleet (most people did), and then, carrying his case, approached the house, knocked, waited, was swallowed up.

Bertram went along the front. 'Yes, I've made a sketch or two,' he rehearsed for the landlord's benefit, 'blocked in the skyline . . . interesting cubist effect these groups of buildings . . . but then the light went.'

In the window of the Waxworks was a showcard announcing in shadowed lettering the latest attraction – 'The Duke and Duchess of Windsor'; there was some faded crinkled paper, too, and some mice-dirts.

Passing the smell of paint, he had the feeling that the air trembled and waited, and then, yes – light swung out boldly from the lighthouse . . . flash, wink, pause . . . endorsing what the artist had already decided, that the day was gone.

'We are now frying God,' Bertram read aloud off the café window, then stopping, mystified . . . 'Oh! Cod!' He laughed and turned into the pub.

The harbour, in its turn, observed Bertram. There had been other artists, but with easels, half-circled by children, and not so much before the season began. This man they half-suspected. He had none of the paraphernalia. The beard was naval, not

Bohemian. They watched behind curtains from shop and house, and Mrs Wilson at the Waxworks looked out from her top front window and wondered if he was a spy, forgetting that the war was over. When she saw the light swinging over the water she felt terror and desolation, the approach of the long evening through which she must coax herself with cups of tea, a letter to her brother in Canada or this piece of knitting she had dropped to the floor as she leant to the pane to watch Bertram, the harsh lace curtain against her cheek, the cottony, dusty smell of it setting her teeth on edge.

Tory Foyle unwound the black chenille scarf from her hair. She was what was once held to be the typical English Beauty, her pink face, bright hair and really violet eyes.

'I had a letter from Edward.' She took a small piece of lined paper from her pocket and smoothed it.

Beth poured tea and waited, her heart-strings all ready to be plucked.

'Dear Mummy,' Tory read, 'I hope you are well I am. Please send envelopes. It is not very nice here. And stamps. I have a bad throat. Other boys have pots of honey. I am having a lovely time. Regards. Yours truly Edward.'

'Oh, dear,' said Beth. 'They just don't think what they're saying. They write what they can spell. I remember when Prudence went away once. She wrote: "I am in agony. I cannot say what." When I telephoned I discovered that she couldn't spell diarrhoea – indeed, who can? – and was better anyway long before the letter arrived. I shouldn't worry.'

'At least I can send some honey.'

'Yes, they measure affection by what comes in the post.'

Beth's younger child, Stevie, stood by the table, one hand on her hip, drinking long and steadily the milk which Tory had brought for her. As she drank, her eyes became unfocused. Beth and her daughters had large, beautiful, but astigmatic eyes.

'Put your beaker down and blink.'

Stevie did as she was told. She stood blinking, wearing a creamy moustache from the milk.

'I read in a book that it relaxes the muscles,' said Beth, pushing her spectacles up her little nose. She looked virginal, Tory thought, not even the mark of a kiss on her mouth.

'The holy printed word,' said Tory.

'You can stop blinking now.'

The child took a deep breath and began to drink again.

'Where is Prudence?'

'She is doing the cats' ears. I had a wonderful idea. I thought I would ask Geoffrey Lloyd to stay for a week-end.'

'I don't know Geoffrey Lloyd.'

'I think you must do. You remember Rosamund Dobson at school?'

'Only too well. When we were about twelve she told me that when one has a baby one's stomach bursts open' – Tory threw her hands apart – 'and has to be stitched together again afterwards.'

'Well, Geoffrey is her son.'

'Then I hope he was born in the normal way. She must have been pleased and surprised.'

'I thought he would be company for Prudence. He is stationed just outside the town in the Air Force.'

'Why go on having an Air Force when it's all over?'

Tory stood up and began to wind the shawl over her head.

'It might start up again, I suppose.'

'It only will if you talk like that,' said Tory, laying a great responsibility upon her friend. 'Ask him to tea first to see what he is like. I am sure he won't be any good.'

'He is only a lad. And Prudence has no friends.'

'I'll leave the jug until the morning.'

'Thank you, my dear ... I don't know what Stevie would do ...'

'It's nothing. I hate milk. If I kept it I'd only wash my face in it. I believe you are match-making, Beth.' She turned her head away. 'Find someone for me.'

'Dear Tory, I wish I could. I don't know any men. If I did, they wouldn't be good enough.'

'I must go.'

But she had nothing to go home for, except to get out of Beth's husband's way.

She let herself out of the large, untidy house and into her own beautiful, hyacinth-scented one. She sat down in the bay-window of her bedroom and combed her hair before the mirror. She took it all down and built it up again, but there was no one to see what she had done.

Mrs Bracey liked a coarse jest, but the girls didn't. In the room behind the old-clothes shop, Iris was getting ready for work and holding a pair of stockings before the fire. She turned them primly. Steam rose from them. Her mother, lying on the bed by the wall (paralysed from the hips down), shook with laughter. 'Yes,' she repeated, wiping her eyes, '"Don't be so damn familiar," he said. "You and your kissing!" And all the time he was ...'

'All right, Mother,' said Maisie, coming in from the kitchen. 'I think we've had enough of that word for one evening.'

'What could be more familiar than that, I ask you?' Mrs Bracey went on, laughing still. 'Depends how you look at it, I suppose. Bloody class-distinctions even over ... all right, all right. You'll be late, Iris,' she added sharply.

'You're telling me!' She drew the stockings on carefully.

'Five to six already. You'll be crippled with rheumatics before you're forty,' her mother said in a pleased tone.

Iris crammed her feet into her shoes and was off.

'Ta-ta,' her mother shouted, but got no reply. 'No one to have a good laugh with,' she sighed. 'What're you doing with that coatee, Maisie?'

'I thought I'd press it up a bit. Mrs Wilson at the Waxworks said she'd give me five bob for it for the Duchess of Kent.'

'Not showy enough for Royalty. Let's have a try on of it. Where'd it come from?'

'The Vicarage. The cook brought down a lot of things.'

'Shouldn't fancy it then. That's no way to treat velvet. Put the iron underneath and the steam'll run up through the pile.'

'And me standing on my head while I do it, I suppose?'

Mrs Bracey folded her hands and sighed with elaborate patience. Bored, she was, frustrated; not only her body, but her mind, her great, ranging, wilful imagination. In the old days, on summer evenings, she had liked to sit outside the shop on a chair in the doorway, watching the boats go out, or chatting with people on their way to and from the Anchor, shouting innuendoes at the fishermen, taking sides in children's quarrels. Now the brilliance, the gossip, had gone from life. When Iris returned from the Anchor she would flop into a chair and pick up her serial story, waiting, her feet out of her shoes, for Maisie to bring the cocoa.

'She's had nearly five hours of the outside world and don't bring me back a crumb,' her mother would think, waiting nervously for the tit-bit that never came.

8

'Who was in to-night, Iris?' she would ask at last, exasperated, yet humble.

'Oh, the usual,' Iris would say, turning a page.

'She don't give a crumb of it away. Thinks I'm being nosey. Let her wait for her turn.'

Mrs Bracey waited with optimism for others to have their turn.

'These girls nowadays,' she thought, as she watched Maisie so calmly working. 'What do they believe in? Nothing *in* their lives.' She was obscurely annoyed always because her blasphemy left them unmoved. 'Bloody little atheists. Don't even believe sex is funny. Get told the facts of life too early, before they can appreciate the joke. All this so-called biology. Takes the flavour out of it, makes it uninteresting. O Lord, why didst Thou not inflict that Mrs Wilson, for instance, instead of me? She don't want to do nothing but sit indoors and look out of the window. I would always've visited her, very good to her I would have been. "Good morning, Mrs Wilson, I just run round to see was there anything you wanted. I brought a drop of my veal broth" – turning the cup upside-down to show how solid with richness was the jelly – "I'll hot it up on the gas for you. We got to bear one another's burdens like Our Lord said. What's religion worth if it's all bloody talk and no *do*? While you drink that I'll just sit here and have a chat. No, I'm in no hurry. There's a good one I heard along at the Anchor last night about a Duke and a chambermaid" ...'

'What're you grinning at, Mother?' Maisie asked, shaking out the velveteen jacket.

'Me thoughts.' It was like a blow to find herself lying on her own bed instead of sitting beside Mrs Wilson's. 'It's a damn shame, Lord. No doubt I deserved it in many ways, but no

9

worse than the others. Strike down some of the sodding little atheists, I say, not one of Thy servants who could have been out in the world doing useful work. Such as sitting out on me chair poking me nose into other people's business or drinking a nice draught Bass in the bar,' she added, for she was no humbug. 'I'll get me reward in heaven. Wonderful comfort I'll get seeing the tables turned, having worked out me own salvation in pain down here. Well worth waiting for, seeing Iris's face, hearing Our Lord say: "What good've you done? Just sit there night after night reading your drivelling little *Women's Chat* without a civil word in your head." If I was in me last agony, she'd finish this week's instalment before she run out for Doctor Cazabon.' Her hands plucked at the hem of the sheet as her thoughts raced on.

'Yes,' said Bertram, 'I blocked in the skyline, just a sketch, you know.'

They were drinking light ale in the bar. Iris sipped Guinness, wiping her lips with a lacy handkerchief.

'We never had an artist in the winter before,' said Mr Pallister. 'One or two might turn up during the season, but that was before the war. They make for anything old. I always think the New Town round the Point, that should make a nice picture, pier and all, and the Italian Gardens. But for the harbour, we'd be finished. Mrs Wilson along at the Waxworks, how she keeps going beats me; lost her hubby in the war, too. But what does she get out of it? People go in out of curiosity, to poke fun. How long's that going to last? Then the Fun Fair. That's shut up, of course. Every season I wonder if they'll come down or not. Flashy London people they are, don't belong down here. Mrs Wilson, she does. Her man took over from his father, same as I did from my Guvnor. In those days this was a resort, bathing-machines under the sea-wall. Why, a concert-party we had once. Remember, Iris? Remember that chap in the pink and white striped blazer and the straw hat? Forget his name.'

'Why, I was only a kid, Mr Pallister,' Iris said, surprised. But Bertram could see that she did remember, that the pink and white striped blazer had been one of those visions which quicken the child's imagination, that she remembered his name, too.

'But that's all done,' said Mr Pallister. 'People don't care so much for the smell of fish nowadays. You're a sailor, that's different.'

'I don't see what being in the Navy's got to do with fish,' Iris put in. 'Besides, Mr Hemingway was an officer.'

'You can't get away from it,' Mr Pallister said. He put a block of wood on the fire, and when he shifted it with his boot little green flames shot up all round it. Red serge curtains covered the windows, yellow varnish shone stickily. 'We Do Not Recognise The Possibility of Defeat' a soiled card announced, hanging crookedly over the bar.

'Quiet to-night,' Mr Pallister went on. He said it nearly every night except Saturday, when he altered it to 'Quiet for a Saturday.' He still contrived to sound surprised.

'Now, here's a little picture for you,' he said, unhooking something from a dark corner. 'Oil painting,' he explained reverently, handing it to Bertram. 'I should like to have an expert opinion on it. A Mr Walker did it one year. He was staying here at the time, had that same front room as you, and when he went he gave that to me.'

'View of the Harbour,' he read, peering at the bottom of the canvas.

There was the lighthouse, the harbour wall, the lifeboat shed, all painted in brown gravy. Peering closer, Bertram could distinguish a sepia boat and a bird. The waves, out on the open sea, mounted up thickly in rows.

'Yes,' said Bertram, handing the picture back. 'I must paint you a little companion for it.' 'Glue and mulligatawny,' he thought, and saw his own picture shimmering with light. 'A little gem by Bertram Hemingway.' 'Who is the lady with the jug?' he asked.

'He means Mrs Foyle,' said Iris.

'Ah, Mrs Foyle from next door. She slips round for her beer at dinner-time. Lady with a black scarf?'

'Yes.'

A little silence fell over them. Iris glanced up from picking at the chipped varnish on her nails. 'Lovely colour eyes,' she added vaguely, thinking of Tory. Oh, God, how dull life was! Suppose the door suddenly opened and Laurence Olivier walked in, down here, perhaps, on location. 'For nothing else would make him come,' she thought bitterly.

The fan of light stopped short near the land. It swept far over the sea, it raked the sky. Lo! it said, and was gone. Prudence knelt in the dark at her bedroom window, her arms on the dusty sill. Yvette and Guilbert, her Siamese cats, pushed their heads ecstatically against her knees, roving, thrilling, purring ceaselessly. Her face, under the heavy Trilby fringe, was like a piece of paper in the moonlight that now illumined the front of the stone house and the scabrous plaster façades along the harbour. Below, various lights spread out over the cobblestones, the lamp above the door of this house, the doctor's house, and the pavement shining red under the serge-draped windows of the

Anchor; nearer the sea-wall, lamps cast down circles of greenish light encompassed by blackness. And always there was the sound she no longer heard, since she had been hearing it from the beginning, water slapping unevenly against stone, swaying up drunkenly, baulked, broken, retreating.

Out on the quay two old men stood under a lamp talking about a boat. The lamplight painted the folds of their dark jerseys with silver. A piece of newspaper was taken up by the wind and went dancing idly forward, to be impaled upon a coil of wire and hang there quivering. When the pub door was opened a river of yellow ran out across the cobblestones. In it Bertram stood for a moment before he shut the door. Prudence watched him, leaning a little forward, her bare arms upon the rough stone of the window-sill. Did her thoughts about him make him look up, for she saw his face lifted in her direction, she could see his beard and, as he walked away, a little ring of paleness at the top of his head where his hair had thinned. He joined the two men under the lamp and added his voice to theirs. He was asking them about her, she guessed, and they would shrug and say 'The doctor's eldest girl' or something of the kind, since she was nothing to them, only a child who had grown up under their eyes. But Bertram – she did not know his name – had looked up at the exact moment when she stopped being a girl and became – she felt dizzy with her power – a woman. That he was an old man was not important, for it was her own power to distract with which she now experimented for the first time.

'Prudence!' her father called – the voice came winding up the stairs – for she was subject to bronchitis and not allowed to lean from windows at night, taking all the dampness into her lungs.

13

'I am twenty,' she thought, 'and I have never been kissed in love!'

'Prudence!' The voice came spiralling up more clearly. He had reached the first floor. She tiptoed to the door and switched on the light and then going out to the landing leant over the banisters, looking down the core of the house.

'Yes, Father?'

He stopped, with one foot on the bottom stair.

'Don't stay in your cold bedroom. It's time for supper.'

'I was doing my hair.' She put up her hand and smoothed the fringe.

'You haven't made much headway,' he observed, wondering why his children were both of them such liars. 'Beth and I,' he thought, descending the stairs again, 'so literal, so truthful. Where do they get it from? Where do we fail?'

He was always worrying about something, and this did to go on with as he went into the dining-room, where the gas-fire roared unevenly in its broken ribs, and the magazines had been cleared from the large table so that supper might be laid there. But although the magazines were put away, the ghosts of patients still sat upon the leather-covered chairs, waiting their turn. The room was full of them.

Beth sat at the table, waiting, too, her hands in her lap, her eyes vaguely dreamy. He kissed her forehead and put his hand on her short, curly hair, which was so soft, so untidy. The gesture meant nothing to either of them.

'Is Prudence coming?'

'She said she was.'

Beth thought that perhaps the shrimps in the sauce might make it look less lumpy than it really was.

'Did you do any writing?'

'Oh, Robert, one thing after another happened. Twice I sat down and the telephone rang and then Stevie came home early from school and I had to get tea and Tory came in . . .'

'Tory!' He whipped out his napkin from its ring, took it by a corner and waved it open. 'What did she want?'

'She had more milk than she needed and brought it for Stevie . . .'

'But don't you see, the child has enough milk. Her appetite is poor because she drinks so much.'

'She loves it,' said Beth, not thinking. 'I shall have to write to-night instead.' But she was glad, so comfortably glad, at the thought of shutting herself up with her books until one o'clock, two o'clock.

'I thought we might have gone to the cinema.'

'Tory thought *she* would go.'

He ate his fish without answering.

'Why not take Tory instead?'

'I certainly shall not.'

'I wish you could like her. There is so much I feel we might do, and she's lonely. *We* have one another.'

'Tory is frivolous,' he thought. 'Tory is frivolous.' He looked at his wife's serious little face. 'Damn it, where *is* Prudence?' and he sprang from his chair and began calling up the stairs once more, angrier with his daughter than was justified.

Prudence came running downstairs, her fringe jumping on her forehead, her breasts springing boldly, arrogantly under her jersey, cats leaping at her heels. But her haste brought on a fit of coughing; in the hall she was checked, her face suffused with red so that her eyes shone with vivid green in contrast, a thick vein standing out on her brow.

'Steady, Prue,' said her father and, with his arm across her

15

shoulders, brought her into the dining-room, without a single grumble about the cooling food, and sat her in her chair.

Bertram had seen Prudence at the window and had been startled by her white face, wondering why she sat at the window of a dark room. He had asked the fishermen about her, just as she guessed. Smiling, they had tapped their foreheads, but would say no more.

Now, as he walked the length of the quay before bedtime, he wondered about this. 'Life breaks through,' he thought. 'There is the pain of it all one's life and now, with old age impending' – in his mind it would always impend, never reach him – 'one expects peace, expects curiosity to be laid aside, its place taken by contemplation, by easy abstractions, work. Cut away from all I knew, in a strange place, I thought I could achieve all I have dreamt about and intended since I was a young man beset at every turn by love, by hate, by the world, implicated always, involved, enfolded by life. Then I shall be freed, I thought. But even now, two days in this place and the tide creeps up, begins to wash against me, and I perceive dimly that there is no peace in life, not' – he had reached the lifeboat house and stood looking down at the black, spangled water – 'not until it is done with me for ever.' Since his egotism was great and his hopes of immortality small, his fear of death was thus overwhelming and he chose to disregard it, to think instead of life, the woman with the jug, for instance, and now a figure moving in a greenish-lit room, behind lace curtains, up there above the Waxworks.

Iris came out of the pub and walked quickly homewards, keeping close to the walls of the houses.

'I must go back,' he thought. 'Old Pallister will be winding the clock, putting a handful of darts in a tankard on the shelf, saying: "It's been quiet to-night, but I feel tired just the same."'

He began to saunter back, the wind behind him now. The doctor came out of his house, bareheaded, wearing no coat. He walked to his car at the kerb and for a moment stood there on the pavement, looking up at the house next door, where no lights showed; then he got into the car and drove it round to the back of the house to the garage.

As Bertram reached the Anchor, the doctor came trotting back again, his head bent against the wind, his hands in his pockets. Standing on the doorstep, he sorted keys in his hand and, glancing once more, very quickly, at the dark windows next door, he let himself in and disappeared.

Mr Pallister stood in the bar with the darts in his hand. 'Like a final beer?' he asked.

'No, thank you. I'm off to bed.'

'If you weren't a sailor I'd say the sea air tired you. That's what visitors always notice. That and the appetite.' He was a white, unhealthy-looking man who rarely went out of doors.

Just as Bertram was getting into bed he heard the quick tapping of high heels along the pavement, and he went and peeped out from behind the curtain. It was Tory, coming home from the cinema alone.

'What a perpetual going and coming there is,' he thought crossly, getting in between the rough twill sheets. He lay there looking out at the curdled, junkety sky. Lo! said the lighthouse, sweeping across his room. The painted ewer on the washstand stood forth, then vanished. He thought of the fishing-fleet crouched far out upon the dark waters. 'And I, ashore, sleeping in a bed, like a woman.'

*

'Who was in to-night, Iris?' Mrs Bracey asked at last.

'No one much,' said Iris, standing before the mirror and rolling her hair. She spoke indistinctly, a row of hairpins between her lips. She did not mean to be unkind to her mother, but in her mind Laurence Olivier kept opening the saloon door and coming into the bar. As soon as he approached Iris and began to speak, he grew hazy and dissolved, for she herself could not think of anything for him to say to her. Just then Maisie brought in the cocoa.

Mrs Wilson locked the bedroom door against the ghostly company downstairs. When Bob was alive she had not minded; now she was ever conscious that they stood grouped there, unmoving, eyes glittering as the lighthouse beam winked upon them, their arms crooked unnaturally or knees flexed slightly in everlasting informality, a disintegrating glove draped between the fingers of Royalty, the unfamiliar faces of forgotten murderers turned to the door, Mrs Dyer, the baby-farmer, with dust upon the backs of her hands.

She lay coldly in the stuffy bed, to one side of it, as if at any moment Bob would come and lie down beside her, and she prayed that sleep might carry her through safely to the morning.

2

Beth sat at breakfast among her press-cuttings. 'Her perception,' she read, 'her broad humanity.' She held the strips of paper high, sipping her coffee, rather pleased with the picture of herself which was suggested.

'I shall be late for the register,' Stevie said.

Robert put down his newspaper. 'Beth, what about Stevie?'

'Run and wash your face, then, dear,' said Beth.

'I don't want to go alone.'

'Prudence, you go with her.'

Robert could see the child was tensed-up ready for a scene. When she returned he knew that Prudence had worsened the situation, rushing her into her coat, tightening her little pigtails until she could not have closed her eyes. Suddenly she broke down and stood there, feet apart, fists in her eyes, her mouth squared.

'What *is* the matter?' Beth asked in amazement.

'She popped the elastic under my chin.'

'Oh, good God!' cried Prudence, flinging herself back into her chair.

'Well, it can't still be hurting now. Where's your handkerchief? Don't go to school with red eyes.'

But Stevie had no intention of stopping for quite a time. Steadily, relentlessly, she roared.

'There's not even a red mark,' said Beth, running a finger along between fat chin and elastic.

'I should have thought it was quite obvious,' said Robert, speaking in a low voice and pushing back his chair, 'that the elastic has nothing whatsoever to do with it.'

Prudence knew by her father's saying 'whatsoever' that he had lost his temper. When he had gone out Stevie's crying dropped into the minor key.

'Could you tell me what is wrong?' Beth asked politely.

'I don't see why I can't believe in God like the other girls,' Stevie sobbed. 'I wish I did. I wish I did.'

'Then do so, do so,' Beth said coldly.

'You said it wasn't true.'

'It was only my opinion. You came home with all this nonsense about hell-fire. Naturally, I have to explain that it *is* nonsense.'

Prudence, who played for safety, thought her mother tempted Providence rather unnecessarily.

'I'd much rather believe in it.'

'Why start all this just as you're leaving the house? There's Robert bringing the car round now. Come here, my love, and let me dry your eyes. Be a good, sensible girl and you shall believe in God as much as you like, and the Immaculate Conception, and Transubstantiation and the Grotto of Lourdes and all the rest of it ...' She spoke with a fastidious sarcasm.

'I only wanted to believe in God,' said Stevie sulkily, 'so that I can go into Prayers.'

20

Robert sounded the horn.

'Now run along, or Robert will get impatient.' She kissed Stevie's throbbing face and went to the window to watch her get into the car. It was a grey and blue seaside day. The sky looked like a child's painting. Robert waved and drove away.

'I wonder why they don't have miracles in England,' said Prudence, still thinking of religion.

'Who is "they"?' her mother asked, at the window-sill. No warmth fell from her over her children. Even their ages, the fifteen years between Prudence and Stevie, suggested that they were haphazardly conceived, incidental to her, strange unexpected flowerings.

'A visitor already?' she now said, watching Bertram as he crossed from the pub to the water side.

'Let me see!' Prudence came running to the window and stood at her mother's shoulder, her bosom pressed softly against her. Beth moved a little, without knowing.

'Oh, yes! I saw him last night. What a lovely white handkerchief!' They watched Bertram blowing his nose. 'And here comes Tory.'

'How dressed up she is!'

Bertram had turned, put the handkerchief into his pocket, and bowed. And they saw Tory smile suddenly and warmly, but as she came towards the house her face looked puzzled.

'Do I know that man outside?' she asked, bringing fragrance into the room.

'He is staying at the pub,' said Prudence.

'Beth, dear, I'm going to London. Is there anything you want?' She was all in grey, her hat feathery.

'To London!' Beth repeated, as if that were an act of one in extremity.

'That house maddens me. I shall let all the clocks run down, I think, so that I can't hear them ticking.'

'You miss Edward. It's always like that the first term.'

'It isn't right to miss children so frantically. I must get something of my own.'

Prudence gathered up her cats and went out. They heard her opening the front door.

'Such as what?' Beth asked, fogged.

'A new hat, perhaps.' Tory laughed. 'A new spring hat.'

'But you have dozens of hats and hardly wear them.'

'I know. The old black shawl.'

'You could have come in with me for the day if you were lonely and restless.'

'You're busy. And there's Robert.'

'What about Robert? He's only here for lunch.'

'Robert and I . . .' Tory hesitated. 'We don't . . . hit it off, whatever that may mean.'

Beth began to protest, but in an insincere and social way.

'Oh, do let me!' said Tory, picking up one of the press-cuttings. 'Isn't it lovely seeing one's name in print?'

'No,' said Beth. 'It makes no difference either way.'

'But when they say nice things?'

'It always comes too late, when one's indifferent. And often they say nasty things. And that doesn't matter, either.'

'You have a secret life.'

'We all have,' Beth said awkwardly, and began to stack up crockery on the breakfast-table.

'"Perception",' Tory read aloud. She put down the paper and went to look in the mirror. 'Have you perception, Beth?'

Beth always blushed like a girl when she was asked about herself. 'I suppose one knows one's to be a writer from very early on. And trains oneself. Noticing things ...' She always became incoherent, too.

'What is it, Tory? You look troubled.'

Tory smiled at herself in the mirror. 'Do I? I don't *feel* troubled.' She ran her finger along an eyebrow. 'I must be off.'

'If you *do* see any of those cream socks,' Beth began. 'But only if you're in the shop.' She followed Tory to the door. Prudence was out by the water's edge, talking to Bertram, her cats in her arms. The cats looked self-conscious, turning their heads away from the conversation as if they knew that they were being discussed.

'Yvette Guilbert,' said Prudence. 'You see they look as if they were wearing long black gloves. My father has a picture of her in a book.'

'You breed from them?' Bertram asked, not really interested, his eyes on that front door.

'No, they don't like one another, you see.'

'Awkward, rather.'

'Yes. Especially as Yvette gets very difficult at times.'

'Naturally.' His mouth twitched, out came the white handkerchief again.

At that moment Tory came out of the front door and waved. They watched her go.

'She is off to London,' said Prudence.

'Is she ... she is a widow?'

'No. Divorced. Her husband went off with one of those women officers ...'

'Please,' said Bertram. 'I am a stranger. I have no right to know.'

Now the harbour from its look of peaceful tidiness broke up

and became disorganised by people beginning a day's work. Ladders appeared outside Mrs Bracey's and the first stroke of wet chocolate paint was laid over the salmon-pink; a mop twirled from Mrs Wilson's top window; the men returned and stood about among the whorls of rusty wire which were full of hanging black seaweed and tatters of rag and paper, broken bottles, too. The café door shot open and the Guvnor threw out a piece of coconut-matting and began to sweep the floor, with the chairs standing neatly upon the tables.

'The Guvnor,' said Bertram to Prudence, smiling. She shrugged. Her mind stretched out with restless tendrils, here, there, fastening upon and relinquishing, the question always 'What is of use to me?' Obviously not the Guvnor, the dingy, hard-working man who looked like Charlie Chaplin.

Only the pub slept, drowsing in its own beer smells. Bertram's window was flung open, the curtains wildly agitated. This always alarmed Mr Pallister, who had spent much of his life keeping out the sea-breezes, tacking felt at the edges of doors and hanging thick curtains at his windows. Reverence for fresh air seemed to him an inland fad and was not to be expected in an old sailor.

Mrs Flitcroft, the daily help as she thought of herself, descended the steep flight of steps at the side of the Waxworks, came rocking along on her famous bad legs, her apron rolled up in her basket. As soon as she saw Prudence she began to wave her arm towards the house and was soon shouting to be heard above the wind and the sound of the water.

'Get along inside!' she cried. 'Indoors with you!'

Prudence turned her head away, her throat flushing. The cats, too, patrician, affronted, removed their gaze.

'You with your chest!' shouted Mrs Flitcroft, coming up close.

The blood rose from throat to cheek and then, her whole face darkening, Prudence began to cough.

'No coat! I don't know what your mother's thinking of. Better get inside as quick as you know how.'

Prudence moved her head in misery, the cats hampering her. Bertram gave her his nice clean handkerchief.

'Don't,' he wanted to say. 'Don't be humiliated to yourself, for you are not so to me.'

They watched Mrs Flitcroft's progress round the corner to the Cazabons' side door, and when she had gone Prudence held out the crumpled handkerchief and smiled. 'Silly old tart!' she began, her voice unsure. 'She must be humoured.'

'No, that is not the way,' he thought, liking women, even very young women, to be gentle. This brittle gallantry vexed him. The young imagine insults, magnify them, with great effort overcome them, or retaliate. A waste of emotion Bertram thought, forgetting how much emotion there is to spare.

'Good-bye,' he said.

The cats lay against her shoulder, their gentian eyes wide, their silken nostrils quivering a little at the hated outdoor air, the wind blowing their fur into little divisions. They yearned to get back indoors, to lie on the radiator in the surgery or at the bottom of the linen-cupboard. As Prudence carried them back to the house they looked over her shoulder at the sea contemptuously.

The men among the barbed wire whistled at Iris as she stood outside the Anchor waiting to be let in. She stared in front of her at the frosted-glass door panel.

'Good morning,' said Bertram.

'Good morning.' An ex-officer, she thought. ('This is my

young brother' – for her dreams had flown ahead, skipping a stage or two – 'How do you do?' She was wearing a grey suit like Mrs Foyle's and a diamond clip. His sleeves were hooped with gold braid. She was on the other side of the bar. They drank pink gin.)

Ned Pallister opened the door, wearing shirt and trousers. He had finished shaving but lather remained near his ears. Iris glanced back at Bertram walking along the quayside. He was beautifully clean in his neat navy blue suit and dazzling shirt, but pinkness showed through his hair. And if he had a brother he was sixty at least (she entered the subfusc beeriness of the saloon bar) – at the other end of the earth, the Canary Islands, she thought, or Panama.

She drew back the curtains but knew better than to open the window.

Lily Wilson sang as she shook her mop out into the glittering air. She was thinking she wouldn't have to cook for herself, but go down to the café and have something there. This decision made her seem to herself adventurous and reckless and she forgot to feel a sense of loss when dusting the photograph of Bob on the chest-of-drawers.

Going downstairs carrying her shopping-basket she was light-hearted, knowing that the spring would come soon and then the lengthening evenings – the same daylight when all these wax figures remained what they were now, shoddy and unreal, and she could go out in the evenings to the cinema or for a chat with Mrs Bracey without fear of walking back in the dark and entering the tall, creaking building alone.

She passed the glass panelled pay-box and unbolted the door. Bertram was looking in at the window although there was nothing to look at but the dirty-coloured paper and the old showcard. She felt ashamed and began to make resolutions, nettled by his look of curiosity. She pulled the door after her and nodded when he said good morning.

Bertram strolled on towards the lifeboat house. It seemed to him that he did nothing but wander about saying good morning to people. He fingered the sketch-book in his pocket and looked out to sea. A little yacht appeared round the Point, white-sailed, trig, something from another world.

The lifeboat house was deserted. He went in and walked round the boat as if it were someone lying in state. On the walls were painted the names of rescued vessels and the dates: the *Scarborough Belle*, the *Bounteous Sea*, *Pride of Lowestoft*.

The day seemed empty to him, he must at last acknowledge, because Mrs Foyle had gone to London. He remembered what Prudence had said of her. Divorced. Her husband had run off with what the girl had called 'one of those women officers'. Odd how men did that so much. Women in uniforms were not women at all, he felt, could not move him, excite him. It was a pretty hat she had worn, he thought – grey with feathers. He liked a bright-haired woman in grey, so long as she kept to grey, resisted the little touches of other colours, no bits of red like a harlot. *She* had kept to grey. So she divorced him.

'Will you divorce me, my dear?' 'But this is so sudden!'

He walked along the arm of the harbour and presently stopped and leant against the wall, looking down at the scum between the little boats, and the gulls putting beaks into their feathers. He took out his sketch-book and laid it on the top of the wall, then his pipe and filled it. 'Voltaire,' he thought, 'started late in life. Sixty or so – if I remember correctly.' Then he found that the point of his pencil was broken and began to search without any success for his pen-knife.

Lily Wilson went up the steep cobbled street past the church, the fish shop, the second-hand bookshop, the palmist's, the old furniture shop with its crest china, its cracked, riveted plates painted with fruit and a glass dome full of broken shell-flowers. All the new shops were in the New Town round the Point. Here were the lees of a life which had receded and which no new life revived. In the shops of the harbour lay objects which, being still, taken from context, became important as symbols of the vanished life, suggestive of something greater, as a rock-pool is a microcosm of the sea; and significant as they could not be seen waveringly through crowds. Quite still, they lay, enlarged almost, like stones underneath water.

But Lily Wilson saw nothing thus, although she had reason to be bitterly aware that life was gone from the place, life and livelihood. She saw the strings of faded postcards against the window of the tobacconist's, the Presents from Newby, the bald china head, mapped out and numbered, in the palmist's window and the sign (behind which a light used to throb on and off): *Phrenology, Palmistry, Crystal. Highly Scientific and Occult*. She saw and set against it all the glitter of the New Town, to the detriment of the old.

In the little school, in the dimness filled with shifting chalk-motes, children chanted a lesson and a woman's voice, domineering, without love, prompted them. On the window-sills hyacinth bulbs trailed cottony threads into jars of water, erupted a little into leaves: as if authority had tried to bring beauty inside and have it teach a lesson at the same time, an idea which Lily understood, for to her learning meant 'a bringing indoors' and education the insinuation into children's heads as painlessly as possible of a substance which might later turn out to have money-making properties.

'Charles the First, Sixteen-twenty-five,' the children were chanting as Lily turned into the Public Library. 'Commonwealth, Sixteen-forty-nine,' and then – something final and triumphant – 'Charles the Second, Sixteen-sixty' – as if they were all concerned militantly with the return of the monarchy. Hesitation followed, they fell into a minor key, for was he not the last real king for a long time; they paused briefly as a salutation to lechery and humour and eccentricity, qualities the English revere on the printed page or across a distance of time. As Lily closed the door of the Library she could hear the children, having refilled their lungs, trailing unevenly down the incline into the confusions of the House of Hanover.

The Library was part of the Institute. Behind a counter was an old man with an ink-pad and a large oval stamp, with which he conducted a passionate, erratic campaign against slack morals. His censorship was quite personal. Some books he could not read and they remained on the shelves in original bindings and without the necessary stigma 'For Adults Only'. *Roderick Random* stood thus neglected, and *Tristram Shandy*, vaguely supposed to be children's books. *Jane Eyre*, bound and rebound, full of loose leaves, black with grease, fish-smelling, was stamped back and front. *Madame Bovary* had fallen to pieces.

The Librarian who performed this useful service to readers had certain fixed standards before him, as he sat there skimming through the pages, one hand fingering the rubber stamp. Murder he allowed; but not fornication. Childbirth (especially if the character died of it), but not pregnancy. Love might be supposed to be consummated as long as no one had any pleasure out of it. There were single words whose appearance called for the stamp at once. 'Oh, God!' the characters might cry in their extremity, but not 'Oh, Christ!' 'Breast' was not to be in the plural. 'Rape' sent the stamp plunging and twisting into the purple ink.

Lily went flicking through one book after another, but listlessly; for the choosing of the book brought the thought of the quiet evening when she would read it. The books themselves with their thick greasy boards sickened her, but gave escape into the land of the living. 'Audley Court,' she read, 'lay low down in a hollow, rich with fine old timber and fertile pastures.' In the spell of these words she sank deeply as if under an anaesthetic, away from empty and makeshift reality; she went down willingly and pleasurably, relinquishing with eagerness the gritty irritations of the harbour streets, the smell of fish, the dusty shops with their cast-off clothes and furniture.

She took the book to the old man at the counter and stood there silently while he did a great deal of clerical work about it.

'That's a fine and powerful story,' he said. 'No need to be prejudiced against lady novelists. In literature the wind bloweth where it listeth.'

He would not give the book into her hands and she was compelled to listen, but looked vaguely beyond him at the dirt-marks shoulder high on the flaky wall where for years people had leant, bewildered, misled, searching for pornography in *Jane Eyre*.

'*Robert Elsmere*, for instance. That's a serious book. Who could object? No!' he said, as if she had contradicted him. 'Ladies – and you notice I say "ladies" – have their own contribution to make. A nice domestic romance. Why ape men?' He put (at last) the book into her hands as if it were a prize she had won. '*Under Two*

Flags,' he added, as she walked away, 'that's another matter. That's something of a very different complexion.'

Lily, without knowing why, was always conscious of something salacious beneath his Puritanical conversation, and found this old-fashioned prurience boring as well as disgusting, worse than Mrs Bracey's Rabelaisian stories. She carried her book away, holding it with loathing, for it was warm still from his hands, and she climbed to the top of the hill for a breath of air.

Here, where the houses stopped, was slippery turf and the sudden wideness of the sky all round and below, and, stretched out on her left as she faced the sea, the long, curving glitter of the New Town: the white hotels, the cliffs of boarding-houses, the broad esplanade and the gardens and pier; all planned and clean and built for pleasure.

And then, below on her right, steeply huddled, the harbour buildings, children running out of school up the narrow streets, playing on the flights of steps, the sea, still, locked in the embrace of the stone wall, dotted with little boats, and, far out on the horizon, smudging the sky with smoke, escorted by wheeling birds, the fleet coming back.

She pressed fingers against her eyes, closing her lids against tears, and turned away from the sight of the place which only love had made tolerable. When her eyes were cleared of tears she opened them again, looking deliberately at the long sands on either side of the pier and the waves creaming over in silence far below.

Beth had been happy all the morning. Ink filled the nails of her right hand. She sat with her back to the window and thus, the words pouring out of her own darkness, she had taken her characters for a nice country walk and brought them back successfully, drawn them together at meal-times and let them talk (but not eat) and now, her eyes burning hotly, was hoping to have an only child dead before luncheon. 'Oh, God, save her!' cried the mother, wringing her hands, and Beth would have wrung her own if they had been less busy. Instead, she wept, but was relentless in intention. She had never seen a child die, but did not need to ask Robert about it. This was how God might have felt, called upon to watch His children suffer, whom He might have saved but would not. Beth, however, was an atheist.

'What is it?' she asked suddenly, sharply.

Her own child stood in the doorway.

'I am home from school,' said Stevie simply.

But with the dying child still on her mind, Beth could not bring herself to welcome this living one.

'Then run and wash your hands,' she said.

'What Mrs Foyle does is no concern of mine,' the curate said to Mrs Bracey.

'We are all members one of another,' she replied. 'The strength of the chain is that of its weakest link.'

'But why is Mrs Foyle a weak link because I met her on the station? What weakness is there in going on a train?'

'The destination. I've watched that woman for years. By that, I mean I *used* to watch her, before God took away the power.' She looked briefly at God's deputy and then went on. 'There isn't a man who comes within sight of her can withstand her ...'

'This one can,' said the curate untruthfully.

She despised the men who fell under Tory's spell, but she was more contemptuous still of those who didn't.

'A clergyman should have no thoughts for women.'

'I don't see why not,' said Mr Lidiard, who had a great many.

'Did you hear that one about the parson who went on a cruise?'

'Mother, for heaven's sake!' said Maisie.

'Yes, I did hear it,' Mr Lidiard said quickly.

'When I was in hospital that time I noticed the Catholic priest visited every day. Yes, they told me twice a week regular he's round calling on the sick in their homes. Twice a week.' She ruminated upon this. 'There's something in a religion such as that.'

'You belong to God. You cannot auction your conscience between two clergymen to see which bids higher.'

'I'll auction my conscience to the devil, if I choose, and not ask your permission either.'

'Would you like a cup of tea, Mr Lidiard?' Maisie asked.

'I should like one very much, please,' and he turned to her while he spoke and his voice was no longer boisterous, not tugged at by laughter as when he was speaking of Mrs Bracey as a child of God or trying to circumvent her stories.

'Where else'd she be going but London? If you ask me, she's always been a bloody sight more partial to the big city than this place. What's kept her here so long, I wonder?'

'Perhaps the fact that it's her home.'

'Perhaps not. You can call them men in, Maisie, for a cup of tea.'

The painters came in and stood in the doorway while they drank.

'What's going on this morning?' said Mrs Bracey, exacting payment for the tea.

'Nothing much.'

One of them said: 'Nice little craft out there just now. Come round the Point. Right out to sea.' Having made this effort he seemed to sink down from the desultory conversation, drinking his tea with his face kept close to the cup.

The other said: 'Who's this old codger with the beard always strolling up and down and in and out of the Anchor?'

'He's a retired naval officer,' Maisie said. As she poured tea she rested the other hand on her hip. 'Staying there.'

'Staying where?' her mother asked sharply.

'At Mr Pallister's,' Maisie said quietly. Their eyes met. She saw her mother's look, empty, fretful. Her own was calm and warning.

'Why don't I get told nothing?'

'Iris can't remember everything.'

'No, of course not. I forgot the Anchor was like the bloody Leicester Lounge with half London flocking in and out. Of course she can't remember.'

Maisie's warning look always failed.

'You are indefatigable in your determination to think us all in a conspiracy against you,' said Mr Lidiard.

'And *you* can shut *your* trap. I was talking to my daughter.'

'Mother!'

The two decorators seemed draped on either side of the door, leaning there, in their whitish aprons, looking into their cups. They were of Mrs Bracey's generation and did not mind a row.

Mr Lidiard put his cup very carefully into its saucer and stood up. 'I must be off.' He made a little bow to Mrs Bracey. 'I shall call next week if I may.' His glance included Maisie.

'I shall most likely have gone over to Rome by then,' said Mrs Bracey.

34

The decorators made way for him, drawing back a little in contempt for his cloth.

'And you can bring me a book next time,' Mrs Bracey suddenly shouted after him. 'A travel book. A nice book about the South Sea Islands.' She chuckled. 'Some of the tricks these natives get up to, the dirty monkeys!' But all her face softened with tenderness and affection.

Lily ate fish and chips at the Mimosa Café, her book propped against a bottle of sauce. The fleet had come in and up at the market the floor was deep with fish, blue and black-barred, a mass of dinted silver, crimson-eyed. At the Anchor Iris was busy for once, with not a minute to wipe down the wet counter or to collect glasses. All over the harbour waters was a frenzied screaming of gulls. Mrs Bracey waited with impatience for her dinner and for her daughter to return at closing-time. Smells of stew crept round the kitchen. She trembled with exasperation, imagining the greyish meat slipping off the bone, the rings of onions, the pearl-barley, the golden sequins of fat glinting on the surface. And she thought too of the jug of draught stout Iris would bring back and her hands plucked peevishly at the bed covers.

They were late, too, at the doctor's house. In the end Beth said they would wait for Robert no longer. She ate vaguely, her daughters on either side; Prudence, sulky, with cats on her lap, forking up shepherd's pie with an expression of contempt, and Stevie, absorbed, thinking of school.

'Miss Simpson! I mean, Mummy!' she began, 'do you know what happened this morning? Millicent was very naughty.'

'Your mouth is full.'

'Your mouth is full, too.'

'I spoke because I had to correct you. Not from choice.'

'Oh!' Stevie appeared to think this reasonable. After a while she went on: 'After prayers we were doing our frames ...'

'Doing your frames?'

'Learning to lace-up and tie bows. It's on frames. And Millicent said "Please, Miss Simpson, may I be excused?" and Miss Simpson said "Yes" and she went to be excused ...'

'Excused from what?'

'She means going to the lavatory,' said Prudence shortly.

'Then say so, dear, another time.'

'Being excused is what we call it.'

'But that is not what the word means.'

Stevie's eyes grew large with tears. 'Miss Simpson means it to mean that.'

'You'd probably be expelled for saying "Can I go to the W.C.?"' Prudence said coolly.

Beth looked worried.

'Well,' Stevie went on between mouthfuls, 'when she put up her hand and said "Please may I ..."'

'Do you really have to put up your hand and ask to be let out, as if you were cats?'

'Cats don't put up their hands.'

'What happened to Millicent in the end?'

'She didn't get there in time.' Stevie laughed carelessly.

'In time for what?'

'Mother!' Prudence cried, exasperated.

'She wetted her knickers,' Stevie said.

'Darling, don't be disgusting. I don't want to hear about hateful Millicent's wet knickers when I am having my lunch.'

Stevie looked slyly at Prudence and smiled. Their mother seemed unreal to them.

'And so Miss Simpson said . . .'

'Your mouth is full again.'

When Mrs Flitcroft brought in the semolina Prudence turned her shoulder and looked disdainfully out of the window.

Presently Robert came home. He kissed the top of Beth's head as he went to the table.

'Do any writing?' he asked mechanically.

'Yes, my dear, thank you.'

'Good.'

'May I be let off?' said Stevie.

'Have you been eating sweets?' Robert asked. 'Or drinking milk before lunch?'

'No, there *is* no extra milk to-day,' said Beth. 'Tory has gone to London.'

'What the devil for?'

'To buy a hat,' said Prudence, lolling in her chair, fingering the cats' ears.

'Really because she is depressed,' said Beth.

Robert had looked quickly from his daughter to his wife and then at his plate. 'Depressed!' he repeated angrily. 'What has *she* to be depressed about?'

'We all think we are the only ones with any right to be depressed,' said Beth.

'I don't think anything of the kind.'

'She leads a very lonely life.'

'May I go to school now?' asked Stevie.

'Run and wash your face, then. Prudence, see to her, please, my dear.'

'If she is so lonely, why does she stay here?' Robert went on. 'Why not go and *live* in London?'

'It would be difficult to sell that house now, I daresay.'

37

'Not at all. Very quaint place. Kitchen like a slum, no garden, cobbled yard like a mews, all very fashionable nowadays,' said Robert, his eyes resting upon his own mahogany sideboard and the empty decanters with their huge cut-glass stoppers. The shepherd's pie seemed very dry and he waited for the cheese to be placed before him.

'Your nails, Beth!'

She curled them into her palm, flushing like a schoolgirl, pushing her spectacles up with her knuckles.

Soon Robert went off to the hospital and afternoon settled upon the house. Prudence had cooked two cods' heads for the cats. She lifted the lid off the saucepan and out rushed an evil-smelling steam, and two pairs of boiled, reproachful eyes stared up at her. She flopped the heads on to a dish and put it outside the kitchen door. The cats walked round it, thrilled and entranced, snuffling delicately, going round and round, until the steam vanished, until they could put their noses into the gluey, boney mess.

Bertram had made a little sketch in water-colour, but was dissatisfied with it. The sky looked as heavy as lead behind his two-dimensional church, the plaster peeled from the Mimosa Café in improbable shapes, the sea lay in a hard line against the wall. He took it into the bar, where Iris was rinsing glasses, and held it under the tap. It looked better then.

3

Bertram was worried about his shirts. He liked to rough it and to mingle, as he was this evening, with men who wore coarse jerseys and smelt of fish and tobacco, as long as he could be sure of a drawerful of what is called dazzling linen somewhere off-stage, something he could return to when he made his exit. Ned Pallister had talked vaguely of 'doing up a bundle sometime', but Bertram distrusted this attitude towards good poplin and cambric, and had done nothing for a day or two, so that this evening, for the first time in his life, he entered the bar feeling conscious of his cuffs, which did not dazzle.

Iris was busy again. The sawdust which had once lain in great whorls over the floor was scuffled and trodden, the air blue and dense. Already Bertram had his cronies, one or two characters who were prepared to be racy and eccentric for the price of a pint. They played dominoes. Bertram bought most of the beer and they called him 'Sir' a great deal, laughing immoderately at his jokes.

Lily watched them from her corner, where she sat on a high stool close to the bar, cut off from the rest of them as if she were there only to talk to Iris, her brown ale standing before her almost untouched and her misery amounting to panic as the time went by. Disliking beer, she shuddered at each sip. She wanted the warmth of another personality, as if her own warmth were not enough to sustain her, but she had no one, and nowhere to go. Mrs Bracey she avoided – there was a coolness between them, not warmth – since the time when Lily's husband was sent overseas and Mrs Bracey had told her about the brothels of the Orient and other soldiers' entertainments which she had read about in a book the curate had lent her.

'I never expected *my* man to be faithful to me in the last war,' she had concluded.

'Well, I'm faithful to *him*, aren't I?' Lily had cried, desperately alone and in love.

'I should bloody well think so,' Mrs Bracey had said.

She thought of this now, wrenching down a little more of the cold beer. In the end, it was better to face the long evening at home than to be made wretched all the time she was out by the fear of returning on her own. She had tried going to the cinema, but it was worse then, her emotions tautened to breaking point. Once she had met Mrs Foyle and they had walked back along the echoing and empty streets together. When Tory had laughed the sound seemed to return to them from the walls of the old houses. Only too soon Tory reached her own house. She said good night and went in and at once lights sprang up in the windows behind the frilly curtains. Lily had walked on down the quay and stood in the shadow of the lurching building where she lived. She took out the key and let herself in. As she passed her hand over the wall for the light-switch the lighthouse swung its beam over the room and the eyes of the waxworks seemed to flicker into life, so that she felt as if they were all standing there waiting for her.

Iris came now and leant an elbow for a moment upon the bar beside Lily. 'Drink up,' she said, 'and have a short one.'

'No thanks.'

'Our new lodger,' said Iris, nodding her head at a young fisherman playing darts.

'Looks nice,' said Lily vaguely. 'Perhaps I could get a lodger,' she thought, 'or would people talk?' She decided that people would talk and took a mouthful of beer, shivering.

'Go on, have a short one,' said Iris.

'No, really, thanks.'

'Mr Pallister sent him along this afternoon,' Iris went on, still looking at the young man. 'Nice hair, isn't it?'

'Very nice.'

It was straw-coloured, streaky. When he turned round, Lily saw his face was brick-red in contrast. He moved in a slouching, insolent way, his shiny trousers tight across his behind. When he glanced at Iris he winked mechanically, unsuggestively. He was singing all the time.

'What's his name?'

'Eddie. Eddie Flitcroft.'

'What, that old Mrs Flitcroft?'

'Nephew. Been in the Navy.'

'You'd think he'd live with her.'

'Not if you knew her, you wouldn't,' Iris said over her shoulder, moving away to draw beer for Bertram and his friends.

'Good evening,' Bertram said to Lily. He drew himself up when speaking to a lady, she noticed, as if he made a little extra effort. 'I saw you this morning.'

'Yes.'

41

'I wait with impatience for the waxworks show to open.'

'Oh.' She scarcely knew what to say, thinking he was making fun of her.

'They fascinate me.'

'It isn't really anything much. Once we meant to do the thing properly, and then the war came.'

'What are you drinking?'

'Nothing, really. I've got this beer.'

'But you don't like it. Have something to warm you.'

'I don't know what to have. I don't really drink. I only come in here for company. I'll have a small port, then,' she said in desperation, pushing away the glass of beer.

Iris brought it without surprise, although Lily had refused her a few minutes before. She took it for granted that it is better for men to pay if they will and that women do so only when they must.

Bertram stayed with Lily while she drank.

'Better?'

She nodded and flushed.

'You come in here for company and then sit all by yourself and speak to no one.'

'I'm not used to it. Coming in alone. I couldn't do it, only I know Iris. It's someone to talk to. When my husband was alive I used to go out with him a lot. That was different.'

'Your husband is dead?' he asked in a low voice, and he spoke kindly, although he used that brutal, forbidden word 'dead'. 'I'm sorry,' he was saying.

'Oh, just one of those things,' she said, as she had once heard a woman say in a film. She shrugged her shoulders.

'People no longer know how to mourn with dignity,' he thought. 'Do you live there all by yourself?'

'Yes.'

'Rather lonely, isn't it?'

'Yes.' She raised her eyes and he saw that she was afraid.

'Have another one of these.' She had finished her drink.

'No, I couldn't.'

'Who sees you home?' he asked, beckoning Iris, who refilled Lily's glass.

'I go home by myself.'

He saw the idea of being rescued light her eye. But 'With all these young men about?' was all he said and, lifting his glass to her, walked back to his cronies. She hated him then, knowing that he had led her to betray herself.

'This is Eddie Flitcroft,' Iris said, leaning over and pulling at his jersey, dragging him round. 'Mrs Wilson!'

'Lay off! Unhand me! Pleased to meet you, Mrs Wilson. I remember you. When I was a kid at the Sunday School Treat.'

'Do you?' she said listlessly.

'When I used to come and stay at Auntie's. Young Iris was in her pram, of course.'

'I thought you were a stranger here.'

'Me? No, little Eddie's no stranger. I was bred all round these parts.'

'I bet you was,' Iris sniggered.

'Well, what's yours?' he asked, looking at her glass. Girls do not introduce you to their friends except for you to buy them a drink.

'No, no more, thanks.'

'No?' He didn't try to persuade her, but sauntered away, whistling. Iris seemed fascinated by his swaying buttocks.

'Little show-off,' Lily thought.

'Time, *if* you please!' Ned Pallister shouted, glancing up at the clock.

In twos and threes they straggled out on to the pavement. Lily put down her glass and slid down from the stool. 'Good night, Iris,' she said quietly.

'Good night, dear.'

'Good night, Mr Pallister.'

'Good night, Mrs Wilson.'

She felt humiliated, being turned out on to the pavement on her own at closing-time.

'Don't run away,' said Bertram, crooking his elbow for her to take. She put her hand timidly on his sleeve and they walked along the pavement together.

'This is it,' she said, stopping in the doorway. 'Thank you very much.' She took her hand from his sleeve and began to search for the key.

'I will let you in. I will make sure the house is free of burglars.'

'I am not afraid of burglars,' she said truthfully.

He followed her in and shut the door, smelling camphor and stuffiness. The light, when she switched it on, was a poor illumination; half the bulbs had been taken or broken.

A red rope was looped round the stands of exhibits, and Bertram stepped over it and began to peer close while Lily stood back smiling, wondering how such a lot of nonsense could ever fill her with dread and loathing.

'Crippen, I recognise,' said Bertram, 'and there are Thompson and Bywaters. An interesting case that. And this – who is this?'

'That's the Blazing Car Murderer,' she said, with indifference.

'Oh, yes. A Mr Rouse, I remember.'

'There's nothing very up-to-date, I'm afraid. Murderers go out of fashion quickly. That's why you can often pick them up cheap from the big places.'

'It is better to find notoriety some other way, you think? Some

44

men long for a moment's fame at any price. In the old days they would go to their public execution as if they were heroes and had done something to be proud of, and would carry themselves with dignity and courage, feeling the centre of attention for the first time in their lives. They had little imagination. A hanged man is a sorry sight, and a hanged woman a sorrier. It is a great indignity to do to any human body – a sort of blasphemy, I think.'

Lily shuddered.

'So you live here among all these mild-looking men? What is this?'

'It's a panorama. It lights up. But it's getting a bit shabby now.' She switched on a light and he read out: 'A View of Tortures Used in the Middle Ages in Central Europe.'

'It's nothing to what we've got nowadays, is it? This is all rather a morbid background for you, my dear, but I suppose you never think of it. Where are your own rooms?'

'Up those stairs.'

'Run along, then. I will wait for you to get up there and then I will let myself out.'

'Won't you have a cup of tea?'

'Another time. And I'll come back in the daylight to look at the rest. Royalty and Crime. Is that what people like?'

'Yes, I suppose so.'

'Up you go, then.'

At the foot of the stairs she looked back and her eyes were shining. 'You have been kinder than you know,' she said. 'Good night.'

Bertram heard her running up the stairs and opening a door. He had another look at Dr Crippen and let himself out, slamming the door loudly. He walked back to the pub, feeling pleased with himself. Very tactfully he had done a great kindness. When he was kind to people he had to love them; but when he had loved them for a little while he wished only to be rid of them and so that he might free himself would not hesitate to inflict all the cruelties which his sensibility knew they could not endure.

At the Anchor Iris was putting on her coat. She had hoped Eddie would wait for her, but he had gone off at closing-time.

'Iris, dear, what can I do about my cuffs?' Bertram began at once, holding out his arms, his hands drooping miserably. 'Who in this place will look after my linen?'

'My sister would, I daresay.'

'I ask you because you always look crisp and starched yourself.'

She smiled a little into the mirror, rolling her hair with her fingers, looking expectant, as if she were going out for the evening.

'I'll ask Maisie.'

'There's a dear girl.'

'I suppose it was "dear" and "darling" all the way home with Mrs Wilson, too.'

'Yes, of course. I like young women.'

'Oh, you do?'

'Yes.'

'You'll get quite a name for yourself soon.'

'I hope so.'

'I even saw you jawing to the doctor's girl this morning.'

'Yes, a strange girl.'

'A bit touched, I should say. Stayed at school till she was nineteen.'

'I think she is beautiful.'

'Yes, she is,' Iris said fairly. 'Bar the eyes.'

'But her eyes are the most beautiful thing about her.'

46

'That's what you tell *me*. Oh, well!' She turned away from the mirror and became brisk. 'I must be off.'

'You look very nice. But it seems a pity. It must be your bedtime.'

'*You* might think so. Good night, Mr Pallister.'

'Good night, Iris.' He was bringing in a crate of lemonade.

'All these girls talk the same,' Bertram said to him when Iris had gone. 'It must be the cinema.'

'That's right. You seem to get the same answer no matter what you say. They come back at you very sharp but it don't seem to mean nothing. And they all stick out their bust such a devil of a way. It makes you wonder where to look sometimes.'

'Busts come and go,' said Bertram. 'When I was in my heyday they were thought nothing of and the girls all stuck their stomachs out instead. Well, when I say "stomach" you'll understand my meaning. Now, they're all frightened to let their breath go. But I daresay they'll soon be on the wane again.'

'It makes you wonder,' said Mr Pallister, 'how they do it ... Did you get on with your painting to-day?'

'Not so bad,' Bertram began in a sort of bedside manner. 'One of these days you shall have your little picture.' And he walked over and peered at the harbour scene on the wall in the corner.

'Well!' said Mr Pallister suddenly. 'Mrs Foyle never looked in for her supper beer.'

'She went to London for the day,' Bertram said, and turned back to the picture again, counting the waves, which were arranged evenly, corrugated, from the lighthouse to the horizon, and were still breaking a little into Chinese white as far out as the eye could see.

*

After supper Robert went to a nursing-home some miles out about an overdue confinement. He felt tired and bad-tempered and snapped at the matron when he was coming away.

'I did wonder if you would advise an induction,' she said, swimming down the corridor beside him, her skirts, her veil spreading and crackling.

'Too much interference these days. It can stay there till it grows whiskers as far as I'm concerned,' Robert said, opening the front door. 'Good night.'

'Good *night*, doctor.' Her lips smiled but her eyes blazed at his rudeness. He knew she would go hurrying upstairs to punish the patient, and he walked down the path between the laurels feeling ashamed.

He was high on the cliffs between the new town and the old, and inland a little, so that there was no smell of the sea. Far below, the lighthouse winked faintly and above the railway cutting a great plume of fiery smoke rushed along, buffeted by the wind and followed by the trim, gilt, lit-up train, the last train.

He freed the brake and let the car tip silently downhill until he was in the lamp-lit streets again, going slowly still, and only switching on the engine when he was by the station square.

Tory came quickly through the barrier carrying a large paper bag in one hand and her feathery hat in the other. She looked white under the station lights and a curl had sprung loose on her forehead.

He stopped the car and leant over, opening the door for her.

'What's all this clutter?'

'A new hat.'

'Why?'

She didn't answer, settling herself down with a great deal of rustling, pushing her hair up with the back of her hand.

'Been on a case?'

'Yes.'

'Baby?'

'Not *so* far.'

'Must be a bore.'

'I thought women found it exciting.'

'Oh, do they?'

'You're tired.'

'Yes, I feel tired and filthy dirty.'

'You've been to see your husband,' he said suddenly in an accusing way.

'Yes, I did.'

'But why? Why?'

'I get drawn back like a murderer to the scene of the crime, or a dog ... we won't go into that, perhaps.'

'Where did you see him?'

'He goes every day to the same place to lunch and it is also where I go when I am shopping. I see no reason why I should change my fixed habits to oblige him.'

Robert made no answer.

'I *have* to go,' she went on. 'I get the feeling that I must have a look at him to see if he's still alive.'

'Was he alone?'

'Yes. Well, I mean, he was with another man.'

'Did you speak to him?'

'Yes, he came to my table and said, "Good morning, Victoria," and I said, "Good morning, Teddy," and he said "How are you?" and I said "Very well, thank you, Teddy," and he said "That is a mad sort of hat you are wearing," and then he said "Will you excuse me?" and after that he went off.' She laughed. 'I had put on the new hat I'd just bought and it is very lovely,

49

like a little straw dish full of lilac. Yes, mad, of course, but hats should be, and dreadfully painful too. It felt like a crown of thorns and I kept putting up my hand to see if it had drawn blood.'

He swung the car into the garage at the back of the house and switched off the headlights. Tory began to rustle again.

'Tory!' he began, staring at the blackness before him.

'Yes, Robert?'

When he took her hand at once her fingers laced into his twisting tightly, answering him viciously and angrily as if she had awaited the touch too long. The dislike they had fostered, one for the other, had robbed them of tenderness. In the lamp-light from the street he could see a vein running straight down the centre of her forehead, pulsing, and he sat back away from her and looked at her, feeling her hand relaxed in his.

'I don't for one moment see what we are going to do,' he said inevitably and then, sharply, as if reproving her: 'We must go in.'

Feeling for some reason contemptible and undignified, she stood near the lamp holding her paper bag, waiting while he slammed the garage doors. In silence they walked round to the front of the house, where the wind waited for them at the corner, striking suddenly like an assassin.

Prudence knelt, as she often did, at the window-sill in the darkness of her room, wondering if Bertram would come out for his last stroll along the sea front. She knew that Robert would be angry with her for kneeling there in the night air and she did not call out when she saw him come round the corner with Tory.

'I am simply dog-tired,' she heard Tory say. And then: 'No, I want to go indoors by myself.'

In a quick and furious way Robert said suddenly: 'Tory, forgive me!'

'It is both of us,' Tory said, and put her hand up to her forehead – and Prudence, in great fear, drew back into the darkened room.

4

'I suppose Tory will come rushing in in a minute with her new hat,' Beth said at breakfast.

'I daresay,' said Robert. 'Prudence, you were coughing in the night. You must have the vapour lamp.'

'Oh, hell.'

'Don't set Stevie a bad example,' said Beth. 'She would get into trouble for talking like that at school. Who is this letter from, I wonder?'

'Probably from some old lady saying there is too much sex in your books,' said Robert.

'Oh, no! It is a young man's handwriting, I think.' Beth very slowly put on her spectacles.

'Well, then it will be to say there is not *enough*.'

'You *could* open it,' Prudence suggested.

'That is exactly what I intend to do.'

By now they were all on edge about the letter and looked at the Y.M.C.A. paper and the slanting lines of handwriting with impatience.

'Why, it is from Geoffrey Lloyd. Of course,' said Beth at last.

'I had forgotten all about him. And he would like to come to tea on – oh, dear, that's to-day – and if it's not convenient I am to let him know. But I don't see how, for he gives no telephone number. How on earth can I get a message to him at such short notice?'

'But *isn't* it convenient?' Prudence asked.

'Yes, I suppose it is. But I hate being rushed and unprepared.'

Beth glanced with regret at a little funeral picture she had in mind and had meant to describe later in the day. The thud of the clods on the coffin lid and so on.

'Well, then . . .' Prudence said and shrugged.

The old-time funerals were best, Beth thought, as she refolded the letter, the brown sherry and seed-cake, the floating crêpe, the horse-drawn hearse with all its carved black and its frosted glass. When we were children the plain liquorice-allsorts we called Norton's Horses. Norton was a famous undertaker, and his horses shone like liquorice and wore plumes on their foreheads, and in those days there was much to beguile a novelist, 'floral tributes', not merely wreaths – the vacant chair made out of chrysanthemums, or a carnation harp with a broken string, or a lovely pillow of white roses with the word 'Rest' in mauve everlastings.

'You did bring it on yourself,' Robert was saying.

'What a mercy I changed my mind about asking him for the week-end. We are rather out of cake, Prue. Could you knock up a few rock-buns this morning, do you think?'

'It sounds as if he'd do better in the canteen,' Robert said. 'Stevie, get the egg off your mouth and come along.'

'Did you go into prayers yesterday?' Beth asked.

'Yes.'

'What did Miss Simpson say?'

'I forget,' Stevie said, reddening.

'I will take you and wash you,' said Robert and he led her away, determined not to have another scene. Loving her small warm hand in his, he also felt it this morning to be a reproach, a reminder.

'Were you really coughing a lot in the night?' Beth asked Prudence.

'I didn't hear myself.'

'I didn't hear you, either. Robert must have slept not well. He was expecting the telephone all night. I kept falling into those deep, drugged sort of sleeps, full of nightmares, dreadfully tiring. An awful one about your granny. . .' Prudence resigned herself . . . 'I was almost afraid that I should find a letter about her this morning with bad news. I dreamt I was at her funeral and when we were in the church I suddenly noticed that the coffin lid was moving up and down very slightly . . .' Prudence poured herself more tea . . . 'And I called out in a loud voice "This funeral must not go on!" Robert was furious and told me not to be hysterical because unfortunately no one else could see that the coffin lid was bobbing up and down, and at last . . . Teddy Foyle was there, I don't know why . . . and he took one of those packing-case openers from his pocket and prised the coffin open . . .'

Prudence leant her chin on her wrist and looked at her mother, waiting.

'And it was full of a very fine set of Fielding in calf, that I once coveted very much in a shop in London, only it cost twelve pounds. But, of course, it was not to be expected that we should find them in Granny's coffin . . .' Prudence stirred and stirred her tea . . . 'And then Ethel, your Aunt Ethel, suddenly called out in a ringing voice: "I chopped Mother up and put her

54

in the boiler last night, to make room." And your father made a very nice and sensible speech asking us not to panic and saying, "You must all excuse Ethel. She is at a funny age." It seems so very vivid this morning.' She sighed, for the truth was that the memory of her dream funeral had rather spoilt the one she had mapped out for Chapter Thirteen, had made nonsense of it, in fact.

Robert put his head round the door.

'I was just telling Prue of a terrible dream I had last night about your mother . . .'

'I can't stop, dear. Another time. Stevie will be late.'

'No. All right. Good-bye, Stevie.'

Beth put her face under Stevie's large school hat and kissed her.

'How sweet young children are!' she said to Prudence when the others had gone. 'I think Tory won't be coming in for a cup of tea. I expect she was late last night and is lying in this morning.'

'She came by the last train. I heard her go by when I was in bed.'

'Then we'll clear the table,' said Beth, and put one cup into another as if beginning her day's work.

'I wonder what it is like being divorced?' Prudence said, looking at her mother.

'Perfectly horrible, I should think,' Beth said.

The day went on and Tory did not come. Beth remarked upon it several times, and again at lunch when Robert was there, but no one answered.

'I think I must go round and see if she is all right,' Beth persisted.

'All this running in and out,' Robert said. 'Women must live in one another's pockets. No wonder they quarrel so much.'

'I have never quarrelled with Tory in my life, not even when we were girls at school. I have never quarrelled with any woman.' Beth's relationships with people had always been of the most timid. Only on paper did she employ sharp words or risk a conflict. She had a sluggish nature and was lazy physically, but her head was full of clamour, her imagination restless.

'I wonder what time Geoffrey will come?' Prudence asked.

'At ten to four, I expect,' Beth said. 'That is the time I go out to tea.'

'I have never *known* you go out to tea.'

'When I was a girl I went at that time.'

'Perhaps things have changed since then.'

'I went to school with his mother,' Beth said, not irrelevantly.

Robert thought that having been to school with one another meant something special to women. Men never found it of interest, or felt themselves drawn together on that account; but women were entranced at the idea and retraced their steps tenderly together backwards to their girlhood, forever saying 'Do you remember, my dear?', shutting men out, implying (he thought) that it was in those days they were happy, before the world, men, impinged upon them. 'Or perhaps I am jealous of them,' he thought, since to-day all his heart's doings were suspect. 'Jealous of Tory and Beth.'

After lunch Beth put on a coat and went to call on Tory. She rarely went out-of-doors and consequently saw things freshly when she did, as if with the eyes of one released from a prison or sick bed. This was useful to her as a novelist. Everyday things did not become dull. She stood for a moment on the doorstep of Tory's house and surveyed the surroundings: the men on the ladders at Mrs Bracey's, Lily Wilson sitting on her window-sill high up, with her back to the street and the sash drawn down on her knees as she polished, the glass glinting blue, reflecting the dark sky. Out at sea a white sail tipped and turned, scarcely progressing.

Tory opened the door.

'Oh, that yacht!' she said at once, looking beyond Beth. 'It reminds me of Teddy. The old days when he took Edward out and I would keep running to the window to see how long I must keep lunch waiting. I wonder where – if – he sails now?'

Her house smelt of hyacinths and furniture-polish. She led the way into the room, where a little gilt fire rustled.

'Did you have a good day?' Beth asked.

'I didn't get those socks for you. I have only just remembered.'

'Did you get the hat?'

'Yes. I'll fetch it.'

Beth, still with her new eyes, glanced about her. She would have liked to have achieved such a room as this for her family, and felt the old guilt about her writing coming over her, and the indignant answer trying to smother it – '*Men* look upon writing as *work*.' Even if she wished to be released from it, as she sometimes did wish, she knew that she could not. The imaginary people would go on knocking at her forehead until she died. 'Haunted!' she thought. 'I'm haunted. Inside me I am full of ghosts. But I am nothing myself – I am an empty house!' And panic began to rush through her, so that when Tory came back, twirling the hat on her fingers, Beth stood staring, her hand at her throat.

'It certainly *is* a hat,' she said at last, as if hypnotised by lilac. 'What happens when it gets dirty?'

'I shall take it to London in a bag and put it on when I get there.'

She put it on now, standing before the mirror, the black and white striped paper on the wall behind a background to all the white linen flowers and her pink face underneath them.

'We haven't altered ... you and I ...' Beth said, watching her. 'At school you wore even those holland tunics with a difference. You never looked crumpled or inky like the rest of us.'

'*You* were always lying on your belly on the grass writing "Volume One" in a new exercise book.'

'Writing Volume One is easy,' Beth laughed. 'I used to start the book wondering what in God's name would come next. The physical act of writing tired me and I never reached Volume Two. The atmosphere around me ...' she waved her hand above her head ... 'must be full of half alive characters with no hope now of ever being brought to full-term. The best part of writing a book is when you write the title at the top of the page and your name underneath and then "Chapter One"! When that's done the best part's over.'

'You made a catalogue once of all the books you were going to write before you die.'

'Did I? When I think of all the words that have come pouring out of me since I was a child I feel dizzy.'

'A little veil would soften this,' said Tory into the mirror.

'Your face softens it.'

Tory laughed. 'Women pay all the best compliments in the end. And I doubt if men would pay any if we did not put them in their minds first.'

She took off the hat and perched it on a candlestick.

'Geoffrey Lloyd is coming to tea. Come in, too,' Beth said.

'No – I'd rather not. I always loathed his mother, and I hate going out to tea.'

'Did you see Teddy yesterday?'

'Yes, I did, as a matter of fact.'

'Why are you still in love with him?'

'I doubt if I am. But he has become interesting to me for the first time for years. I'm not used to being left high and dry by men, and naturally I'm intrigued by the one who could do it. He has simply flabbergasted me, but unfortunately too late.'

'Tory, I wanted to ask something of you.'

'Of course,' Tory murmured, but seemed at the words to become galvanised, ready to resist.

'It is dreadfully tricky, and if I didn't want it so badly I couldn't ask.'

Tory looked frightened now; her eyes seemed to go instinctively to her hat as if for reassurance.

'For God's sake tell me!'

'I am afraid it will bring up all those unhappy days when we first knew Teddy wasn't coming back any more . . .'

'I often think of them,' Tory said carelessly. 'It won't be bringing it all back. It is here already.' And she touched her breast and then her brow in a gesture of great beauty, Beth thought.

'You remember the time when he refused to answer your letters . . .?'

'Indeed, I do.'

'And nothing would make him. And Robert wrote to him . . .'

Tory frowned, remembering.

'And I sent a telegram . . .'

'And still nothing happened . . .'

'Then we had that idea of frightening him, so that we should *make* him come and talk to you . . .'

'Oh, the blood-stained letter!' Tory said suddenly and snatched a handkerchief out of her cuff and clapped it to her eyes, but it was laughter which had brought the tears, and Beth began to laugh, too.

'Oh, God, yes,' Tory went on. '"Dear Teddy, when you read this I shall be dead." I wrote it with the left hand so that it would seem my strength was failing, and we took it in the larder and dipped it in the meat-dish.'

'A piece of topside . . .'

'When I cooked that I felt as if I were eating part of myself. What fun we had even then!'

'But he did come. He thought you had opened a vein. It only made him angrier than ever.'

'Yes, but I got the chance to say what I wanted. I felt all right after that.'

'Robert was angry, too. He said he had always known that there is nothing women will draw the line at.'

'Yes, Robert was angry, too.' And Tory was suddenly sobered, and she smoothed her handkerchief out on her knee and then folded and refolded it. 'But what do you want to ask?' she said, looking up.

Beth was ashamed again. 'Tory, no one else knows about that, but just the four of us . . .'

'*She* probably knows, too. Teddy's young woman, I mean.'

'Oh, yes, of course. I hadn't thought of that.'

'What is on your mind?'

'I am in difficulties with my book.'

'Oh, I see.' Tory looked relieved and sly. 'You want your heroine to wipe *her* letters in the meat-dish.'

60

'I hardly knew how to ask you. I have got them separated and I cannot find a way of bringing them together again.'

'Suppose I had said "No"?' Tory teased. 'Does it matter more than your friends, more than your children? Or your husband?'

'There are some questions it is not right to ask. Like saying "Out of your children if one had to die, which would you choose?" It is a decision no one should be asked to make.'

'You and I ...' Tory said. 'We are so different. But nothing with men is so good as our friendship. If women love one another there is peace and delight, fun without effort. None of that wondering if the better side of one's face is turned to the light ...'

Beth scarcely knew what to say. The happiness she felt she had with Robert she would not smugly parade before Tory, who had no one. Instead, she said lightly: 'The smart young ones would find a sinister implication in your words.'

'Yes. They would overlook a trivial but everlasting thing about me – that I like to be made love to by men. Shall I get some tea?' She yawned slowly and deliberately like a cat, and closed her eyes, leaning back among cushions. After that Beth could not have answered yes.

'It's half-past three. I'll let myself out. Don't move. I must go and powder my nose,' Beth said, prepared to make this concession.

'Tell me to-morrow what Rosamund's little boy is like,' Tory called after her. She opened her eyes as she spoke, but when she heard the door slam after Beth she closed them again quickly, yet it seemed as if she did it needlessly, for the darkness which rushed over her came not from outside but from within.

At three o'clock the front-door bell startled the silence of the house. Prudence ran downstairs, hooking her frock up at the side, and found a very scrubbed-looking young man on the doorstep. Against the rough uniform his face was rosy and the belt round his middle brilliantly white.

Prudence could not help seeming put out and furious with her mother, thinking of her next-door with Tory. She invited the young man to enter the hall, which he did, turning his cap over and over and then tucking it into his belt.

'I am Prudence,' she said, leading him into the drawing-room, where she had meant to put a match to the fire at three-forty-five.

'My name is Geoffrey Lloyd. Your mother . . .'

'Oh, I know – she will be here in a few seconds,' Prudence said without confidence. She knelt down on the rather matted sheepskin rug and struck a match.

'Perhaps I have come too early,' he suggested.

'Good heavens, no!'

Flames threaded their way through the trellised firewood, and Prudence and Geoffrey sat on the edges of their chairs on either side. They watched the fire growing as if it were of tremendous importance to them.

'You're stationed here?' Prudence asked quickly, to cover up a little bubbling noise in her inside.

'Yes, over in the New Town.'

'Oh, yes!'

Her features became disorganised as she attempted a look of animated interest.

'My mother won't be long now,' she said after a pause.

'I think the wood is damp.'

'Yes, I think it is.' She lifted a log with the poker.

'Our mothers went to school together, didn't they?'

'Yes.'

'I've heard mine mention Mrs . . . your mother.'

'*Mine* mentions *yours*, too.'

'Oh, does she?'

'They were in the same form, weren't they?'

'Yes, I think they were.' He pulled down his sleeves, thinking his wrists looked rubbed and crimson. They could not for the moment find anything more to say about their mothers and sat there staring into the fire as if they were an old married couple at the end of a long life together and everything said for ever.

Suddenly Geoffrey brightened. 'Mine was hockey-captain.'

Prudence started. 'What?'

'My mother.'

'Oh, was she? . . . I hated hockey,' Prudence added.

'I can't believe that,' he said. Feeling that he had boasted about his own mother he went on: 'I have been reading one of your mother's books.'

He had rushed into the town and bought one the day he had received her invitation. It was ill-afforded but could be given to his mother for her birthday.

'What was it like?' But Prudence felt no curiosity about her mother's books.

'Well . . . you know what I mean . . . witty and observant and . . .'

'My mother? She never made a joke in her life. And she's as blind as a bat.'

The door-handle began to wobble and they both looked at it expectantly.

'Oh!' said Stevie. She came in and looked round the room as if she had never seen it before. 'Why is there a fire in here?'

Prudence flushed.

'This is my little sister Stevie,' she said and put her hand out as if to draw the child tenderly towards her.

'How did you get those flowers?' Stevie asked, staring at the bowl on the window-sill and ignoring Geoffrey.

'From the garden,' Prudence said shortly.

'You knew my father said not to pick the hyacinths. He *will* be in a bate.' At last she let her eyes dwell upon Geoffrey. 'Unless it was a special occasion,' she added, staring at him. 'Now I must go upstairs and be excused.'

'Why, Geoffrey!' Beth cried, hastening, unpowdered, into the room. 'How horrid of me not to be here. So you and Prudence have met again at last.'

'Again?'

'The last time, the only other time, Rosamund and I took you back to school to the Old Girls' Tennis Match – both of you in little silk smocks. We only did it to boast of what we'd got, to show the staff that at last we'd got the better of them. We went to the same school, you know,' she explained to Geoffrey.

'Yes,' he said. 'Yes.'

When at last Mrs Flitcroft brought in the tea they were all relieved.

'What darling little cups!' Stevie exclaimed, as if she were a stranger to the house.

Tory had a terrible afternoon, going from room to room of the silent house, trying to still herself. As the light was fading a letter dropped into the hall and for a moment she was afraid to pick it up. 'It is from Robert,' she thought, knowing that it could not be. It was from her son. She sat down on the hall chair and read it.

DEAR MOTHER,

I hope you are keeping quite fit I am. I am writing again as you will see. My father came to see me last Mon. and brought his wife a rather young woman he calls Dorthy, a rather nice woman. Please send honey. I miss you. Also more stamps. Excuse the writing. I am quite fit. A boy here called Henry says bloody and other words better not write them down in case of trouble. If you come to the school concert it would be best not to wear that hat with the red currents. Yours faithfully, E. Foyle.

A few days ago Tory would have run to Beth at once with this letter, worried and complaining. 'Look, Teddy is being deceitful. He didn't tell me he saw Edward. He is trying to take my child from me now.' And Beth would have listened and agreed. They would have hatched a little plot together and drunk some tea and she would have come back steadied and sane.

This evening, she walked up and down with the letter in her hand, feeling confused and wretched. Presently she sat down at her desk to write to Edward, something amusing if she could think of it. She drew a sheet of paper towards her and wrote carefully in script: '2, The Harbour, Newby,' but then in a sudden convulsion she scrawled the words 'Dear Robert, help me!' across the centre of the page. She dropped the pen and sat staring at what she had written, her hands tight together between her knees and her body trembling.

Late that night Iris sat on the bed cutting her toe-nails with a large pair of scissors.

'Don't get those bits in the bed!' Maisie said. She leant

forward to the little mirror which, propped at an obliging angle by a book called *The Madcap of St Winifred's*, gave back her face in a bluish, misty way. With her mouth and eyes wide, she plucked her eyebrows and as she dimmed the glass with her breath she reached up and wiped it quickly with her sleeve.

'I always remember this job the night my maid's out,' Iris said. 'These working-class people, they go off for their own pleasure and never wonder how you're going to manage without them, and not putting out my frock to-night either. She just ran my bath and said: "I'm off, Madam," just like that, and when I get back into the boudoir I can't find the key to my jewel-case and I have to wear my second-best pearls I'd been wearing all day, that single rope I had on my twenty-first . . .'

'Oh, for God's sake!' said Maisie.

Iris breathed heavily, reaching forward to her feet and snipping. She sat on the lumpy double-bed with its three brass knobs. The fourth had been unscrewed and lost long ago when they were children. The wall on one side of the bed was covered with photographs of film-actors. Behind the faded striped wallpaper, the plaster had fallen away unevenly and in places the paper was broken and letting out a little chalky dribble. In one corner was a large china doll with a matted wig and dusty eyelids. On the mantelpiece stood a china clock painted with violets. 'It will do for the girls' room,' Mrs Bracey had said years ago when it had stopped working. A curled-up photograph of Maisie looking more than naked in a wet cotton bathing-dress was propped against a vase of chenille catkins, and two stuffed love-birds sat on a lichened branch in a case which had lost all its glass; their beady eyes were smug as if they were on their honour to remain and would do so.

The façade of the old doll's house swung loose on one hinge

and inside it a headless doll sat up before a meal of plaster lobster and a chipped swiss-roll. Maisie's best dress hung against the wall, its hanger hooked on to a picture of Hope. The rest of their clothes were in a wicker hamper under the bed.

'This is the second night running Mrs Wilson's been in,' Iris said, brushing bits of toe-nail off the honeycomb quilt. 'To-night the old boy took her home again ...'

'Do you think he ...?' Maisie began, leaning close to the mirror.

'He goes indoors with her. Silly old fool. He's old enough to be her father. I've never been kissed by anyone with a beard.'

'Dad had one.'

'I don't remember. I don't fancy it, but she may like it. Tastes differ.'

'I think it's rather a shame,' said Maisie, turning round quickly.

'What's that?' Iris cried, covering her bosom with the blouse she had just taken off.

'Good night, girls!'

It was Eddie Flitcroft banging on their door on his way to the next bedroom.

Neither of them answered. When they heard his door shut they began to talk again, but in lowered voices, and Maisie undressed rapidly and climbed into bed beside her sister.

'Don't tell Mother about Lily Wilson,' Iris whispered.

'Of course not.'

'You're right over my side,' Iris complained, her face to the wall.

'Oh, no, I'm not.' Maisie put up a hand and felt for the middle rail of the bedstead and drew a line down between their two pillows. 'It's you,' she said, hitting Iris's behind.

'Shut up!'

'Don't kick.'

'I didn't.'

'Now girls!' came Eddie's voice from the other side of the wall.

They lay down quietly. 'Mother'll turn him out if he goes on like that,' Iris said.

They listened to him whistling, the floor creaking as he walked about, both of them sharply conscious of him there in the next room.

Maisie felt wide awake. She lay for a long time quietly, her cheek on her hand. Iris began to snore a little and seemed to uncurl in sleep, sprawling loosely in the bed, arms splayed out. 'Move over,' Maisie hissed, suddenly pushing her. After a while Iris began to snore again. Maisie lay there awake a long time.

5

As soon as Robert had gone off in the morning Tory came hastening round. 'Well . . .' she began, throwing open the door, her face bright with laughter. Then she saw Prudence clearing the table and she put an end to her laughter, which had not been real. 'Was it a nice tea-party?'

Prudence gave her a brief look and went out with the tray.

'Well, what is Rosamund's little boy like?' Tory asked Beth.

'He is rather big. An ordinary sort of boy, shy and fashionable.'

'Fashionable?'

'I mean his literary tastes are all so up-to-date, loving the right ones – Donne and Turgenev and Sterne – and loathing Tolstoi and Dickens. At any moment he will find himself saying a good word for Kipling. He has already said one for Tennyson.'

'So that is what you mean by being fashionable? Is he coming again? Has it led anywhere?'

'Yes. He asked if he might bring some of his own poems and read them to me.'

'What about Prudence?'

'Prudence?'

'I thought it was Prudence who was so lonely.'

'Prudence seems to have no interest in literature.'

'Perhaps she takes an interest in young men. For that matter *I* don't take any interest in literature.'

'Oh, nonsense, Tory. You *have* been *educated*. Girls of Prudence's age seem not to be educated at all. When they leave school they know one play of Shakespeare's inside-out and nothing else.'

'All the same, he might have taken Prudence to the cinema.'

'Perhaps he will.'

'It doesn't sound hopeful. He sounds like the sort of son Rosamund *would* have.'

'What on earth can Robert want?' Beth asked, at the window.

'Robert?' Tory seemed to flatten herself against the sideboard.

'Yes, he's come back.'

Forcing her eyes away from the mirror, Tory stood quite still, as if roots had run down from the soles of her feet. They heard Robert going along the passage and into the surgery.

'He has forgotten something,' Beth said.

'I had a letter from Edward—' Tory was beginning when Robert opened the door.

'It is odd,' she thought, 'for life to fall into such a symbolic pattern at half-past nine in the morning.' There was Beth at the window, dense and dreamy; she herself facing the mirror; over the room a little silence not longer than a second or two; and Robert ... Robert said: 'Good morning, Tory.'

'Good morning, Robert,' she replied, and gave a little stiff, sideways bow, as if she were Royalty.

'I forgot this,' he was saying to Beth, holding up a case. He gave Tory a look, but she did not know what it meant.

'Well!' Beth laughed when he had gone. 'You and Robert are so very formal with one another, it is quite amusing.'

Tory sat down at the table, which was still covered with a crumb-scattered cloth, ringed with cocoa-stains in Stevie's place and littered with torn-open envelopes. Staring at all this, Tory almost said: 'We love one another.' Her fingers gathered up the crumbs on the table, pleated an envelope. She could not speak. 'I love your husband,' she thought she would say. 'So please help me now, as you have always helped me before.'

'Oh, Edward's letter,' she said instead, and took it from her pocket and gave it to Beth. Seeing Tory's face, Beth was prepared for something disquieting. 'She is as nervous as a cat about the boy,' she thought. 'She will make herself quite ill.'

'Teddy is rather naughty,' said Tory disdainfully. She lolled back in her chair flicking crumbs across the tablecloth. 'Rather naughty and deceitful. He promised he would go only once a term to see Edward.'

'But he's his father,' Beth objected.

'He has other things. I have only Edward.'

Beth stood up and handed back the letter. She looked shocked for once.

'Tory, you mustn't make a battlefield of the child. You and Teddy tugging him in different directions.'

'Teddy is not to tug at all.'

'He can't help it. He can't suddenly give up being a father.'

'That's what it amounts to,' Tory said distinctly. 'I didn't ask him to leave us. He chose to. If that frumpish young woman means more to him than I do' – she glanced again in the mirror – 'or his home here, and his son ...' She shrugged. 'He

wants to eat his cake and still have it put out for tea every day.
I shall refuse to allow him to see the child ever.'

'You can't do that. It would be cruel to Edward.'

'Don't you think I know what is best for Edward?'

'No,' Beth said. 'No, I don't.'

They looked at one another with the frightened and astonished expression of people who have never quarrelled before.
Then Tory glanced quickly away. She got up and went to the
door.

'Tory, what *are* you worried about? You are always Edward's
mother. Who can alter that?'

'You talk as if you were Auntie Beth in one of the women's
papers,' said Tory, scornfully. 'You've no idea of what is real, and
how real people think.' She put her hand to her breast, as if she
were saying: '*I* am *real*.' She was suddenly swept away on a tide
of words such as came from Beth only through her pen. 'Writers
are ruined people. As a person, you're done for. Everywhere you
go, all you see and do, you are working up into something unreal,
something to go on to paper ... you've done it since you were a
little girl ... I've watched you for years and I've seen you gradually becoming inhuman, outside life, a machine. When anything
important happens you're stunned and thrown out for a while,
and then you recover ... God, how novelists recover! ... and
you begin to wonder how you can make use of it, with a little
shifting here, and a little adding there, something can be made
of it, surely? Everything comes in handy. At school you fell in
love with the English mistress ... it was the sort of thing ... so
sloppy ... one writhes about it when one's grown up ... laying
bunches of roses on her desk, writing poetry, drawing her name
in golden syrup across your porridge. But it was real then. I could
respect that. For years you tried to forget, and God knows I

72

wouldn't remind you, although I was as likely to fall in love with the gardener's boy as that creature; and then suddenly you start churning it round again, brisk and business-like ... "What can we make of this at three guineas a thousand?"' Beth looked up, as if she were watching a sleep-walker, but Tory swept on: 'Oh, I know! There you flicker into life. "Oh, but it is four guineas," you want to say, or five or ten. Your writing pride is hurt. The only pride you have. Damn the English mistress, whatever her name was – Eirene Crichton, that was it. She spelt it in the Greek way so that there was no mistaking she was different from everybody else – oh, and damn *me*, and your children *and* that boy you loved before Robert, who turned up in the last novel but one. I know you so well. I know you too well. Geoffrey Lloyd. I expect he'll come in handy, too. Damn Prudence and her loneliness. You are so used to twisting things that you can see nothing straight. One day something will happen to you, as it has to me, that you can't twist into anything at all, it will go on staying straight, and being itself, and you will have to be *your*self and put up with it, and I promise you you'll be a bloody old woman before you can make a novel out of that.'

She put her arm up across her face and turned away.

Beth led her to a chair and stood close to her, timidly, her hand on Tory's shoulder, although she disliked touching people.

'Tory, you seem all of a sudden to hate me,' she said in a gentle but perturbed voice. 'I don't know what to say.'

'I don't. I don't,' Tory sobbed, her tears hot through her sleeve. Beth had never seen her cry before. 'I really think I love you more than anyone else, except Edward.'

She lifted her face, and it was still pink and smooth, Beth was surprised to find, rather like a wet rose, certainly not without charm, and not in the least swollen or disintegrated.

She blew her nose loudly. 'I think it is the change of life,' she said, looking haughty.

'My dear Tory!'

'Have you a cigarette?'

'Of course.'

Beth got up and began to search, looking in all sorts of unlikely places.

'We must have a nice talk about our wombs some time,' Tory laughed, dabbing her eyes.

'Yes, that would be fun. Here is a rather bent Turkish one. Cigarette, I mean, not womb. Do you really think all this about me?' Beth asked shyly, holding out the lighted match, her hand shaking.

'Yes, I do,' Tory said. 'But I think it in a quiet way, not crossly like that. I feel you don't live in this world any longer. But your husband and children do. I do, too. You will balls everything up with your indifference one of these days. I sometimes wonder if you love them.' She stared in front of her.

'Love whom?'

'The children. And Robert.'

'But, Tory!'

'You do, then?'

'I should have to be a monster not to love my own children. And Robert? Why, I love him so well I don't even think about it any longer.' She had never been so embarrassed in her life.

'This cigarette is years old,' Tory grumbled. 'It smells of sealing wax and face-powder.'

'Oh, I beg pardon,' said Mrs Flitcroft, halting at the door and then, with a glance at the clock, coming into the room. Gathering up the tablecloth, she shook it over the carpet. 'The

74

sweeper'll take that lot up,' she exclaimed, and began to fold the cloth with one edge tucked under her chin. Tory winked at Beth as she threw the cigarette away, her lashes flicking down, still wet. Beth smiled back, and her hands fell apart in a bewildered little gesture.

Mr Lidiard, the curate, was due at three, and Mrs Bracey leant back with her face turned to the clock, but her eyes shut, for a watched clock never moves, she had long ago decided. She imagined the afternoon outside, the bitter, washed-out sky, the sea slapping down one wave after another on the shore, the grit swirling along the streets. And Mr Lidiard she saw, too, stepping out from the ugly brick vicarage where he lodged and slamming the nail-studded door, under his arm three or four books. She took him through the churchyard for a short cut. Here the old gravestones lay this way and that, dark slabs sunk into the rank grass, but farther away from the church the new granite block with the fancy lettering – 'Alfred Bracey, aged 49' – and a space underneath ... her heart turned over at the thought. 'I shan't go out of here again, save when they carry me feet first,' she often said to people. Now it occurred to her that it was true. 'Oh, my God, let it not be true!' she prayed. She opened her eyes. Five minutes more at least.

Maisie was in the shop with Mrs Flitcroft. Presently they came into the back room to try on a corset. Mrs Bracey watched with interest while Mrs Flitcroft took off her skirt and an old cardigan Beth had given her for polishing rags, next a petticoat and lastly what could only be called drawers. Mrs Bracey lay back smiling, hoping for Mr Lidiard to walk into the middle of this scene, longing to see Mrs Flitcroft making for the scullery in her combinations. Maisie was lacing her up.

'Tighter, dear. I like to feel something in the small of the back.'

'How's the doctor's wife?' Mrs Bracey asked her.

'They're a funny lot. Her and Mrs Foyle had a proper set-to this morning. I come into the middle of it to do the dining-room. Mrs Foyle crying.'

'Not she!' Mrs Bracey said, full of scorn.

'That's right. She was standing up by the door crying. Temper. I never heard the like. Of course I had to creep away and come back later. They never saw me. That's right, Maisie. That seems all right.'

'What was it all about?'

'Don't ask me. "You'll be a b. old woman before you can do something or other," I heard her say. The language was something terrible. I always say it takes some beating when a couple of ladies let fly.'

'Ladies!' said Mrs Bracey. 'I like that.'

'I got nothing against Mrs Cazabon. Nothing at all. You have to speak how you find. Well, I think that's the ticket, Maisie.'

'Suspenders a bit on the long side,' Maisie said.

'When I goes out later in the morning to do the steps,' Mrs Flitcroft continued, stepping into her drawers, covering her colourless, veined thighs, 'there's Mrs F. as merry as a lark with the old boy from the Anchor, and he's cleaning her front-door brass for her. And laugh! You'd never think that an hour earlier she was crying her eyes out.'

'What, old Pallister?'

'No. The old boy staying there. Proper old sailor. Hemingway, that's the name. A beard,' said Mrs Flitcroft, drawing her fingers out from her chin.

'What was he doing that for?'

'Ask me another.'

'There's the shop bell!' Maisie said. 'Oh, it's Mr Lidiard. Into the scullery, dear.' She addressed all her customers as 'dear'. Mrs Flitcroft gathered up her clothes and was bundled away, so that Mr Lidiard could be called in. One way and another it was being a delightful afternoon to Mrs Bracey.

'Good afternoon,' said Mr Lidiard, his face looking bitten by the cold.

'Won't you sit down?' Maisie asked, fussing.

'There's Mrs Flitcroft's cardigan. Take it out to her,' said her mother. 'She's putting on her drawers in the washhouse,' she explained to Mr Lidiard.

'Oh, yes.' He seemed to take it for granted that this should be, refusing to let her ruffle him or surprise him. 'Where's Iris to-day?'

'She's laying down on the bed. Just finished her dinner. Her feet ached.' ('If that silly fool's coming, I'll take my book upstairs,' was what she had really said, going off in her stockinged feet, and taking a handful of toffees and *Woman and Beauty*.)

Mr Lidiard put two books on the bed and edged back again on to his seat.

'What's this? *Little Dorrit*? I don't get on with Dickens, he's too vulgar. *Hakluyt's Voyages*. That looks better.'

'It belongs to the Vicar, so don't spill your dinner on it.'

'You can take back the other,' she said ungraciously. 'I like a nice true book, something you can get your teeth into. If there's any make-believe to be done, I can do it myself, out of my own head. *Foxe's Book of Martyrs*. I enjoyed that. And *Seven Pillars of Wisdom*. But that was a bit tiring, to hold up I mean. *The Newgate Calendar*. Did you ever read that? And what was the other book I liked? Maisie!'

'Yes, Mother?' She came out of the scullery, followed by Mrs Flitcroft, fully dressed.

'What was the book I liked so much?'

'How do I know?'

'Well, I said at the time. "A pity they don't write a few more of the same kind," I said. About one of the Gaiety Girls married an old titled gentleman. Her life story.'

'I couldn't say, I'm sure,' said Maisie.

'I've got no patience with all these novels Iris sticks her head into. Everyday life. That's good enough for me. Are you comfortable, Mrs Flitcroft?'

Mrs Flitcroft nodded hurriedly.

'I hear Mrs Foyle's getting herself talked about again,' Mrs Bracey went on, turning to the curate.

'Mother, don't gossip.'

'Let him see her in her true colours.'

Mr Lidiard stiffened. He would have spoken up for Tory, but he realised it was useless. With Mrs Bracey there was nothing to do but wait for her to die, which she would probably do long after her time.

'Did he go inside with her afterwards?' she asked Mrs Flitcroft.

'After what?'

'Cleaning the brass.'

'I couldn't say, I'm sure,' Mrs Flitcroft said, very off-hand, for the curate's benefit, but nodding behind his back.

'There's the shop again, Maisie. When you've finished serving we'll have a cup of tea.'

But it was not a customer. It was Bertram, carrying a bundle of shirts under his arm.

'Good God!' he thought, checked and confounded. 'The

78

things I let myself in for.' His eyes went at once to Mrs Bracey and hers to him, as if each recognised in the other something above the stature of curates, charladies and young women. 'Beauty in vile ugliness,' he told himself, imagining he looked at her with the eyes of Rembrandt.

'Oh,' said Iris, coming into the room in her stockinged feet. She didn't like Bertram catching her off her guard, with holes in her heels, her skirt crumpled. She looked reproachfully at her sister, who should have warned her.

'I am getting to know everyone,' Bertram was saying, and began to count them by name on his fingers: when he mentioned Mrs Wilson, Iris and Maisie exchanged glances; when he said 'Mrs Foyle' (and he said her name last) they all looked down. 'And the place that's shut up? Who lives there?' he asked.

'No one,' Mrs Bracey said. 'Not local people at all. Bloody interlollopers from London. They been coming down every summer for years and taking the fat of the land and soon as the weather gets bad they hop it.'

'Well,' said Mrs Flitcroft (and she got a look from Mrs Bracey for butting in), 'you can't blame them. No visitors, no money.'

'Are there visitors, then?' Bertram asked, but he did not know how deep this question went with them, nor how little they cared to give an answer.

'There used to be,' Mrs Bracey said, after allowing a little silence to rebuke him, 'when I was a girl' (she saw herself, black-stockinged, the white wings of her pinafore standing up on her shoulders, playing hopscotch, or patting a ball against a brick wall, or running out with a jug for a pint of vinegar), 'when I was a girl this was shipbuilding country. And for years before that. Building yards where you're sitting this minute. Out in the washhouse there's an old mooring-post. Iris!' she said suddenly, raising her voice, 'take this gentleman to see the post.'

'Oh! Mother, he doesn't want to see that.'

'Yes, he does. Don't you? And leave off picking at your nails like that, Iris. If you must put that muck on them for God's sake leave it be.'

Iris sighed theatrically and stood up. 'You'd better come,' she said to Bertram, 'for peace and quiet.'

He stood up eagerly, for Mrs Bracey was right. He did want to see. Curiosity about what was out of sight had always dominated his life and led him into difficulties, disasters and much boredom. He wanted to see not so much the mooring-post but what was behind the door, and he went out into the dark scullery with Iris and looked round quickly. 'Yes,' he said to her, 'that's interesting.' But what he found interesting was the cracked mirror above the sink, Iris's dinner plate not washed up, Eddie's shaving brush on the window-sill beside a flower-pot all overgrown with maiden-hair fern, and the tap dripping into a bowl of water. Iris stood by sulkily, dissociating herself from all her mother's doings.

'Yes, that's interesting,' he repeated for Mrs Bracey's benefit, returning to the kitchen, his head bent as he came through the low doorway.

'My mother remembered when they used to carve figure-heads on the boats, great women with big busts and drapery and crowns on their heads. Painted.'

'That's right,' said Mrs Flitcroft, nodding.

'And then the industry died out or shifted?' Bertram asked.

'Went up north. Then they opened that hotel on the hill. "The Newby Bay." Visitors started to come. We had a concert party every summer.'

'Yes, I heard about the concert party,' Bertram said.

'Oh!' Mrs Bracey glanced at her two girls.

'Then the New Town began to grow round the Point?' Mr Lidiard, a foreigner, suggested.

'Yes. It's milder there. More sheltered. They got a pier and Italian Gardens.'

'Ice Cream Parlour,' said Mrs Flitcroft.

'Cinema,' the girls added.

And then a little silence fell over them.

'What happens at the Fun Fair?' Bertram asked.

'Slot-machines and pin-tables and those funny mirrors.'

'I hate them,' said Mrs Flitcroft.

'Every summer I think they'll make it their last, but they always turn up. One morning it's peaceful, and the next they're in and the shutters up and music coming from one of those penny-in-the-slot machines all day long.'

'You hear it right out over the harbour, my man says,' Mrs Flitcroft put in.

'And *he* stands out the front with his arms folded and bawling his head off London ways. Fair people, I always say they are. And pigging it in those upstairs rooms.'

'When do they come?' Bertram asked.

'You'll see. They'll come all right.'

Mrs Bracey thought how it would be: one morning she'd hear the braying, tinny music and would know the summer had come. And though she pretended she hated it, she would always call to Maisie to leave the shop door open, and her heart would quicken, feeling life stirring outside.

Bertram guessed that the opening of the Fun Fair had some especial meaning to them all, as if they could not face a time when the London interlopers did not come, when they would be abandoned. It was, perhaps, to them the measure of the outside world's recognition.

He stood up to go and, bending to take Mrs Bracey's hand, he picked up the book from the bed. '*Hakluyt's Voyages*,' he said aloud, holding the book as if he were judging the weight of it, and looking at her with eyes which seemed to judge her, too. 'I could do so much for you,' he thought, and the old desire to make himself felt, to make himself indispensable, came over him. 'Shall I come again?' he asked her.

'You can please yourself,' she said.

'Well, then, I will.' He laid the book down on the bed again.

'Good day to all of you,' he said, grandly, to the other four. Maisie went after him to see him out. As he passed Iris he smacked her hands down, for she was picking her nails again, absorbed.

'Wet Paint,' he read aloud off the pavement and looked up at the half-finished shop-front; then he smiled at Maisie and walked away.

Mrs Flitcroft was favourably impressed. 'Look at the quality of these shirts,' she said, leaning over quickly to finger his bundle of washing. 'I only hope Maisie does them justice.'

'My Maisie knows how to wash and iron,' Mrs Bracey said calmly.

'So friendly,' Mrs Flitcroft marvelled.

Mr Lidiard was called upon to agree.

Mrs Bracey withheld comment, but when Maisie brought in the tea she gave a smooth, pleased sigh. 'It's been a nice afternoon,' she said, smiling round at them all, but she had to add, 'for once.'

*

Lily Wilson sat behind the lace curtains with *Lady Audley's Secret* on her lap, but it was too dark to read. Although awaited, the first flash of the lighthouse was always surprising and made of the moment something enchanting and miraculous, sweeping over the pigeon-coloured evening with condescension and negligence, half-returning, withdrawing, and then, almost forgotten, opening its fan again across the water, encircled, so Lily thought, all the summer through by mazed birds and moths, betrayed, as some creatures are preserved, by that caprice of nature which cherishes the ermine, the chameleon, the stick-insect, but lays sly traps for others, the moths and lemmings. 'And women?' Lily wondered, and she turned down a corner of *Lady Audley's Secret* to mark the place, and stood up yawning.

She banked up the fire with small coal and put on her coat, for 'Why sit alone when I might be in company?' she asked herself uneasily. Downstairs the waxworks seemed to stand in a greenish, submarine light. She hurried between them and, opening the door, was struck by the buffeting wind, which she took into her lungs with relief.

'Each evening I go a bit earlier,' she thought, hurrying along to the pub. 'Bob wouldn't like it.' ('But he shouldn't have left me,' the little voice in her breast whispered, the little voice the bereaved try not to hear, for it is full of reproaches to the dead, who have forsaken them but are beyond blame.)

During the evening Prudence met Bertram on the quay and walked with him beside the rocking water, complaining of her life and how, as soon as she made plans, bronchitis overtook her – and it had been the same always as long as she could remember.

'Oh, the young!' he thought. 'The egotism of the young.'

'It is hateful,' she said, meaning her youth, her life. 'The old ones keep everything to themselves.'

'Except the things they cannot keep,' he said. 'Beauty, the unwrinkled eyelid, the round cheek, the bright hair.' He continued the catalogue to himself, looking at her in the lamplight.

Passing Tory's house, she had the feeling of having touched something loathsome unexpectedly, the quick recoil and the will summoned to make an effort of forgetting, and she looked away from the lighted window as if some frightening image might be printed upon the thin curtains. She had such a feeling that her father was in Tory's house, that when he drove up at his own front door she felt shocked.

Bertram said good night and strolled back towards the pub, and Prudence was forced to arrive at the doorstep at the same time as her father.

'What are you up to?' he asked, sorting out his bunch of keys.

'I went for a breath of air.'

'And did you get it? Who is that man?'

'Mr Hemingway.'

'For God's sake, Prudence, don't go wandering round the harbour in the dark. It's the worst thing for you.'

'Don't fuss me.'

He opened the door and let her in. His first movement was always towards the telephone-pad, which he read with absorption and annoyance.

Prudence felt that the shabby, badly-lit hall was unbearable in its changelessness. It was, perhaps, a desire to explode its calm dreariness, the feeling that all alteration must be for the better, that made her suddenly say: 'Mother and Tory had a quarrel this morning. Would you believe it?' she added, laughing in a frightened way.

He looked up from the pad in his hand and stared at her. She could not believe that she was looking at her own father; his expression was for a second incredulous, full of panic. 'He is afraid to ask me about it,' she thought.

He unhooked the old-fashioned telephone with a movement so agitated that he might have been trying to get the fire brigade. Running his tongue between his lips, he waited, and at last gave the number. Prudence walked past him and upstairs, and as she reached the half-landing she heard him saying: 'This is Dr Cazabon and I want Matron, please.'

Now, later, she lay in bed, naked, as she liked to be, with a cat on either side; silken fur against her flesh; cold, padded feet upon her. She felt oppressed by the sudden view of her parents as human beings, a view she had not formerly imagined possible. To a girl who had taken for granted that her mother and father were sub-human creatures, from whom might be expected no emotions stronger than irritation or anxiety, or a calm sort of pleasure, this sudden view opening out was not easily to be borne. She felt shame and disgust and terror. She was not prepared to pity her mother, whom she had always rather despised, nor to despise her father, whom she had loved. That he deserved to be despised she did not for a moment doubt. At the first signs of her house cracking, she saw it lying in ruins, and that he was false to her mother and had lived with Tory (her mother's best friend) in adultery (and by 'live' she meant 'popping in and out of her house at odd times') for years and years, she believed without hesitation. Her parents had encouraged the idea of themselves as stoics, they had never displayed affection for one another in front of the children and, although sometimes they bickered slightly, they had always stood together and hidden any deep displeasure. 'We are the meal-providers, the rule-makers,' they seemed to say. 'Do not embarrass us by demanding more.' Prudence could not imagine her mother crying or using harsh words. She had listened to Tory's muffled sobbing and raised voice with incredulity that morning, standing by the kitchen dresser hanging up cups, and feeling her wrists weaken and terror strike at her. She lay in bed remembering all this. Then she saw another picture, of the day Stevie was born. She was fifteen. She came in from school, and her mother was telephoning in the hall, wearing her old dressing-gown. She heard her say, 'Good-bye, Robert. Don't hurry,' and there was a ring of whiteness round her mouth, but she turned and smiled at Prudence and said: 'Hullo, dear. Did you have a good day?' as she always asked when she was not busy writing. She looked different, and yet her voice was carefully the same. 'Do you want tea here or with Tory?' she had asked. 'I'll go in with Tory,' Prudence said, knowing the rules of this game. 'She must have been in pain,' she thought now. 'And then, when her books come out, perhaps she is excited after all, perhaps she feels it is a special day, different from the others. And perhaps she is sometimes frightened or disappointed. And now may be grieved.' But her new picture of her mother was no more like the real Beth than the old one.

She gently lifted the cats' claws from her bare sides and they came burrowing through the bedclothes until their cold noses were thrust against her neck.

The real Beth was undressing. She put on a wide, old-fashioned nightgown, which Robert called Big Top, and began to brush her hair.

'We forgot Prudence's vapour-lamp,' Robert began when he came in.

'Oh, so we did. But she seems better.'

'She was out this evening. It really is maddening.'

'Stevie seems tougher than poor Prue.'

'She's not tougher in her mind.'

'No. At tea-time we were just having a cosy time, and she suddenly said: "Which do you want to be when you're dead? Burnt or buried?" I hope she is not going to be morbid.'

'What did you say?'

'Oh, I said it didn't matter either way, because when you're dead you're not there.'

'She wanted an answer.'

'What would you have said?'

Beth looked so worried now, sitting there looking at him through the mirror, that he laughed.

'I should have said that both were so delightful I wouldn't know which to choose.'

And then she laughed, too, and began to brush her hair again.

6

As the days went by it seemed to Lily Wilson that her very happiness was staked upon Bertram. The pattern of her life was reversed and all her days bent towards the evening. No longer did she fear the light failing and all those wretched thoughts about the future, about loneliness and old age, about money, seemed not to accompany her into bed if she were warmed with wine. Her mind would go backwards over the evening, not groping timorously into the future. In the warmth of Bertram's kindness her personality seemed to unfurl; she became, she thought, someone different, someone she would always have liked to have been. His curiosity melted her reserve. He was an inquisitive old man, she knew; but his interest in her life gratified her, so that everything she did had importance now and she fell into the habit of remembering incidents for him, and all that occurred to her during the day she tried to see with his eyes and would furbish every turn of phrase for his delight. She knew that he would not stay for ever; but 'surely he will help some miracle to happen to me before he goes,' she would think, so deeply did she now rely upon him.

In the evenings at the Anchor she still sat by herself upon the stool and he still played dominoes with the old men, but from time to time he came over and bought a drink for her and for Iris, and always at closing-time he offered his arm to her and carried her off with such grandeur that they might have been going down the aisle of a church together. When they reached her home there were little jokes about Dr Crippen and Mrs Dyer, and upstairs, cups of tea and Bertram going up and down the room, picking up ornaments, peering at old photographs, talking, asking questions, explaining things to her about her own possessions, things she had never wondered about – how the ship got into the bottle, how the glass paper-weight became full of bubbles, how the bead-work stool was made. A kitchen chair became something different as he took it up and described how the legs were turned, how the back was bent, when it was made and from what woods. Then it stopped being the kitchen chair and became an extension of his personality. He was everywhere in her house and whispered from every corner, from the lustre jug, which she had never thought beautiful before, and the picture painted on glass with its look of a thunderstorm which she had not found as funny as it was. Even Bob's mother's wedding photograph she smiled at now as she would scarcely have dared to do before – the bride who looked, Bertram thought, so like a little girl dressing up in lace curtains for a charade, and the bridegroom less real than the models downstairs, beneath their feet a strip of rucked-up carpet and behind them apparently rocks of a great height and a cascade.

Bertram belittled her discontent, dismissed her ambitions. 'My dear child, of course you don't want to go and live in the New Town. There you are nobody, here you have a place among people who know you. There, everything is artificial, here there is character.' So character began to be something she comforted herself with; it compensated for everything, he implied, comfort and luxury and cleanliness. She saw that there was much to laugh about in her life, for just so long as she might share her laughter.

He talked, and drank his tea, and went, and since she had no reason to be ashamed of their relationship she innocently believed she would not be gossiped about, especially as he was old enough to be her father, as Iris had said.

Once he called in the daytime to see the waxworks, but then she felt awkward and shy, finding nothing interesting to say and evading his direct questions. She did not know why. He looked out at the harbour from her front window and found all the buildings arranged differently. From here – for the foreshore curved slightly – the Cazabons' house stood forward, a square stone house, built, said Bertram, about seventeen-forty, its slates tucking down under a parapet (even the slates had names to Bertram – Duchesses and Countesses and Queens) and two front windows blocked in to save the tax (Lily had sometimes wondered why); this curiosity did not extend merely to those who now lived in the house but to the ones who had built it and all those who had gone in through its front door in so many different kinds of clothes from seventeen-forty onwards.

This view of life was novel to Lily, who had always thought of the past in two sections – what seemed to her to be living memory, and then the great stretch of darkness behind that curtain which had come down so finally, so sharply-dividing, on January the first, nineteen-hundred. Now, people began to peek through this curtain at her, and she found herself wondering about them.

'*Lady Audley's Secret*, forsooth!' Bertram said one day, picking up her library book. 'What do you want with this?' For he, like Mrs Bracey, found life richer than fiction.

Next day Lily took her book and changed it, so that she never found out what Lady Audley's secret was, although she sometimes idly wondered. Instead, she took home a book about Queen Anne, in whom she felt a vague interest, for she reflected Bertram faintly, the poor Queen; she was stupid and was bullied, and all her children died, he said. But the book was rather dull, and was not given colour, as Bertram's talk was, by gossip, by irrelevancy, by trivial but beguiling detail. On the whole she rather regretted Lady Audley.

The Librarian had been nonplussed. 'What's this? Non-fiction?' he had said, warming the book in his hands as he always did. No one read non-fiction, apart from the book on poultry-keeping. (Mrs Bracey would not have library books in her house, for they carried infection, she said. Germs, which she imagined as rather like invisible tadpoles, were her sly and lively enemies, and Maisie was always made to inquire carefully about the clothes she bought from people, especially the wardrobes of the deceased, as her mother called them. 'I've known folks take leprosy that way,' she sometimes said, fright-ening the girls.) When at last the Librarian put the book into Lily's hand he felt as if he gave something of himself with it, and the idea was delightful to him – indeed, he did give some warmth, but Lily quickly drew on her knitted gloves.

Now, after tea the days were prolonged a little and the blue veils came down later over the harbour. In the country at that time of the year the birds sing, staking their claims upon every branch, but at the seaside there were only the gulls, and these walked stiffly on the quayside or rose up, their yellow claws to their bellies, at the approach of the fishing trawlers, wheeling over them as they slowly came in from the sea, their holds full of fish, the waves combing away on either side.

Lily took a little walk before turning in at the Anchor. She almost went in to see Mrs Bracey, knowing it was time she did, but the evening air seemed so sweet that she was reluctant to leave it. She abhorred ill people, pity could never overcome her shrinking. 'The longer I stay away,' she thought, 'the more courage I shall have to find in the end. If it were me I should think it a very little thing for anyone to do.' But then, she could not imagine people ever shrinking from herself. It was different.

She walked for a little along the sea-front to where the path ended under the cliff, with its stunted trees and the slate-coloured stone among which valerian grew in summer, and which shone now with recent rain. When she went into the Anchor Bertram was not there. She ordered her drink and sat alone, for Iris leant over the bar at the other end, watching Eddie Flitcroft playing darts.

Lily would not ask about Bertram, so she sat still and sipped slowly, and pretended to watch the game and waited. Each time the door opened, which it seldom did, she turned her head.

'And so you loved your husband?' Bertram asked.

A pinkish light came through the fluffy curtains as if it were left entangled in the muslin after it had gone from the outside world. Tory sat on the sofa with her feet up and her lap full of fashion papers.

'At least there was a history of passion behind us,' she said calmly, looking at her shoes. 'He was rather a stupid man,' she added, 'but, then, I am rather a stupid woman.'

'Is he no longer stupid, then?'

'No, I don't mean his stupidity is a thing of the past, but that he himself is. At least, as far as I'm concerned.' She turned and looked at him and laughed. 'You insinuate yourself into people's lives,' she said, and moved her hand to and fro so that it looked like a fish weaving its way through weeds.

'Yes,' he thought to himself, 'they will all remember me. Years after, they will say to one another, "that was the summer *he* came," like the man in the concert party who wore the pink-and-white striped blazer and whom they all remembered and so often talked about. Where was he now? But wherever he was he had left something of his personality in the place as other visitors had not, a thumb-print, something not tangible like Mr Walker's oil painting hanging in the Anchor, but the very gentlest of mementoes, a stirring-up of the imagination merely. And I will leave both,' Bertram decided, 'the tangible and the intangible, the souvenir and the memory itself, the thumb's pressure and the painting in the bar parlour.'

'I am a painter,' he suddenly said to Tory, who had been thinking of her husband.

'A *real* painter?' she asked, looking up.

That was the question. All at once he felt like telling her the truth as he glimpsed it at that moment, that he was not a painter and never would be, that he would have no immortality, leave nothing to linger after him, had no hope of greatness, day-dreamed merely, frittered time away, let curiosity beguile him. But he could not bear the truth, even for a second, not for himself, still less to share.

'That is not for me to say,' he replied primly. And looked old suddenly and exhausted.

But he soon recovered. He began to walk about the room,

93

examining all the little treasures, as he did at Lily Wilson's, turning the Dresden china upside-down so that Tory laughed and asked if he expected to find the price written on the bottom. 'He is a goatish sort of man,' she thought to herself, 'a mischievous, a prying kind of man.'

Bertram still thought about his painting as he went restlessly from one ornament to another, and he stood with a piece of Bristol glass in his fingers and said: 'Unlike Picasso,' – and he gave what he considered a dry laugh – 'I do not *trouve*, nor even *cherche*. I merely hope to get overtaken.' He could bear as much of the truth as that and could even add: 'I am devilish lazy.'

'And I,' Tory said, yawning into her two hands.

'It is odd for a woman like you to crop up in a place like this,' he went on, looking at her grey, draped frock which he knew to be fashionable as well as beautiful.

'Crop up!' she repeated. 'In what way do I crop up?'

'I should expect a woman with untidy hair and a fisherman's jersey and trousers to live in such a place.'

'It used to be our holiday house. My husband liked sailing. He was inclined to be rich.'

'Is that a thing which still goes on, or has it stopped as far as you're concerned?'

'He pays me money, as he should and must. A man cannot be allowed to reserve a woman's beauty for himself until it is gone, and then throw her on to the market again with nothing left to sell.'

'You are trying to hurt yourself,' he said gently. 'Thank heaven, a woman's beauty is different from a flower's. Her petals do not drop as soon as she reaches perfection. She remains at that stage – at your delightful stage – for many a long year.'

'Her petals do not drop,' Tory conceded, 'but little lines appear here and there, at the corners of her mouth, between her eyebrows' ... she put up her fingers and smoothed her forehead ... 'and then the edges of her face grow vague, the skin wrinkles ...' she pinched up a little of her arm, which was scattered unevenly with freckles like a linnet's egg ... 'Young skin doesn't wrinkle.'

'If that is the worst that will happen ...' Bertram began.

'Oh, but it isn't. It is only the beginning. The invisible enemy against which one slaps on cream, and massages, and tries out all the little tricks these books ...' she tapped her fingers on the fashion papers in her lap ... 'put one up to. To stave it off for one day longer, to have one day more of looking beautiful.'

'You talk like a courtesan,' he told her.

'Every birthday one wonders: "Shall I go out of this year as I entered it?"'

'Oh, birthdays!' she thought to herself. 'Birthdays on my own. Trying to be gay for Edward's sake. Beth giving me some bloody silly present because she is full of absurd notions such as it is the thought that matters, not the gift. And the evening going slowly by, full of memories – memories of parties, of toasts, of little jokes, of cakes with too few candles, of the glossy brown and pink deckle-edged cards Teddy always found, pictures of nineteen-eighteen flappers, curly roses, kittens with hand-painted eyes – "To My Dear Wife" and then a little verse.' Her bosom rose sharply in a sigh and then she laughed.

'I must polish this old knife-box for you,' Bertram said. He lifted the lid a little. It was full of papers. 'Oh, I beg your pardon. The best thing is a soft cloth wrung out in hot water, and then an even softer cloth to bring up the surface.'

'You have lived in ships far too long,' she said. 'If I make a little omelette, would you slip in next door for the beer?'

She swung one foot, then the other, to the ground and stood up stretching, her hands clasped behind her head. 'The pink jug on the hall-table,' she added.

'So now I'm the one who carries the jug,' Bertram thought, going along the pavement in the gathering darkness.

The bar was very quiet. Lily sat on her stool and she turned her head as he opened the door.

'Now, what are you going to drink?' Bertram asked her, coming up briskly.

'No, I couldn't really,' she said quietly; and her glance slid uneasily from the pink jug he had put down upon the counter. She took up her glass of beer and drank it bravely, trying to smile at him.

'Why must we drink this flat beer?' Bertram asked, flopping some out into a glass where it stood without a bubble upon it. 'Why can't I get some bottled ale?'

'It gives me wind,' Tory said. When she cut the omelette in half grey mushrooms fell out. It was delicious, he thought, but not enough. Women never give one enough to eat, he decided, taking more bread. God knows why men ever marry any of them.

'If you are a painter you ought to meet my friend, Beth, who lives next door,' Tory was saying. 'She would love a nice chat about Picasso or anyone of that type.'

'I did meet her daughter.'

'Oh, yes, poor Prue!'

'Why "poor"?'

'I don't know. But what a dreary life for a girl! A little dusting for Mother, a little cooking, a lot of mooning about. She was going to start a job, but then she got bronchitis. There doesn't seem to be anything for girls to do nowadays, to enjoy themselves, I mean. When I was young it was so different. Or, to look back upon, it was – a perpetual summer, like all those plays with young men in blazers coming through french windows – so many of them and all the same. It always seemed to be the week-end. And I suppose we, the girls, all looked the same, too – shingled hair, sashes tied round our behinds, no waists . . .'

'No bosoms,' Bertram cut in eagerly.

Tory gave him a quick haughty look and then laughed. 'I had a peach-coloured georgette frock, all hung with silver beads, and it showed my knees, in very shiny pink silk stockings. It was called 'sleeveless' and that was precisely what it was, just like a dress with the sleeves taken out.'

'It sounds as if you were rather fast.'

'And if it ever *was* the winter I wore a fur coat made of squares of fur and big bobbles of fur for buttons, and a collar like a bolster.'

'And a hat like a jelly-mould, I daresay.'

'How long ago it was, and the only problems we had were which of the striped blazers to marry, not that it would make much difference in the long run.'

'No war.'

'No, we were the lucky ones. Our young men were just the very ones who'd escaped by a month or two. And yet we had come to the point of being grown-up in that world of telegrams, of girls rushing into their bedrooms and slamming the door. Perhaps we all got frightened of being left on the shelf as our elder sisters looked like being. Beth married when she was younger than Prue is now.'

'The doctor? I've seen him, I think.' He felt as if a jig-saw puzzle was falling into place.

'Yes, I expect so. Would you like some prunes?'

Bertram could not really be bothered with a lot of stewed fruit, but he took it because at least it was something to eat.

'What is he like?'

Tory feigned absent-mindedness. She turned to him and asked: 'Who?'

'The doctor.'

'Oh – a tallish man, dark, rather pale, thin.' She moved her hand sketchily, with impatience.

'I know what he *looks* like. I meant what is he *like*?'

Tory, having deliberately turned the conversation to embrace Robert, could not endure it now that he was mentioned. She felt that even by saying he was dark and thin she was betraying him.

'I have never known him well,' she said. 'He is rather taken up with his work.'

'This year, next year, sometime, never,' Bertram said aloud, spreading his prune-stones round his plate. To himself, he thought: 'So she can describe everyone, but not him.'

'Do prunes give you wind, too?' he inquired in a polite voice, for she ate nothing, sat there with her fingers laced together in her lap.

'If I could tell him,' she thought. 'If I had someone I could tell, some good friend. But Beth is the only real friend I ever had. And I cannot tell Beth.'

'No,' she laughed. 'Not prunes. Only bottled beer.' She put her finger-tips upon the edge of the table and stood up. 'Why, it is quite dark,' she said.

*

Lily Wilson let herself into the dark house. She moved quietly as if there were those inside who slept. When a mouse stirred – and she knew that there were mice – fear rushed through her, she felt as if fingers were locked tightly round her ankles. She went stealthily to begin with, and then with a little rush up the last few stairs into the room whose door she could lock. She switched on the light and crossed to the window to draw the curtains. Sweat had sprung from her and now felt cold at her armpits, the backs of her knees.

The view outside calmed her – the light falling on the cobblestones, and the peace of the quiet buildings. Iris came out of the Anchor and walked along, her hair swaying on her shoulders. When she reached her home, Lily saw her put up her hand to protect her forehead curls from a gust of wind. Then the street was empty except for an old man – it looked like the old Librarian – strolling along beside the water, his hands clasped behind his back. Yes, it was he, for as he drew level with Lily's house he looked up and she could see his face in the lamplight – even his lips curved moistly above the square-cut beard which gave him, Lily thought, the look of Elijah.

She did not care to be seen peering out of the window, and put up her hand and drew down the blind.

Tory had let her room sink into darkness and silence; only the fire shifted the shadows round the walls. Bertram still sat on one side of the fire, she on the other, her feet up on the sofa. 'I hardly know him,' she thought, 'and yet there can be this long, lazy silence between us, as if we have the rest of our lives together for talking.' His presence laid a surface of calm over her nerves, but under that surface something raged inside her. Even sitting still she was conscious of the violence of the emotion which assailed her, as if it had an origin outside and away from her. Yet, although she felt that this violence would remain beyond her control, tormenting her forever, she also felt that she would never be overthrown. She was sure of herself, like a good sailor on a bad sea.

'Well!' Bertram began, slapping down his hands upon his knees, meaning that it was high time he went.

She switched on a lamp and half of her little room, with its white paint and blue glass, sprang back into existence.

'Life is full of surprises,' Bertram said, standing now with his back to the dying fire. 'Yes, it is full of surprises. Something odd round every corner.'

'Am I an odd thing round a corner, do you mean?' Tory asked.

'Yes.' He took her hand as if he were going to kiss it in the most formal way but changed his mind and, turning it over as it came near his lips, he put the kiss into her palm instead. 'Yes, you are certainly something rather odd.'

'You don't mean it cruelly, I know, but "odd" means someone who is left over when the rest are divided into pairs.' She sat with her head bent, sliding a ring up and down and changing it from one finger to another.

'My dear, when I say "odd" I mean someone – remarkable, someone strange, someone out of the ordinary.'

She struggled for words, could not speak, made a little gesture with her hand, as if cutting the air. At last she said: 'Forgive me. I tried to be clever at your expense.'

'At your own expense,' he said gravely. And then in a different, brisker voice, he went on: 'I shall be coming in to polish the knife-box, to do the copper saucepans. You will not easily get rid of me now, not until I go.'

She felt she did not want him to go and said good night to him with some reluctance, confronted once more by the ticking clocks, the empty house, standing there in the hall, shivering.

She went into the kitchen and filled the kettle and stood by the gas-stove waiting, her hot-water bottle in her hand. Going to bed on her own, in silence, was even now strange and dismal to her. For Teddy had been what is called a good husband, who danced attendance, who waited hand and foot, who filled water-bottles, for instance, and heated milk, and brought early-morning tea; and, in short, himself did for her all those things which in war-time money had been unable to do. 'Until he suddenly sheered off,' she now thought, lifting the kettle and pouring the boiling water into the bottle with such a reckless gesture that the water bubbled upwards, overflowed, and poured over her feet. She put the kettle down and groped behind her for a chair. The pain was cold first, then blisteringly hot. 'My poor feet!' she thought, 'my best stockings!' and fell forward in the darkness, her hands grazed upon the coconut matting.

7

As Robert had remarked, there had always been a good deal of running to and fro between Tory's house and his own, which is often so between friends who live close together, especially when one is as vague a housewife as Beth. Robert had a masculine dislike for all these little errands and messages, the borrowings and gossipings, the shared letters, the little screws of salt and butt-ends of loaves; even the gifts irked him – the titbits and samples of Tory's cooking, pats of cream-cheese and bowls of lemon-curd. His own mother had taken a pride in never finding herself without supplies.

He tried to explain to Beth the usefulness, for instance, of a slate on the kitchen wall on which she might jot down oddments as they dwindled. 'What a very good idea!' she had exclaimed, wondering why no one had ever thought of it before. She hung the slate up at once and wrote 'pearl barley' upon it. After six weeks Stevie took her slate back and rubbed off 'pearl barley' and did a drawing in its place.

'Prue, darling!' Beth called suddenly in the middle of her morning writing. 'Will you pop into Tory's for a spoonful of mustard?' Her mind seemed to divide sometimes and run forward along two different tracks, so that now, with her imaginary family sitting round listening to the reading of the will, she could still find herself thinking about lunch. 'Robert will hate his cold beef without any,' she went on and as she spoke she wrote the words: 'When Allegra turned away to the window, the lawyer's voice became a faint . . .' She crossed out 'faint' and wrote 'vague'. But a vague *what*?

'Isn't there any?' Prudence asked in a grumbling tone. 'And the toilet roll's finished, too, in the downstairs lav.'

'There are plenty more in the linen-cupboard.'

'No, there aren't. I looked.'

'Well, in the boot-cupboard, then.'

'There aren't any,' Prudence said distinctly.

'Oh dear! Never mind. These things happen in the best regulated houses, so naturally they happen much more often in ours.'

'Yes, but what are we to *do*?'

'Use your brains, dear. There are those paper serviettes with the Union Jacks on we had for Stevie's party. You really must be a little more resourceful. You have got spoilt by living in the lap of luxury. What do you suppose our soldiers did at the front?'

'I haven't the least idea,' Prudence said disdainfully.

'Well, fetch the mustard, dear, and give Tory my love. I will pay it back when the grocery comes.' She dipped her pen into the ink. 'Vague *what*?' she began to wonder once more. 'This isn't writing,' she thought miserably. 'It is just fiddling about with words. I'm not a great writer. Whatever I do someone else has always done it before, and better. In ten years' time no one will remember this book, the libraries will have sold off all their grubby copies of it second-hand and the rest will have fallen to pieces, gone to dust. And, even if I were one of the great ones, who, in the long run, cares? People walk about the streets and it is all the same to them if the novels of Henry James were never written. They could not easily care less. No one asks us to write. If we stop, who will implore us to go on? The only goodness that will ever come out of it is surely this moment now, wondering if "vague" will do better than "faint", or "faint" than "vague", and what is to follow; putting one word alongside another, like matching silks, a sort of game.'

'There is a green hill far away,' Stevie sang coming in from school, slamming a door. 'Without a city wall.'

Prudence had knocked on Tory's door and presently heard her coming very slowly along the passage. She wasn't in the least prepared for the metamorphosis of Tory, with her hair loose on her shoulders, her mouth colourless. She forgot all about the mustard in her agitation. 'What is wrong? Why are you in your dressing-gown?'

'My legs,' Tory said faintly, and sat down on the hall chair. 'I scalded them last night.'

'Last night?'

Tory inclined her head as if words were now beyond her.

'Why didn't you ...?' Prudence began. 'I will fetch Mother.'

Tory began to count to steady herself. Beth was there before she reached thirty.

'My dear pet, don't worry. Robert's here. He is just coming.' She knelt by Tory and took her hands and began chafing them. 'You're frozen. Poor dear Tory!'

'Not Robert!' Tory said. 'Please not Robert.'

Robert came into the hall and saw Tory looking up at him with the strained and anxious expression of a hurt child.

'What is it, Tory?' he asked rather sternly.

'Her legs are scalded,' Beth said.

'Some of the skin came away with my stockings,' Tory began, and then she retched a little, her hands over her face.

Robert put down his case and lifted her. He carried her into her little sitting-room and put her on the sofa.

'Beth, would you remove this child,' he said angrily, for Stevie had come in, and was insinuating herself into a good vantage ground.

'Yes, I will sit her up at the table and let her begin her lunch or she will be late back to school. I will come back later, Tory. You are in safe hands, my dear. Robert will know more than I what to do. I have put two kettles on,' she added proudly, feeling like a doctor's wife in a novel. Stevie went unwillingly, for her father had now lifted Tory's gown and was peering at the watery, puffy skin.

'Tory, what is the meaning of this?' he asked presently, his head bent over his case while he snipped at something she could hear, with some little scissors. She tried not to imagine what he was going to do.

'Oh, I was filling my bottle and I suppose I was dreaming . . .'

'I didn't mean that, as you know. But why did you not come in last night?'

'I couldn't. I fainted,' she said proudly.

'But as soon as you could? And all this morning. Surely you have deliberately stayed away.'

'You insist on an answer because you know it is one it will give you pleasure to hear. You want me to tell you I didn't come because I am in love with you. Only the very words and me saying them will satisfy you. You deserve to be struck off the roll, or whatever it is.'

He shut his case and went out without a word. 'I am playing merry hell with him,' she thought complacently, her head a little lightened, empty, with fatigue and nausea. When he came back, though, he looked very calm and not in the least mortified by her words, and was carrying a hot-water bottle which he laid to the soles of her feet.

'I'll send Prudence in to make you a cup of tea,' he said, and he looked very stiff and formal, except that he had one of her shoes in each hand. 'And I'll come in this evening after surgery.'

'What time will that be?' she heard herself asking.

'I have no idea,' he said coldly.

She bowed.

And then Beth came hastening in with a cup of hot soup.

The day seemed pleasantly disorganised to Stevie. As there was no one to spur her on with her dinner she leant back in her chair, her eyelids at half-mast, her head on one side. It sickened her to look at such a quantity of food that must be got inside her, unless by a miracle, by her own craft or the weakness of adults, she might be let off.

When her father came in she squeezed a couple of tears, one from each eye, and forced them down her cheeks.

He was clashing the carving-knife against the steel but suddenly stopped.

'Stevie, put out your tongue.'

She put it out and the tears accumulated beautifully and spilt over; she felt them everywhere, in her throat, behind her nose, her breast was full of them, her eyes overflowed.

Her tongue, however, was nicely pink.

Robert came round the table and wiped her cheeks. 'What is it, then, my dear?'

'I didn't like. Tory's legs,' she sobbed. A voice outside her seemed to whisper to her the right things to say.

'You had no business to be there. Can't you eat your pudding?'

'No, I don't think I can.'

'Would you like something different just for this once?'

She thought she would very much like a chocolate biscuit, but the voice outside warned her against saying so.

'No, I don't want anything.'

'You can get down, then. Sit quietly in a chair and look at a book until you feel better.'

'Couldn't I just pop up and be excused?'

'Yes, of course.'

He carved himself some beef and tipped salad all over his plate. Upstairs in the lavatory Stevie sang loudly:

'Jesus bids us shine
With a pure clear light
Like a little candle
Burning in the night.'

He could hear her banging her heels against the pedestal and then yards and yards of toilet-paper being unwound.

'In this world of darkness
So we shall shine
You in your small corner
And I in mine.'

She gave a great kick and then there was a brief silence and the cistern being flushed.

He glanced at the plate of cold rice pudding, knowing he had been fooled. Now she was in the bathroom, running water into the basin. She was muttering to herself, as if engrossed, sometimes singing a snatch of a hymn but in an absent-minded way. 'Playing with the water,' he thought; but, deliberately turning his mind away, sat chewing the greyish beef and wondering about Tory's behaviour and her words. 'I am a middle-aged doctor. I am a father' – here Stevie broke loudly into song once more – 'Crown him! Crown him!' – and the water went hastening suddenly down the pipe as if drawn by a great parched throat – 'A father,' Robert continued to himself, 'weighed down by a mass of routine and habit and daily duty, never again to be free of it. I am not,' he thought, reaching for the mustard-pot, 'some young Shelley, capering about with old-man's beard in my hair, breaking women's hearts to left and right.'

The mustard-pot was empty. He left the lid off as a protest.

'I must get surgery over quickly to-night,' he decided.

Prudence made a cup of tea for Tory as her father had told her, and carried it in on a tray, standing by rather grimly as Tory lifted the cup out of the saucer which was half-full of slopped tea.

'You are as bad as Beth,' Tory laughed, holding the cup carefully because of the drips.

'How dare you!' Prudence said suddenly.

'How dare I what?'

'Speak of my mother in that way.'

'My dear child!'

'And I shouldn't rely on that too much, either.'

'Rely on what?'

'My being a child.'

Tory put the cup down and looked carefully at Prudence. 'Are my legs affecting my head, do you think?' she asked. 'Am I really hearing you say these things? And if so, what does it mean?'

The young have few weapons against coolness. Prudence became surly and incoherent. Despising herself, getting out of depth, she mumbled: 'You know what I mean all right.'

But she could not frighten Tory as she had frightened her father. Tory merely looked back at her as if fascinated, a kind of look she kept for people who had views she disliked. She would never fly into a rage with her opponents, but let them state their case in such silence that they would eventually flounder and then notice the dreamy little shake of her head, the eyes, fascinated, smiling, as if she were saying: 'I would never have believed it if I hadn't seen it myself,' incredulous, bemused, with the look of someone gazing at a cage of mandrills. This did not help Prudence to get her mumbling coherent and she snatched up the empty cup and hastened back to the kitchen.

As soon as she had gone Tory stopped smiling and sat very still, frowning at her bandaged legs.

Maisie Bracey had no high-flown ideas about life as her sister had. She laughed always at Iris's make-believe, teased her during her bouts of hero-worship – that man in the concert party, to begin with, with his straw hat, his face smooth, unreal, with number nine grease-paint; then, later, Ronald Colman; now Laurence Olivier. Maisie had never pinned up photographs of film stars on the bedroom wall or woven dreams (how John Gielgud, coming out of the stage-door one night suddenly raised his hat and said: 'I am sorry, but I *have* to speak to you,' and the lines from his nostrils to his down-curving lips seemed more nervously beautiful than could be borne). For Maisie, what her mother said insincerely was really true, everyday life *was* good enough for her. She did not care for any devastating romance and knew that she would do her own hair till the day she died, and her own housework as well; that no one would wait upon her unless she were ill, and perhaps not then; that she would grow to be an old woman and say 'I didn't go to stay at Claridge's after all,' and not care in the least, as Iris would. She knew what she wanted and in the end it was only two things. She wanted to get married and she wanted her mother to die. When Eddie Flitcroft, whom Iris despised, had asked her to go to the cinema one afternoon, her mother had become fretful and importunate.

'What's to happen to the shop?'

'Iris will be here.'

'And if Iris is in the shop, what happens to me?'

'The same as what happens when I'm here alone with you.'

'Why should you want to go to the pictures? I haven't known you go for years.'

'That wasn't because I didn't want to,' Maisie said quietly.

'So I stand in your way, do I? Perhaps I'd be better dead. Isn't it bad enough for me to be lying here year after year without you forever rubbing it in that I'm a nuisance to you?'

As the argument had gone beyond reasonable discussion Maisie said nothing. Her mother's hands trembled on the counterpane. Deep inside her a little voice told her to let the girl go, that she had been a good daughter and had done nothing to provoke the vicious lashing of her tongue. And it was words merely, her suggestion that she should be better dead, for her egotism told her that she was still indispensable, that the world and all that is therein would fall to pieces any day that Rose Bracey failed to draw a breath. Yet she hushed the little voice of reason, or overrode it, and her words reared and plunged away like a wild horse.

'It's that Eddie. We were all right until he came. What does he want with you? You're old enough to be his mother, anyway.'

'Only if I'd had him when I was four,' Maisie said.

'Don't be disgusting. You'll let this business slide. I know. And then come grizzling to me when there's no more left to live on. I didn't work my fingers to the bone building up a nice little connection just for you to throw it all away on boys. All my hard work all these years and you'd let it go without a murmur. Without a murmur. And I must lie here helpless and watch you do it.'

'I only wanted to go to the pictures. I'd have been back by half-past five.'

'Time's nothing to you. It's only those in pain know how heavily even a minute goes by. I can't manage any more,' she added, pushing aside her dinner-plate with a few fish-bones left upon it.

Maisie took the plate and went on eating her own meal calmly, but the tears were deep down in her breast.

'All right, go then,' her mother said presently, in a different, broken voice. 'You can tell me all about it when you come back. It will be something for me to look forward to all the afternoon.'

'I shan't go,' Maisie said.

'Yes, you go, girl. I don't mind. You're quite right, just because I can't have any pleasures myself I mustn't stand in the way of yours.'

'Some people just say to themselves: "I'll go to the pictures" and then go,' Maisie marvelled to herself, but she said nothing.

'You'll be late if you don't hurry,' her mother said sharply.

'I'm not going.'

'Oh, if you're going to sulk and be a martyr. Your father used to be just the same. You can't expect happiness in this life if you're not prepared to make a little effort. Everything's too much trouble.'

Maisie took the plate out into the scullery and stood gazing at the pot of maiden-hair fern. She took up a jug and poured some water into the muddy saucer, but she did it like a sleep-walker. 'I wish she'd die,' she thought. 'I wish she'd die.' The idea was at home with her now and could not shock her as it once did. She let it come bubbling up easily to the surface of her mind.

When Eddie came in and raised his eyebrows at her, she shook her head. He frowned quickly in annoyance, but she could only shrug her shoulders.

'This is a lovely cup of tea, Maisie,' her mother said, having had her own way.

Stevie had her own world, down among the skirts, the trousers of the grown-ups. These skirts, these trousers constantly impeded her. She dodged among them, avoiding the glances of the eyes above her, the faces swimming moon-like overhead having less meaning to her often than all the inanimate things she encountered on her own level – doorknobs, railings, flow-ers. She was acquisitive. She liked picking flowers and collecting old envelopes and wearing her jewellery – she had a gold cross threaded on a piece of wool, a string of corals and various brooches and rings which Tory had worn in plays when she was a girl. There were arguments in the house about her jewellery, because she liked to wear it to school and Beth would not let her, was quite shocked at the idea. 'She's only five,' Robert would say. 'Bless her heart, let her get it out of her system while she is young.' And, although Stevie hated the look of distaste on her mother's face at the diamond and emerald brooch pinned in the middle of her Viyella smock, she could not resist the glory of it.

At school she fell into violent adorations of bigger girls and mistresses, even cherishing their defects; stammering a little like one girl; blinking like another; closing her eyes while she talked, as Miss Simpson closed hers. As soon as she reached the school gates and said good-bye to her father she unwrapped a piece of wire from her handkerchief and fitted it across her front teeth, in imitation of a girl in the Second Form. She desperately desired to wear spectacles but too deeply to be able to speak about it. She also told lies – about dresses she did not possess or deeds she had never done; how she had been a bridesmaid at a wedding, was recently vaccinated, was learning to play the violin. She also had a baby sister called Rosie who cut teeth when she was a few days old, but after that did not seem to progress. Miss Simpson forgave her her lies, even the one about being cruelly treated at home, because her mother was a writer, and where there is bad blood, as they say, it will out. 'Well, that *is* a lovely story!' she would exclaim in her bright, sane way, having listened to a description of Robert's and Beth's wedding, with Stevie one of the bridesmaids in red silk and pearls.

Prudence, at school, had been quite different; a little backward, kind people might have said, when she was still trying to matriculate at the age of eighteen, and not managing it. Slow she had been, with a strange lack of co-ordination, Miss Simpson explained in her reports, between brain and hand, reason and action, a girl who made neither friends nor enemies, always standing a little outside the edge of the crowd, not yet quite alive.

Nothing ruffled Miss Simpson. She could deal with everything – new girls who sobbed for a week, children who used bad language or kicked her on the shins, little girls who told lies. 'She is going through a funny little phase,' she would say, smiling calmly. Even children who passed from one funny phase to a funnier, could not disturb her. 'We can cope,' she would tell the mothers. 'We can cope.' Then the mothers who could not cope, who sometimes at home gave a sharp slap instead, felt ashamed, as if they must seem tawdry and hysterical in her eyes. They did not realise that she could even cope with mothers.

When Robert returned to the house at six o'clock he found a great scene going on and Stevie passing through a very funny little phase indeed, clinging to the banister rails and howling.

'What *is* this?' he cried, striding forward in great urgency, for it was time for surgery.

'She won't come to bed,' Prue said, and as fast as she uncurled the little fingers from the banisters they gripped it again.

'Where is your mother?'

'She is in with Tory.'

Tory seemed to have upset his day in every way she was able. He sat down beside Stevie on the stairs.

'What is wrong?'

'I haven't done my homework.'

'It's all nonsense,' Prudence put in quickly. 'She doesn't have homework at her age.'

'I do. I do. It's a punishment.'

'Stop screaming!' Robert said. 'Why were you punished?'

'I said a rude word,' Stevie improvised, not realising that Robert was leading her up the stairs.

'What did you say?'

'Just rude.'

'I saw a new baby to-day.' He was tired or he would have known that this was a useless change of tactics. At once, Stevie, sensing the red herring, began to howl and clung to the banisters again.

Beth came hurrying to the hall. 'Stevie, darling! What is the matter?'

Robert straightened up suddenly. He resented the way Beth came hastening to her child as if he had been treating her brutally.

'You'd better deal with her,' he said crisply. 'I've work to do.'

'But what is wrong?'

'I don't know.'

'Perhaps she is overtired.'

'I know *I* am overtired. She has exhausted Prudence and me. Perhaps, coming freshly to it, you will have more success.'

'It's my geometry,' Stevie sobbed. 'I've got to do my geometry.'

'Of course, darling one,' cooed Beth. 'We shall do it together when you are in bed. You shall sit up and we'll pin some drawing paper to the pastry-board and do a nice lot of geometry.'

'What is geometry?' Stevie asked, crossing the landing.

'You shall see. As soon as you are in bed. You shall see.'

Taps were turned on, their voices drowned.

'Well, I could have got out of it that way,' Robert thought, going into the surgery and tipping the cats off his chair. 'The child is thoroughly spoilt, I suppose.'

*

This evening Mrs Bracey was in a good humour. She even did a little mending for Maisie, but her geniality was tentative and spasmodic, like the approaches of a child who has been naughty and is not sure of being forgiven. Eddie had gone out in a huff; Iris was at work. The little room was brightly stuffy, in contrast to the chilly darkness of the shop with its rows of hanging clothes, the lighthouse beam glancing there on a paste buckle in a pile of old shoes or on the moonlike bowl of water Maisie had set on the floor to absorb the smell of paint.

'What's for supper?' Mrs Bracey asked.

'If you don't mind being left for three seconds I'll slip along to the café for a bit of fish,' Maisie said coldly.

'I could fancy a nice piece of skate,' her mother agreed, instead of grumbling in the usual way that she'd had fish for her dinner and soon would be looking like a fish, with fish-bones sticking out of her bodice and a bloody fine fish's thirst in her throat.

So Maisie unlocked the shop door and stepped out on to the pavement and went along to the café, where a dim, yellowish light lay over the tiled tables and Bertram was eating a plate of sprats the size of safety-pins.

Stevie sat up in bed, drawing circles round egg-cups, which was Beth's notion of geometry. She covered a great many sheets of typing-paper in this way, then suddenly tired, she climbed down out of bed and padded across to the window.

'Stevie!' Beth called from her own bedroom down below.

'I am only on my pot,' Stevie shouted, standing by the window and looking out at the sea beyond the low parapet – for her bedroom was tucked high up under the roof. Between the tiles grew little plants like stiff rosettes, and gulls had left long chalky splashes on the slate. It was almost dark, and the sea looked taut and smooth, like silk stretched in a frame. Looking out at the lighthouse, she murmured: 'Please send me a nice dream about new-born babies and me being a nurse. Or if I can't be a nurse, let me be a lady. And have corsets. Amen.' She stood quite still by the window, shivering, and when at last the lighthouse threw its hurried beam over the water, she could feel that her prayer had been noted, and trotted back to her bed.

'Your surgery was over quickly,' Beth said, pouring out coffee in her own reckless way. Prudence looked at the swimming saucers and then at her mother with anxious, searching eyes.

'Did you do any writing?' Robert asked.

'Yes, but I have one of my characters in bed with pneumonia, and it is always dull writing about illness. It has been done so much before. This evening, thank heaven, we are through with the crisis.'

'How did it go?' Robert asked politely.

'Oh, badly, thank you. How long before I can let her die, do you suppose? Two or three days?'

'There is no need for anyone to die of pneumonia these days,' Robert said in a rather high-handed and unhelpful way.

'I'm afraid she must.'

'The average expectation of life in your novels can't be high. In fact, the death-roll is quite alarming.'

'You might as well let her get it over,' Prudence said, flicking over the pages of a rather dull medical journal and then throwing it on one side. 'What's her name?'

'Allegra. Like Lord Byron's daughter.'

'How funny. I didn't even know he got married,' Prudence said.

'I should never dare to give a name like that to a child. It is too much of a challenge,' Robert said. 'She would be almost sure to grow up fat and flat-footed and terribly Andante.'

'Yes, like a girl at school called Honor Collins, who was an awful liar and told tales,' Beth said. 'Are you going to see Tory to-night?'

'Yes, I said I'd look in. Are you coming?'

'No. Tell her I'll look in directly after breakfast. Geoffrey Lloyd said he'd bring some of his verse to read to me this evening.'

'How awful for you!' Prudence said suddenly.

'I have some mending to do. It doesn't matter. But you'll be here, dear, won't you?'

'Good heavens, no. I loathe poetry. Especially the sort people have written.'

'Oh, dear! I thought you would like it.'

'I can't imagine why.'

'Where are you going, then?' Robert asked sharply. 'I don't want you out of doors after dark, you know.'

'Don't you?'

'What a pity!' Beth was saying. 'He seems such a nice lad.'

'Is his poetry any good?' Robert asked, and glanced at the clock.

'Well, my dear, I am only a wretched novelist,' Beth said proudly. 'I don't understand about poetry.'

'I must go,' Robert said. 'Funny how inferior novelists feel – from Jane Austen down.'

Prudence had the idea that his mind proffered one set of words and his tongue another. She watched him as he leant forward to kiss her mother's brow, just as Beth bent forward suddenly for the coffee-pot. Nothing came of the kiss; it scarcely happened and certainly Beth was oblivious of the attempt. 'If there's anything Tory wants . . .' she was saying.

'Teddy would foam at the mouth if he were to see us drinking this,' Tory laughed.

'Damn Teddy!' Robert said, putting his brandy glass on the table.

'There's one advantage in being the one who is left. It means a great loss of face for the other to go round gathering up possessions. I did quite well out of Teddy. All his things were here at the house when he was bewitched and he never could get them away – not with any dignity, that is. I gave a lovely Harris tweed suit to my young brother and sold the rest of his clothes to old Mrs Bracey. He must have found that the course of true love never does run smooth.' She paused. 'Which it does not,' she added quietly.

He found unnerving the way in which women can drop from nonsense into a passionate seriousness. 'What can I say to her?' he wondered. 'How can I begin to talk?'

'Don't you want to look at my bad legs?' she asked.

'No.'

'Then why did you come?'

'To talk to you.'

'What have you done with Beth?'

'Done with her? Do you imagine I've hacked her to pieces with a meat-cleaver?'

'No, I didn't think that, actually.'

'She's in there' – he made an impatient gesture in the direction of the wall – 'with this young man, listening to him reading his poetry.'

'Drink up your brandy.'

'I don't want it.'

'Just because I said it was Teddy's!'

'I always hated him. I've just this moment realised how much. I'll certainly not drink his brandy.'

'The most sensible thing to do to people you hate is to drink their brandy.'

Silence fell once more. They were desperately uneasy.

'And is Prudence sitting at her mother's footstool, breathing in this fine literary air?' Tory inquired.

'I worry about Prudence ... Everything has turned out so differently from what I planned. I'm no feminist, but I do believe in girls having lives of their own. I've always disliked the idea of their wasting time while they wait to be married-off. But she is even less fortunate than those girls used to be ...'

'You mean there's no marrying-off.'

'She has the worst of two worlds. In a place like this what is there for her?'

'Good evening,' Prudence said to Geoffrey Lloyd, passing him in the hall on her way out.

'Her bronchitis is a pity,' Tory was saying.

'Bronchitis!' Robert exclaimed. 'That's merely an excuse for something I daren't put into words, even to myself.'

'Say it to me!'

'You know it already. She could never do a job because her mind is empty. She moves through normal life and seems normal herself; but inside her there is nothing.'

'I think you are quite wrong.'

'Remember what she was like at school. Impossible.'

'At lessons perhaps; but that's not everything.'

'It's the same sort of thing as earning one's living. Where it all went wrong for her, I don't know, or when it was I began to see that she was being left behind. Neither Beth nor I are complete fools ...'

'Beth at school was a bit one-sided ...'

'Of course. Literary people always do suffer from an aversion to mathematics. The sight of figures upsets them. Notice how often they write a number rather than make the figure ... But I was good at maths when I was young.'

'So you had it planned that all your mathematical cells, or whatever they are, would coincide with Beth's literary ones in equal proportions and produce a fine all-round sort of child ...'

'It looks as though Beth's mathematical cells have coincided with my literary ones ...' he admitted. 'The result is nothing, as it was bound to be.'

'I think we are not being very scientific.'

'No. Children are a great disappointment.'

'Stevie has her wits about her. And I think you are wrong about Prudence. If you are not going to drink that brandy, please hand it over to me. Carefully!'

'Why do you think I'm wrong about Prue?'

'Because she has intuition and perception, perhaps all the keener because her head is not a rag-bag of bits of knowledge.'

'She is still a child.'

'She is not. What does Beth think about all this?'

'Beth?' He walked up and down. 'Don't ask me what goes on in Beth's head.'

'She was already a writer when you married her, you know,' Tory said accusingly.

'I didn't count on it going on so long – not having books published, for instance. I thought when she had children ... but even then she used to sit up in bed scribbling. A confinement is a fine chance to finish off a novel, she thinks. When she was feeding poor Prue she wasn't thinking about her. It's a disease, a madness.'

'Perhaps in the end it is what she was intended for ... perhaps her writing is the Beth-ish thing. Not the children.'

'Oh, nonsense!' he said, tiredly. 'It's a disease all right. I ought to have cured it, but I could not.'

'She is about the only happy person I know. Don't you see how she is to be envied? Nothing people do can ever break her.'

'Writers can be broken just like everybody else. Look at Keats and Chatterton and ... Oscar Wilde. And all the others who were beheaded and locked up and shot.'

'What I mean is that the thing that is precious to them, that they are staked upon, is always safe inside, can't be got at or violated – only by themselves.'

'I didn't come here to talk about what writers are or are not,' he thought.

'Am I trying to tell him that whatever he and I do to Beth we cannot really destroy her?' Tory wondered.

'Why did you say Prue has perception?' he asked suddenly in alarm.

Tory thought carefully. 'Nothing special,' she lied.

'Nothing about us?'

'How could it be? There isn't anything about us, is there?'

'No.'

He knelt down beside the sofa where she lay and took her in his arms.

'Right up to the moment when he kisses me there is still time to go back,' Tory thought in a panic. 'Let us not!' she said aloud.

'Too late,' he said calmly, and took her head between his

hands and turned it a little sideways so that he could kiss her. She shut her eyes and felt that she was dropping backwards through endless space, that hard though he might kiss her, he would never be able to follow her to the end or catch her up.

Geoffrey Lloyd sat down, holding his folder of manuscript, and waited. He had looked forward to this evening for, apart from loving the sound of his own voice, he liked the titillation of what he thought of as spiritual relationships with older women, liked the safe excitement.

'You don't mind, Geoffrey, do you, if I do some mending while I listen?'

Although this was not what he had planned, he could not dissent. Beth glanced round for her work-box and he jumped up and fetched it for her. When she had swung her feet up on the sofa and he had made her comfortable with a cushion at her back he shuffled with the manuscript and paused.

'The Zones of Pleasure,' he presently announced. He read calmly and with confidence. After a moment or two Yvette and Guilbert got up and stretched and walked contemptuously to the door, where they stood waiting.

'Oh, dear,' said Beth, beginning to gather together her wools and cotton-reels, but Geoffrey sprang to the door and took the poor creatures and threw them somewhat violently into the hall.

'I'm so sorry,' Beth apologised when he returned.

After this he read for a while in peace.

'I am rather bad at saying "How nice", or "How nasty", after each poem,' she said artfully as he turned a page. 'So I will just listen and say nothing, and you can read without interruption.'

'I wonder where Prue is?' she thought uneasily. 'And what can

123

have upset her. I plan a pleasant little evening for her and she just disappears.'

The verse was of a kind she found embarrassing to listen to. It was a great deal about sex and revolution, and the atmosphere in the room seemed to become sultry. An almost overpowering desire to laugh swept through her. 'Don't let me!' she prayed to no one in particular, weaving grey wool in and out of Robert's socks. 'Don't let me! Please don't let me!'

> 'Loving this world and for its sake
> The hymen of the future we shall break,'

Geoffrey read, and Beth cut off her wool with a little snap and blushed. His hand flicked over the page and he began again.

She was safe now. The moment of hysteria had passed and she felt she would not laugh. She darned peacefully, not listening. She composed a kind and critical little speech for the end and then fell to scheming about her book; sorting out snippets of dialogue, planning death-beds. She rolled up Robert's socks into neat balls, very pleased with her work, and then took up a frock of Stevie's she was lengthening. The button-box fell with a crash. 'Geoffrey, I am so sorry. How very rude and clumsy.'

They were on their hands and knees on the floor, gathering up needles and buttons and buckles and many other oddments, when the door opened and Robert came in.

'Curse, sod, damn, and worse,' said Geoffrey to himself, standing up and shaking hands.

Maisie washed at the sink in the scullery before going to bed. The curtain was drawn over the small window; the only light was from a small oil lamp. She stood in her petticoat and her hair was pinned to the top of her head. Leaning over the bowl of water she soaped her arms. In the kitchen Mrs Bracey snored.

The door from the yard opened and Eddie came in. Furiously, dripping wet, she snatched at the towel.

'Sorry!' He shut the door and stared at her. Then, as he went towards the kitchen door, he suddenly put out his hand and stroked her polished-looking shoulder, touched her soapy arm. He hesitated and came back to her, his face changed, darkened.

'Why wouldn't you come this afternoon?'

'I couldn't.'

'Wouldn't, you mean.'

'Mother . . .'

'That was an excuse.'

'You don't know her.'

'I know you're a fool if you let her ruin your life.'

'My life isn't ruined just because I don't go to the pictures with you,' she said proudly, and tried to escape from his exploring hands.

'Come here.'

She shook her head. He took her arms and drew her closer. 'Please, don't!'

She laid her hands flat against his chest and tried to push him away.

'Next time will you come?'

'I don't know.'

'Iris would, I bet.'

'You'd better ask her.'

'I wanted you. Weeks before I have another chance perhaps.'

Mrs Bracey turned in her sleep, groaning, and Maisie put her fingers to her lips warningly. 'I must go to bed. She might wake.'

Without a word she put her blouse round her shoulders and lifted the latch. Eddie, who was frightened of her mother, scarcely breathed as he followed her through the kitchen, creaking up the stairs. 'Damn Iris!' he whispered as she reached her bedroom door. He ran his hand down her thigh, detaining her.

'Good night!'

When she opened the door she found that Iris was still awake.

'What's all the whispering about?'

'I was only saying "good night" to Eddie.'

'Why whisper?'

'Mother's asleep.'

'Put the light on.'

'No, I can manage.'

Her arms felt stiff with dried soap. She hurried to bed, lay beside her sister, her thigh, her breasts, still with his touch upon them.

'What have you been up to?' Iris asked.

'Don't be silly. I'm tired.'

'Has he been kissing you?'

'Why shouldn't he?' Maisie said angrily.

'All right. All right. I don't know how you could, that's all.'

'Why not?'

'Well, he's so . . .'

'What?'

'Such a kid . . . shows off so . . .'

'All young men show off, unless there's something wrong with them. I've seen you making up to him yourself.'

'I wouldn't let him kiss me.'

'I suppose you're still waiting for Noel Coward.'

'Someone a bit better than Eddie, certainly . . .'

'Better?'

'You know what I mean. Look at his great, red hands. What else did he do?'

'If only I could sleep alone!' Maisie thought. 'If only I could keep my secrets to myself!'

'Passion seems to be in the air to-night,' Iris said sarcastically. 'That old fool Hemingway and Lily Wilson. He took her home again. It must be the spring. I shall have to see what I can do for myself; perhaps old Pallister . . .'

'Damn Iris!' Maisie thought.

When he had taken Lily home Bertram went for a walk along the waterfront. A soft wind blew in from the sea, waves swirled in and broke in great swathes beneath the lighthouse. Lamplight, lights from the windows, fell over the uneven cobblestones. He walked along past Tory's house, which alone was in darkness, and beyond the Cazabons' house to where the cliff rose up, thrusting itself out into the open sea. The path here, at high tide, was wet with spray. He walked slowly, reluctant to go in. Below him, as he paused to lean on the railings, the waves flogged the sea-wall, flecked with long trailing foam, floating seaweed. Above him was a smell of dusty trees, an atmosphere of great darkness, and the faint crepitations of dead leaves.

Also leaning over the railings a little farther on was Prudence, with her hair tucked into her upturned collar, and her hands thrust up her wide sleeves for warmth.

'Hallo!' she said as if, he thought, it were midday.

'What are you up to?'

'The same as you, I expect. Out for a walk.'

'Have you quarrelled with your young man?'

'I haven't a young man.'

'How long have you been here? You look frozen.'

'I don't know.'

'You're a strange girl. A very strange girl. So beautiful, too, and not to have a young man!'

'Beautiful!' she echoed in a startled way. Then she laughed, dismissing the idea. 'I'm not beautiful.'

'Indeed you are.'

'I'm cross-eyed.'

'Nonsense. Your beauty is imperfect, moving. The only kind worth having.'

She turned away from the railings, dropping her hands, staring at him.

'I'm going back now. Are you coming?' he asked her. Without answering, she began to pace along beside him. They went slowly, their heads bent, a wide space between them.

'You're unhappy,' he said, and he remembered what Tory Foyle had said about the girl's lonely, dull life. 'What about this young man?'

'What young man?'

'The one you say you haven't got.'

'I shan't ever have a young man.'

She was agitated. She even stopped walking for a second, and then moved on more briskly than before, wringing her hands.

'Why do you say that?' he asked gently, as gently as he could above the noise of the water and the buffeting wind.

'Because ...' She lifted her white face and looked briefly at the sky as if for help. 'Because ...' She gave up; she shrugged. 'I hate love,' she said in a quicker, different way. 'I don't ever want to fall in love or for anyone to fall in love with me. Surely there is more in the world than that?'

'I have never found it so disagreeable that I wished for much more,' he said.

'You're laughing at me.'

'Yes, young people always imagine they've said something one can laugh at. Oh, my dear, I'm sorry. Why am I rude to you? And what has happened to you, I wonder, that you talk in this way.' He thought: 'I suppose she has been jilted.'

'Nothing has happened to me,' she said, and he noted the hesitation at, the stress upon the last word.

'You don't want to go home, do you?' he asked, for her step slackened as she came near the house. 'Are you in some trouble there?'

'Of course not.'

'This is not the first time I have delivered you at your doorstep.'

'No.'

'Well ...' He hesitated. Obviously something more seemed to be demanded of him. 'Don't let yourself be distressed about a young man who doesn't even exist.'

'No.'

Still staring at him, she drew her coat collar up to her chin and shivered. 'I wish ...' she began.

'What do you wish?'

But young people feel they have the right to begin sentences and never finish them, to leave their listeners stinging with curiosity.

'Good night.' So little sound came from her moving lips. A great pressure of fear lay over her, he thought. If she had not been beautiful, he would have felt exasperation and impatience at the annoyance of becoming involved in her troubles, whatever they were, even when he was involved only to the extent of curiosity or pity. 'Bed-ridden old women,' he thought (having spent an hour with Mrs Bracey early in the evening discussing some of the more disreputable kinds of behaviour in remote parts of Africa), 'young women who are frightened of waxworks, girls who are frightened of God knows what, themselves possibly.'

But he said 'Good night, my dear,' in his gentlest voice and walked on past Tory's house. 'Now there's a woman,' he decided, glancing up at the dark windows, 'a woman who is frightened of nothing, who needs nobody's help, who can take a blow on the chin' (he liked this manly figure of speech) 'without flinching.'

The lighthouse now interrupted the run of his thoughts with its fleeting gesture, and in his mind's eye, his painter's eye, he saw the two men sitting in the little building which crouched in the shadow of the tower; there they were, in shirt-sleeves, fans of greasy cards in their hands. In silence they eyed one another, one card went down, then the next, and so the night wore on.

He turned in at the Anchor. 'What is that child frightened of?' he wondered. 'If I were a young man I would have taken her into my arms and kissed away all her misery.' He had always had great confidence with women and a tendency to kiss them better, as he called it; only when he had gone, their fears, their anxieties returned, a little intensified, perhaps, but he, of course, would not know of that, and remained buoyed up by his own goodness.

'Like a final beer?' Mr Pallister inquired.

As usual, Bertram began to refuse and then, 'Yes, I will. I think I will,' he said and came and waited by the dying fire, spreading his hands out over the dull coals, his mind haunted by the girl's white face, the bewildered, frightened eyes.

'That doctor's girl,' he began, taking his drink from Mr Pallister. 'A queer girl, that, walking along by the sea-wall just now. All alone.'

'Yes, a queer girl,' Ned Pallister agreed. 'And them dratted cats of hers. Unnatural devils. She thinks the world of them, you know.'

Bertram drained his glass. 'Well . . . I feel like bed. Getting old.' He laughed.

'We don't get any younger,' Mr Pallister agreed.

But Bertram had not spoken seriously. He knew he had nothing in common with this dim, grey man, who had probably looked the same age for years and years. He climbed the steep staircase, with its walls covered with pictures of boxers, of ships in full sail, photographs of choir-outings, of bowling clubs, all undusted, unobserved for many a long year. As he opened his bedroom door the curtains seemed to be sucked backwards towards him; there was a great rush of sea air and, when he stood still to listen, the interminable turning over of the waves far out to sea.

8

Spring comes last of all to the seaside. The tight buds of those shrubs which seemed to kneel upon the cliff-side looked as if they never would unfurl. Out in the country, fields, hedgerows, woods exulted with green; birds sang. In London, barrows were stacked with rhubarb and daffodils. But at the harbour only the light changed and the days gradually lengthened.

Tory went to Edward's school concert, properly dressed, she thought, in a grey suit, a grey felt hat, and found herself looking like all the other mothers, which pleased her son and disciplined her own vanity.

Driving up in a taxi towards the school, she dissolved a peppermint in her mouth, suddenly terrified of the gin-and-french she had taken before luncheon at the Station Hotel.

She made a great effort to remember all the things which she had read in boys' school stories, that she must beware of Christian names and not seem pleased to see her son, not inquire after his health nor set his tie to rights, nor, in fact, behave exceptionally in any way. But boys' schools seemed to have changed since Tory's days of reading Gunby Hadath, Richard Bird and *The Fifth Form at St Dominic's*. Edward even hugged her and seemed put out by her own off-hand greeting. He spoke of his friends as 'Hugh' and 'Martin' and 'Angus'. He stood still while she had a quick look at his ears, especially the curly bit at the top.

'Matron gave us a good do-over,' he explained. 'And we all had our hair cut.'

Then she saw that the special effort was not all on her side.

'I'm glad you haven't made your nails red,' he said. 'All the boys here hate it. Look at old Martin's mother. Just like a tart. He must feel sick about it.'

'A what?'

'A tart.'

'What a delightful way to speak of your friend's mother!'

'Oh, he doesn't mind. All his sisters are, too. Go to dances and ride in point-to-points.'

'Good gracious! Who is that handsome boy over there, with the curly hair?'

'Boy?' Edward at once became the victim of that delightful sort of laughter which is paroxysmal, muffled, dangerous and half-painful. 'My God! that's Mr Vincent. He's a master. Oh, my God!' He held his stomach, lifting one leg, then the other.

'I should like to meet him,' Tory said. 'Try to be a little more civilised, Edward. Let's go over and you can introduce him to me.'

Edward's laughter stopped suddenly. 'Don't be silly. He's not my form-master. We're only allowed to introduce to form-masters.'

'What an annoying rule!'

'It's not a rule. It's just a thing we don't do. That's my form-master, over there.'

'Oh!'

'He's a decent sort.'

'Is he, dear? I'm so glad.'

Every boy who passed surreptitiously lunged at Edward, dug an elbow at him, crooked a knee at his behind.

'Perhaps he is very unpopular,' Tory thought, although Edward himself seemed not to notice.

'Do you want to be introduced to old Thirsty?'

'To whom, dear?'

'My form-master.'

'Oh, I don't think so. We seem happy where we are.'

When the play began she was astonished at the beauty of the little boys dressed up as girls, wigged and rouged, their thin shoulders angular and touching, feet astride beneath long gowns, the crooked and incongruous ringlets emphasising the delicate line from cheekbone to jaw.

Edward scarcely distinguished himself, aimlessly tapping at a triangle in the percussion band, looking vacant, even mental, his eyes wandering vaguely over the audience.

'I shall see you in a week,' Tory said when it was over. 'I will be at the station to meet you.'

'Good-bye. And thank you for wearing your best hat.'

'This wretched thing!' she laughed, but his eyes shining up at her moved her heart over. She felt shy and awkward, not knowing how to take leave. Martin's mother, for sure, was smothering her son in camphorated furs and bits of trailing veil, kissing him without shame; but Martin's mother had, it seemed, a dowry for doing what was incorrect – varnishing her nails and bringing her daughters up to go to dances. So Tory put a hand for a second on his shoulder and smiled, as if her greatest delight lay in saying good-bye to him.

'It's a pity Father couldn't come,' he said.

'This station hath an ancient and fish-like smell,' Bertram said, taking her elbow as she stepped from the train.

'What are you doing here?'

'I met the train before this and meant to meet the next.'

'Oh, I'm so tired.'

'We will take the station car.'

'I couldn't do that. It's such a little way and people never do. It will cause comment.'

'Very well. There are two dozen oysters for your supper.'

'Two dozen!' she said faintly.

'And a bottle of Guinness, if it will not give you wind.' She began to laugh, feeling braced, her tiredness falling away from her.

'How was your son?'

'He was well; but how mad and wearisome little boys are. They cannot forget their arrogance for one moment. Even on their best behaviour one is conscious always of a surreptitious scuffling going on. When I pay the school bill I think how expensive it all is and then when I go there I think "How cheap!" Twice the money couldn't make up for living in that hell, cleaning their ears, separating them when they fight, enduring their noise – little boys have a peculiar smell, too, as if they have been clutching pennies in their hot hands all day.'

'You do rock along on these cobblestones.'

'They ruin all my fine shoes.'

'You mustn't look, but there is the old palmist peering out from behind her lace curtains, gathering up every little crumb.

135

Now, if you go in to have your hands read she will tell you you are going to marry an elderly man with a beard.'

'But I am not going to.'

'Of course you are.'

'But indeed I am not.'

'You'll find you will.'

Standing at her door rummaging in her bag for her key, Tory smiled and nodded at Lily Wilson, who came hurrying along and turned her head away at that moment as if she did not see them. Indeed, it was almost dark by now.

'And what have you been doing all day?' Tory inquired, stooping to pick up a couple of bills from the door-mat.

'I've been listening to Mrs Bracey's life story.'

He followed her down the dark hall into the little blue and white room.

'That old harridan!'

'An artist sees human nature differently – with different eyes,' he explained, feeling (which it was death to him not to feel) that he was a little out of the ruck of ordinary people.

'For a painter, you do very little painting,' she said, and she put the bills up behind the clock and surveyed the room.

'Painting!' he exclaimed. 'Look at outside! There has been mist all day, gauze hanging over everything since early morning.'

'I didn't mean only to-day. And you could have painted the gauze. Why don't you paint my portrait?' She saw herself there, for all time, in her grey dress. Or her green?

'Women always want to be painted and then when they are they don't like it.'

'And the great Mrs Bracey? What of her life story?'

But she wasn't interested and was fixing up the electric fire and making no pretence of listening to what he said.

'Imagine what it must be like, a woman of her vitality imprisoned in that unmoving mass of flesh!' he was saying.

'She was always a lazy bitch. I've known her for years.'

'She doesn't like you. That came to me while we were talking.'

'And I don't like her. There, that's better. How cheerless a house is that's been empty all day. With the sort of smell we used to come back to after our summer holidays when we were children, the closed-in atmosphere and the waiting silence and the garden suddenly full of golden rod and those large striped spiders sitting in webs across all the pathways and arches.'

'Shall I fetch your supper now?'

'Our supper, I hope you mean.'

He left her drawing curtains, trying to make the room come alive again. Outside, the gauze hung all over the darkness and the waves turned milkily at the foot of the cliff.

He disappeared into the Anchor.

Far out in the fishing-grounds the men turned in for a sleep. It seemed calm and warm to Eddie, who had only lately come down from trawling off Scotland – a week out at a time, after cod and turbot, and sorting and gutting to be done in the most bitter weather, with frozen, bleeding fingers. ('Look at his red hands!' Iris said.)

Here, the fishing-grounds lay nearer the shore – sometimes even within sight of the lighthouse – life seemed nearer to him and, especially near, his thoughts of Maisie Bracey, whose quiet sense he admired.

He drank his tea and turned in for his short sleep. His uncle, old Flitcroft, snored already, his teeth safe beside him in his empty tea-mug. He was an old hand at this game and knew how to get the longest possible spell of sleep before they would begin again the monotonous work of hauling, knee-deep in water, winding in the bobbins, the winch creaking and the boat wallowing broadside to the waves.

Now there was silence over the calm sea. The lights of the other trawlers made a faint constellation, the buoys bobbed gently on the surface and *The Star of Newby* rose to each wave, light on the water, her hold half-empty still.

'I don't think any food is aphrodisiac,' Tory was saying, and she put down her empty glass with its lacing of tawny froth and stared at it. 'Let us go and sit by the fire,' she said, suddenly moving. 'No,' she went on, still disposing of a fallacy, she thought, 'I am sure that is an old wives' tale.'

'An old wives' tale!' he laughed. 'Very apposite. Very apposite and gruesome indeed.'

'Well, you know what I mean. This is nice and peaceful. I should be very grateful to you for your kindness except that I know you simply can't resist making yourself indispensable.'

'I cannot resist your beauty.'

'Mrs Bracey is not a beautiful woman.'

'Bother Mrs Bracey! Tell me about your son.'

'Oh, he's just a very ordinary little boy,' Tory said proudly; and then, not altogether irrelevantly: 'I wonder if people gossip about me. Not that I care.'

'Gossip in what way?'

'Oh . . . I haven't really the least idea, so please forget it. You know, I have come to the conclusion that the real purpose of marriage is talk. It's the thing which distinguishes it from the other sorts of relationships between men and women, and it's

138

the thing one misses most, strangely enough, in the long run – the outpourings of trivialities day after day. I think that's the fundamental human need, much more important than – violent passion, for instance.'

'You are even convincing yourself,' he marvelled.

'It's true.'

'All right. All right.'

'And coming home after a day out with no one to pour it all out to.'

'I was there. I am still here.'

'I know. I'm sorry. I sound ungrateful and . . .'

'Seeing your son has depressed you, I think.'

'Yes. Yes.' She frowned pettishly. She thought: 'Soon he will be home for the holidays,' and she felt that she was not ready to have him back or devote herself to him, and felt torn in two with guilt and anxiety.

'I daresay I shall marry you quite soon,' Bertram said airily. 'Then there will be someone to talk to again.'

'You are as likely to marry Mrs Bracey.'

'I do not marry easily. In fact, I have never done so before. You are the only woman who has made me inclined to it, and for that reason I do not intend to be fobbed off with a lot of excuses.' ('When I talk to her I have only half her attention,' he thought, 'she is distracted in the first sense of the word.') Aloud he said: 'I am getting on, you know. Time I settled down.'

'But not with me.' She smiled.

'With her as my wife, I'd *paint*,' he suddenly thought. It came to him in a bright flash. 'Yes, I'd paint then. It is what I need – background, anchorage, inspiration. All artists need it.'

*

Lily Wilson had a small port to warm herself. Whatever others might say, she felt chilly. 'Mild to-night, summer on the way,' they said in the bar, but she could only shiver.

Bertram had not come, and the port, she hoped, would help her to go home alone. When she stepped out into the dark a faint drizzle fell upon her face. She held her key tightly in her hand and went along quickly, her head bent against the mist, passing Mrs Bracey's, where lights from the kitchen came faintly through the shop. She wished she could turn in there for the night, until darkness was past, so painfully did she yearn for human contact. With tears of terror on her face she went forward, her key ready in her hand, and stepped into her own doorway and into someone's arms.

She fell back in horror against the rough wall, her hands stiffened before her as if she had run them into blood.

'There is nothing to be afraid of,' a voice now said, and when she could make herself look she saw the beard, the moistened lips of the old Librarian. He took off his old-fashioned curly trilby hat and held it to his chest.

She stayed where she was, panting, against the wall, her fear neither lessened nor increased, but the shock over.

'I beg your pardon, but I was only sheltering from the rain. I had no idea you were going to run full tilt into me.'

'Rain!' Lily echoed, looking quickly out of the porch, for she had forgotten that drizzle, the drops which hung in the air, scarcely even falling.

'I will bid you good night,' he said, and he touched his tie-pin with a crinkled, veined hand and then, carefully putting on his hat, walked away.

'Oh, God, I can't go in,' Lily sobbed, staring after him, crouching against the wall. It used all her strength, the courage only the nervous know about, to impel herself through that avenue of waxworks, past the glittering eyes, each sinister, still hand, and up the stairs to her room. As always, she went at once to the window and looked out. It was so peaceful. No one stirred. Light fell from the frosted glass of the Anchor over the cracked pavement. The cobbles were scarcely wet. 'It wasn't rain for anybody to shelter from,' she thought, a little puzzled. And then had a sudden feeling that he had returned and was waiting again in the porch below. She dropped her hand from the curtains, glancing back quickly at the door of the room.

'I can't bear one more night alone,' she thought. 'This must be the last. Whatever I do, however I sink my pride, I'll go mad if I ever have to be alone here again.'

She tried to draw the curtains quite noiselessly and sat facing the door, her ears strained to catch sounds which her reason would deny. There was no commonsense left in her, and she was too afraid to go to bed.

'Good night, my dear,' Bertram said, taking up the empty Guinness bottles.

'Yes, it will be nice to go to bed,' Tory yawned. 'It has been rather a day. All very nice, but tiring. It is tiring, you know, pretending to be a boring, sensible old mum, the salt of the earth and all the rest of it.' She looked at her pale fingernails and sighed. 'So good night, Bertram, and thank you. I hardly know how to keep my eyelids open after all that Guinness and riding in trains.'

At the door he stopped, bottles in his pockets and under each arm. 'To-morrow morning I'll be working . . .'

'Working?' she echoed incredulously.

'Painting,' he said with severity. 'And in the evening I have a darts match next door. But I shall be round in the afternoon to propose to you as usual.'

'What a busy ...' she began and then checking herself, pretended to yawn again.

He knew she had been about to say 'old man'. 'It is what I am,' he thought. 'I suppose it is what I seem to her, to everyone, except myself.' And he went home after that, rather dejected.

'And don't talk in your sleep to-night,' Iris said.

'Why? Did I?'

'You're always doing it.'

'What do I say?'

'That's the annoying thing – I can never make head or tail of it.'

'Iris!'

'What?'

'Those are my stockings you've got on.'

'They certainly aren't.'

'They certainly are. Where did you get them from?'

'As a matter of fact,' Iris said, in a different tone, 'they're one of a dozen pairs I had sent over from Paris.' She sat on the edge of the bed and rolled them down carefully.

'I'd know my darning anywhere. And yours.'

Iris ignored her, stretching her leg out, flexing her foot.

'I was just limbering up on the set to-day ...' she began, but Maisie snatched away the stockings and held them under the light.

'There you are! *You* can't darn like that.'

But Iris put the backs of her hands to her mouth, yawning, her elbows raised and her slip tight across her breasts. 'No one in to-night,' she said. 'Quiet. Oh, my God, deathly quiet. Awful. You just don't know. Old Pallister – "Quiet, to-night, Iris." "Yes, Mr Pallister." "Nice mild evening." "That's right." "Soon have summer here." "I hope so, I'm sure." ... Lily Wilson stuck there on her stool, like a ghost taken to the drink. No sign of the old boy.'

Eddie's bedroom was empty, and they did not lower their voices to-night.

'Now, this summer,' Iris went on, brightening, 'I shouldn't be surprised if someone like Cecil Beaton came down and discovered the place. Well, it's picturesque; it stinks enough. The only trouble is that people who like old places are always such peculiar old fogies themselves, especially the women; well, the men, too, really. But still, I'd make a good photograph, I think, taken in front of that cut-glass panel in the saloon bar, with some of those pots of tongue-ferns lying on their sides. I've seen pictures like that in those *Vogues* Mrs Foyle gave me. Might get on the films that way, you know. Photogenic.' She seemed to like that word and repeated it.

Her silk slip crackled as she pulled it off.

'I believe you're sulking, Maisie darling. All about a pair of stockings.'

She climbed into bed beside her sister.

Maisie wasn't sulking. She was thinking about Eddie, trying to imagine what he was doing at that moment and, for the first time in her life, wondering what it was like out there in the dark.

'Now, remember!' Iris said, as if it were her final word. 'No talking to-night.' And she heaved over, taking most of the bed-clothes with her.

*

Moving stiffly in his oilskins, Eddie had forgotten his brief sleep. His uncle was up at the winch in front of the wheelhouse and they had begun to haul in the net. First the otterboards came over the bulwarks, and then the wooden rollers, and, at last, the great net itself, water pouring from it as it emerged from the sea, and the gulls suddenly gathering from nowhere, it seemed, and clustering above the haul. With a great slithering the net was emptied over the deck, shells clattering down with the fish, bits of wreckage, parts of aircraft – a fantastic cornucopia, starfish, weeds and other rubbish, crabs, plaice, sole, cod.

When the net had gone down again Eddie went forward up the slimy deck among the brown and ice-white of the fish, stooping down in the cold dawn light, sorting good from trash, working hard as he always did. He annoyed the men often enough with his youthful, flamboyant ways; all that crooning, they said, and changing into his good navy suit before going ashore; but while he was on the job he worked, and while he worked he moaned away everlastingly at those self-pitying songs of his, and thought of Maisie and the nice little suppers she cooked, and how smooth her shoulders were when he touched them that night, how sweet she smelled of soap, and how often, through the thin bedroom wall, he heard her turning over in her sleep and murmuring. Or was it Iris, after all? – he suddenly wondered.

9

Mrs Bracey began to sense something which was not visible enough for comment – an assumed silence between her daughter Maisie and Eddie Flitcroft. It was as if they were in a conspiracy to say as little as possible to one another, and for this reason any words that did chance to pass between them were weighted with meaning, something for Mrs Bracey to puzzle over, to unravel for hours at a time. This exhausted her. She felt like saying, quite definitely, 'I'm not having it,' but could not be definite about *what* she was not going to have. If anything more than the most trivial phrases were ever exchanged between them she, with all her searching looks, could not discover it. Yet she knew there was something, and the perpetual bantering between Eddie and Iris did not fog her in the least. 'How long are they going on like this?' she would wonder, and then it would occur to her that they were waiting to be rid of her and perhaps confident of her early death. Before long, Eddie came to symbolise to her the imminence of death, which was a strange thing for him to symbolise, with all his swaggering, defiant ways and lively assurance.

She did not know how to be rid of him, having let him in in the first place, to enrich the scene, hoping he would bring some life in to her; but he had brought only the idea of death.

Maisie had grown quieter, as if she had but to hold her tongue and wait. When her mother grumbled about Eddie – his whistling, unpunctuality, door-slamming, appetite and badinage – she did not answer. When the complaints were made directly to him, a glance from Maisie checked his reply.

Eventually, one afternoon when Mr Lidiard, the curate, had called, a brilliant idea came to Mrs Bracey.

'I see young Foyle is home for his holidays,' he had begun.

'That'll clip her wings,' she said at once.

'He's grown a lot – a nice lad.'

'I daresay, but I'm not likely to see.'

And then in a flash it came to her that she *could* see, for if she moved upstairs again to her old front bedroom, she could see it all once more, a good view of the harbour, too, the waterfront, the little flights of steps, the lighthouse, the people on the quay, and the fishing-fleet putting out and returning, the fish-baskets going up to the market – all the sights she had known since she was a little girl, skipping about those narrow passages, up and down those flights of steps, and which she had never thought to see again.

'I've been thinking, Maisie,' she said (and that was untrue, because the idea had come to her only a second before in that flash of brilliance which artists call inspiration), 'why not move me up to my old room now the summer's coming? I could get a nice view out of the window there, something to pass the time. All I see here is this blasted wall and the basket of tongue-ferns, rain dripping out of it all the winter, too, gets on my nerves; I find myself counting the drops. And that drainpipe, too. I see it in my dreams. Hours and hours I've stared at it, wet and fine. That's no way to spend the last years of my life.'

'Years!' Mr Lidiard thought, depressed. Maisie felt the same.

'But we moved you down because you said you were lonely up there and felt left out of things.'

'It won't hurt Mr Lidiard to climb the stairs.'

He smiled professionally.

And then Iris said, for Maisie would not: 'What about Eddie?'

'Eddie's nothing to me,' her mother said sharply. 'I'm not called upon to consider him. If I want the room he'll have to go.'

No one answered. A little while later Maisie said casually: 'All right, but I don't take the responsibility of moving you till Dr Cazabon's been asked.'

'So that's your way out, sly little madam!' her mother thought, and she was determined that Maisie should not get a word in first with the doctor. She called for the pot of ink and a writing-pad, and, in letters which were duplicated because the pen nib was split, she wrote a little note to the doctor urging him to call at once. She folded this over and wrote 'By Hand' in one corner and then gave it to Mr Lidiard. 'You can drop that in on your way,' she told him, feeling that clergymen, though dense and foolish, are to be relied upon.

'By Hand,' he read out, laughing a little.

'Meaning it wasn't the postman delivered it,' she explained grandly.

'Don't postmen have hands?' Iris giggled.

'You're quiet, Maisie,' Mrs Bracey said. 'What's upset you? The thought of me having a bit of a change, I suppose?'

'That's right,' Maisie said quietly.

'Sarkey little tripehound.'

'Now, come . . .!' Mr Lidiard began persuasively, as if to an ill-behaved child.

Maisie went out into the scullery to get tea, shutting the door so softly that her mother was enraged. She put the kettle on the gas and stood with her hands spread over the warmth, trying to sort out her tangled emotions. She had come to rely on Eddie's support, the feeling that in all her trials he was upholding her by the very fact of being an ordinary person, as she felt she herself was an ordinary person. When he was away she looked forward to his return and liked to feel that he slept under the same roof. She realised now that her mother was determined to get rid of him and that her little inspiration about Dr Cazabon had already been perceived and defeated. Eddie would go, and she could imagine how fractious her mother would become once she had her way, how peevish each time she heard voices in the shop below, how often her stick would be banged on the floor and self-pity force tears down her cheeks. Her own life would become a misery of running up and down stairs, much more of a misery even than it was now. The hope that Dr Cazabon, unless reasoned with beforehand, would refuse to let her be moved was faint indeed, for, as Mrs Bracey's body had reached a standstill, so her age seemed to have done the same, and years added nothing noticeable to her, nor moved her one inch nearer death, her daughter thought. Thus her energy had been stored and had nothing else to expend itself upon but only the evasion of illness, the building up of reserves.

So Maisie made the tea and carried it in, feeling hopeless and suffocated, as if she suffered from a paralysis of nerves and brain, deadened into a clockwork motion only between shop and sick-bed and into ministrations which had become duty only and performed now with hatred and loathing.

Presently Mr Lidiard rose and stood smiling, his fingers tapping gently on the folded paper Mrs Bracey had given him. 'Well . . . I must get this note to the doctor before surgery, I suppose,' he began, thanking heaven for the excuse.

For once, she did not attempt to restrain him: her will seemed to propel him out of the room. So, dully, Maisie gathered the cups and saucers and carried them to the scullery.

The letter came flying through the Cazabons' door soon after tea. In that hall, the heavy chairs, the carved table seemed to crouch in darkness all day long, each tick of the clock sounded as if it would very likely be the last, and smells of English dinners drifted through a pair of plush curtains hanging in an archway. It was so much a house which had been taken over half-furnished from previous owners, and only a gathering shabbiness had been Beth's contribution; for she, often observant of detail, so that her characters might move in significant and vivid atmospheres, quite oblivious of her own surroundings, saw nothing of the sum-total of drabness, was never afflicted by ugliness nor irritated by disorder. When she tripped over the threadbare rugs, she patiently straightened them; pictures remained crooked until Robert set them right, and the books on the shelves were in no more order than the vast jumbles of underclothes and woollies in her chest of drawers, or that surrealist collection in the attic, where waves of rubbish had now reached forward to the door, so that it could scarcely be opened for all the gymnastic apparatus, cracked mirrors, mounted antlers and dressmaker's dummies which arose before it.

The folded sheet of paper fluttered into the darkness and came to rest against the umbrella-stand. Each time a door opened or a skirt brushed by one of its halves lifted and quivered slightly like the wing of a dead butterfly.

'I think,' said Bertram, 'that it would be an excellent idea.' He clapped his hands together to match the heartiness of his words and looked pleased, as if it had been his own idea entirely. 'If you hate it, if you find you have made a mistake, it will still have been a change. As with a holiday, if it ends in your wishing to come home, its aim is accomplished.'

It was only Mrs Bracey's move upstairs he was discussing, and Maisie could not feel that it was in the least his concern, a stranger to the place.

'Doctor's a long time,' Mrs Bracey said, beginning to be afraid that her plan had been overthrown, that Maisie had smuggled messages out of the house under her very eyes. 'I thought he'd have been here by now.' She felt terribly nervous and overwrought, so anxious to look once more at the outside world and to see, moving and in colour, that view of the harbour which had been a grey and white, remembered, half-imagined scene for so long, flat like a picture-postcard view. She wanted to watch the great dappled waves riding in to the foot of the cliffs, breaking and crumbling and scurrying back in confusion, to be conscious of the pulse of the lighthouse, to see once more visitors with folded raincoats stepping into rowing-boats named *Nancy* or *Marigold* or *Adeline*; the moving water, the sauntering people, the changing sky, the wrinkled moonlight on the sea, and fishermen coming out of the Anchor on Saturday nights, standing round the lamp-post singing *Sweet Genevieve*. 'It must be to-morrow,' she thought, wondering how she had existed so long shut away in that back room with her view of the drainpipe and the blank wall, with rain, always it now seemed, falling down it. Yet, powerful as she was, in the end she could decide nothing. Like a baby, she could vent bad temper on them, but could not even move of her own accord.

When he had finished his coffee Robert went out. Beth thought he had gone to put the car away and she took up her work quickly to make the most of his absence. As he passed through the hall Mrs Bracey's note quivered a little in the draught, lying there in the shadow of the umbrella-stand.

'It is worse when Edward is here,' Tory said. 'I feel much worse.' When Robert had kissed her, she went on as if nothing had happened. 'Much, much worse. I don't think we are going to get much fun out of this,' she added.

'Fun!' Robert echoed, rather taken aback by this novel way of looking at serious passion. 'My God! I wouldn't jeopardise the whole of my life, let all my sense of right be overthrown for mere fun.'

'Oh, I would,' Tory said.

'You try to shock me, but I have known you for too long.'

'Tell me how long you have loved me.'

'I admired you and disliked you for years, but, you see, my life had settled into a routine – work and home and bed. I thought nothing would shake me out of it. And then little anxieties about the children or about my work seemed to eat away my vitality, so that I was always tired and felt that other people – especially people like you – were too much for me, belonged to another world which I wouldn't enter any more. You seemed so inaccessible that I never gave you a thought and although you disturbed me a little when I did see you, that was only another reason for avoiding you – for I hated to be disturbed. Your eyes are a deep mauve, you know.'

'Mauve!' She edged away from him in amazement. 'I have violet eyes.'

'Well, violets *are* mauve, aren't they?'

He felt wretchedly at sea and he had wasted time talking, when all he had come for was to experience again that danger and delight of being near her, of drawing her close to him, which he did always with a feeling of throwing himself upon rocks, so little used was he to either the danger or the delight.

'I am afraid I shall have to go.'

'Does Beth imagine you are on a case?'

'Women are so *coarse*,' he thought, wincing at her – perhaps – unconscious brutality. He said nothing, but his face darkened, as she could see.

'Are we never to mention Beth?' she cried. 'Are we so sensitive about the sound of her name that we pretend that she's not there, in case we should feel ourselves cheapened or soiled by what we are doing? Furtive, yet high-minded.'

Since she had abandoned all delicacy of feeling, he felt entitled to do the same, to make her answer a question he had not yet dared to put to her – scarcely to himself. Even so, he had to get up and walk about the room while he asked her.

'For years,' he began, 'you have been utterly indifferent to me. I've walked in and out of rooms without your knowing even, caring still less. You've not even raised your eyes or paused in your everlasting women's chatter with Beth. You came to the house to see her, never once to see me; in fact, you probably left when I arrived because I bored you, or interrupted the gossip and reminiscence. You may say it was the same for me, but I was never indifferent to you. I disliked you, or tried to, as I have said; but I found your beauty exciting just as I found your attitude to life frivolous and shocking. I think I disapproved of you – that was it – but only in the cold, law-making part of my brain. The rest of me, the instinctive side, only awaited one look of recognition from you, one sign, to be completely conquered. But the sign never came. And all the time I was arming myself against such a sign with a catalogue of your faults – how you were selfish and intolerant, often rude to people who had not your advantages, vain, unscrupulous, querulous with Teddy ... no, let me go on ... now I have forgotten what I was going to say ... All this ... and it surely amounted to something, I thought ... yet to be swept away so immediately by the realisation that something had changed, that I myself had changed as a personality in your imagination, that I was no longer just not there, but that you were definitely aware of me, avoiding me, even. How that knowledge gradually came to me I can't remember. Day after day I became more certain, until I determined to make sure and would come into the room and try to catch your glance. I never could. And then one day I did. I caught you looking at me, and before you moved your head quickly away I saw everything in your eyes – anguish and horror and despair. Thank you for listening. What it has all led to is this – Why? What changed you? How does a woman suddenly become aware of a man she has known for twenty years? No, let me tell you the answer. Isn't it because your husband has gone, so that for the first time in your life you are alone and hate it, and must have some man, because your sort of woman does have to? And I am the man, because I am available, the man who never interested you before, who was merely the boring creature your friend had unaccountably married.'

Tory sat quite still, unhurt by his words. She guessed that he was making a final struggle with pride and conscience in order to say to himself at the end: 'And yet I truly love her.'

All she said was: 'You see, we always quarrel. I told you it wouldn't be much fun.'

'I have never behaved like this before, or stooped to such petty deceptions – all so lamentably easy because I am trusted, and so much worse because of that.'

'You imply that I have been at it all my life.'

'It would never have occurred to me. But you are and always have been more frivolous than I.'

'Frivolous? *Do* people still use that word? It sounds so Edwardian.'

'You are a very Edwardian woman, with your pink and white looks and your preoccupation with fashions and appearances and worldly things. And your utter selfishness and lack of care for others.'

'Stop picking up ornaments and putting them down roughly. It is a thing Bertram does and fidgets me very much.'

'Bertram?'

So artlessly, he straightened himself and frowned.

'The old boy who is staying at the pub.'

'Does he come here often?'

'Oh, quite often.'

'I wish you wouldn't, Tory.'

'Wouldn't what?'

He almost said: 'You will be gossiped about,' and she smiled, just as if he had said it.

'I *shall* have to go.' 'Words, words!' he thought. 'We try to put a barrier of words between us.' He took her hands and drew her up from the sofa into one of those embraces they could neither endure nor forgo, which had no ending for them except by the limit of time or interruption from the outside world.

Now Mrs Bracey was convinced of treachery. Perhaps a glance from Maisie had been sufficient to induce the curate to the violation of his trust, the interception of messages, the frustration of her plans. At nine o'clock she sent Bertram off to follow up the note, watched her daughter's face while she gave her instructions, and saw nothing there but indifference.

Bertram went on the errand quite willingly; an opportunity to see inside another door, he thought, ringing the Cazabons' bell.

Prudence looked a little surprised, for no note had arrived, she said, and, half-turning back to the hall as if proving her words, saw the folded paper lying there by the umbrella-stand.

'What a draught!' Beth said, coming through an open door into the hall, loose papers flapping in her hand.

'It is a message for Father,' Prudence said.

'Where *is* your father?'

'I'll fetch him,' Prudence said suddenly, and rushed past Bertram and out through the front door, as if there were not a minute to be lost.

'Well, please do come in and wait!' Beth said to Bertram, with a faintly puzzled air, and she opened the door into the dining-room with a hospitable gesture, at once annulled, he thought, by the cheerless lake of table, the massive architecture of the sideboard, with its tarnished toast-racks and empty decanters.

'If only there were hours and hours!' Tory whispered. 'These snatched-at fragments are death. A lingering death.'

They sat in the firelight, while Robert tried to break away, to make himself leave her; but his reluctance amounted to a physical pain such as a limpet must surely feel, he thought, when it is prised from the ledge of a rock.

He stroked her rounded forearm, laced her white fingers into his, and ran his thumb over her throbbing wrist and the beautiful flatness that came down from the back of her hand. Then the serenity, the delight he felt in doing so would be broken up by a sudden, mutual quickening of their blood, so that their fingers gripped desperately together and in the thickening silence oceans roared in their ears and the room was full of the sound of their hearts beating.

When the door-bell rang they seemed to spin apart, horror between them, and tried to scramble back to everyday life out of a pit of blackness.

Prudence, on the doorstep, noted how the dark windows were suddenly lit up, throwing oblongs of light over the pavement and a lunette of yellow shining above the door. She dreaded the footsteps which came at last along the passage, the quick tap of Tory's high heels and her voice thrown back to someone inside a room.

'It must be Bertram,' Tory had said and opened the door with a sort of bravado she could no longer sustain before Prudence. A mad plan for slamming the door in the girl's face was rejected with an effort.

'Why, Prudence—!' she began.

'I have a message for my father,' Prudence said breathlessly, holding out the note but retaining it.

'Come in, my dear.'

Tory became very grave and preceded the girl into the room so that she could at least meet Robert's eyes with a flicker of

156

warning in her own which made no difference except to reflect alarm.

Prudence came forward with the look of a sleep-walker, the note still held out in her hand.

'What is it, Prue?'

'A note from Mrs Bracey. It has only just been found in the hall.'

'Have you been searching for me?' he asked.

'No, I came straight here,' she said artlessly, telling him what he needed to know.

He had unfolded the note and stood reading it. Prudence kept quite still, looking down at a pale medallion upon the blue carpet, fixedly, as if the rest of the room had some power to frighten her. Tory (oh, so carelessly!) put up her hand and pressed in hair-pins.

'I'll go at once,' Robert said, glancing at his watch. 'Will you fetch the black case from the surgery, Prue?'

'But it's so late,' Tory began, as soon as the girl had fled.

'Mrs Bracey is one of my crosses. She might last for years, but if she is going to die it would be as well for me to be there and not here.'

'How did Prue know?'

'I can't do this, Tory. At times like this, the enormity of it all seems . . . and how hopeless, and cheap, and farcical.'

'I know. I wonder what Beth imagines. And what am I to say?'

'Nothing. Say nothing until I've thought. Just keep out of the way.'

As soon as he heard his own door slammed he went out to meet Prudence, to take the case from her, and hurry off, with nothing but a brief word of thanks to her.

*

'Where did you find Robert?' Beth asked.

'He was just coming in,' Prudence said. 'I met him outside.'

'I'll heat some milk for him,' Beth said. 'He will be dreadfully tired. Poor Mrs Bracey. Are you going to bed, my dear?'

But Prudence had gone already. She walked slowly up the stairs, the cats going up lightly beside her, her hands covering her face and wet with tears.

'What's all this fuss about?' Robert demanded. 'You can change rooms if you want to without calling me out in the dead of night! Or must I carry you upstairs in my arms? Is that it?'

Beth would have been quite astonished by his robust manner. Tory would have been astonished, too.

'Make doctor a cup of tea!' Mrs Bracey called to Maisie, who half hesitated, waiting for his usual refusal. It did not come. For once he seemed in no hurry to be away, and Mrs Bracey, although delighting in this, noted the fact carefully.

He lingered over his tea, had a second cup, ate a biscuit, made a few jokes. When he went at last, she said: 'Doctor's in fine fettle to-night,' and felt she was herself, full of excitement about the morrow.

As soon as he stepped outside, tiredness and depression dropped over him like a damp cloak.

10

Tory was right as well as unusual when she described her son Edward as an ordinary little boy. She did so not only because she believed it to be true, but partly because she was weary of all the mothers of her acquaintance claiming sensitive and highly-strung children, no matter how phlegmatic, even bovine, they might be.

Edward returned from school more or less the same as when he went away; cheerful, rigidly conservative, and lazy with the instinctive, deeply-rooted preserving laziness of a growing boy.

A feeling of wonderful security had enfolded him as he opened his bedroom door. The room seemed much smaller at first; the picture of 'When Did You Last See Your Father?' (over which Tory so grimly smiled) less brilliant in colour, less poignant in anxiety and noble falsehood.

The dormer window was above the cobbled yard Robert had mentioned so disparagingly and to which Tory had given – she hoped – a Continental air, with creeper on a trellis, a bay tree in a tub and two chairs of overwrought iron. Unfortunately, sheets of corrugated roofing, bright with rust, were plainly visible above the wall, on the other side of which they made a shelter for crates and empty barrels at the pub.

After the vast asphalt of the school yard, the flat vistas of playing-fields, it was a relief to have the eye checked, the pace slowed, by cramped surroundings. Detail entrances a child and warms his imagination and at school there is a dearth of detail, so that the imagination loses its glow and often dies. Edward found newly exquisite the prettiness of his mother's house, the collection of blue glass, the copper plates with their pinkish lights, the tongue-ferns lolling out between the stones of the garden wall, and, especially, perhaps, the detail of the food he ate – scatterings of parsley, radishes cut like water-lilies, the fleurons, the garnishings, and all the touches which distinguish private food from institutional.

'And how does your son like school?' Bertram asked, having looked in after breakfast, curious to see the boy. Edward, however, was up at the fish-market, standing on the slimy stone floor and watching the baskets of cod and whiting being brought in.

'He says it is not bad,' Tory answered reservedly.

'In fact, grounds for any other mother to say he has taken to it as a duck to water.'

Tory would not encourage him with a smile. She wanted only to be rid of him this morning so that she could attempt to untangle her thoughts as she had tried and failed to do during the night. She stood very still by the window, obviously waiting for him to go. Her instructions from Robert, to keep out of Beth's way, would be simple enough, for Beth so seldom went out of the house; but she did feel all sorts of compulsions, which seemed to her vulgar and petty – the compulsion of telling lies, not in the grand manner, but in an intricacy of excuses, trivial explanations, distortions, all to be devised beforehand, and complicated by the necessity of making the same explanations and distortions as Robert; all this, moreover, to her dearest friend with whom there had been since childhood only clarity and candour and intimacy, and to Prudence, a young girl to whom it would be lowering to explain anything. Useless it would be, too, she must now admit, having considered during the long night, how hopeless her case was with Prudence, who had guessed at once where she might find her father and must have noticed that careless switching-on of lights before Tory opened the front door. Inadvertently, by her behaviour, and deliberately, by hints, she had shown how she felt herself to be confronted by their guilt.

As she stood there hoping that Bertram would go, she was horrified suddenly by the appearance of Beth, who had come out of her own house and now stood looking at the harbour, where the trawlers, closely packed in a small space, grated against one another, masts and funnels like a forest along the sea-wall.

'Now here's Beth!' Tory said crossly, as if this were entirely Bertram's fault. She felt in a great flurry and tried to will Beth away, moving discreetly from the window as she did so.

'I must go,' Bertram said. 'I have a great job on hand to-day, and I could not mean that more literally. This afternoon young Flitcroft and I are to carry Mrs Bracey upstairs. Perhaps this is the last time you will see me as I am.'

Tory laughed at last. 'It will be a lesson to you not to romanticise yourself, nor to see poetry in people in whom it does not exist. Even Rembrandt didn't have to carry those fat old women about. I could not be more delighted.' She moved to the door as

Beth rang the bell. She was determined now, in spite of having had no time to lay the lies out ready in her mind, to seem at her gayest, most self-possessed, and she crossed the hall and opened the door, still smiling.

Beth's gravity smote her heart.

'Well, now!' said Bertram, coming into the hall after her, bowing to Beth. 'I will go and collect some strength together, prepare myself.'

'What *does* he mean?' Beth asked after he had gone.

'He has to help Mrs Bracey upstairs this afternoon; or rather carry her up as a dead weight. I can't imagine how it is to be done. And as soon as she's there, no doubt she'll want to be moved down again.'

They had drifted back into the little sitting-room. Beth sat down at an angle to the table, suggesting that her call was of a temporary nature. Tory waited, her heart lurching about drunkenly. She turned away to light a cigarette.

Beth launched upon one of her long explanations and was a good way through it before Tory realised that favours were being asked of her, and favours of a safe and trivial kind.

'... And it would mean staying the night in London,' Beth was saying. 'If I were to do any shopping as well ...'

Tory looked blank at her.

'If you could keep an eye on Stevie ...'

'Of course.'

'And perhaps have her in to lunch ...'

Beth floundered wretchedly, awaiting the generous offers she had been so sure of, so sure, that she had not prepared herself for asking each favour separately. Then suddenly Tory warmed and thawed and smiled.

'My dear Beth, she shall come for as long as you like and be welcome every minute of it. Don't dream of coming home until you want to. You deserve a change.'

And then again Beth saw the warmth fade even from Tory's face, which paled. She was like one of those spring days, full of flooding sunshine and curt showers.

'*Whom* did you say you have to see?'

'My publisher,' Beth said, surprised at having to repeat what she had already explained.

'Oh, yes. Then you can make a day of it, as they say, go to the theatre afterwards to cheer yourself up . . .'

'I said "publisher", not dentist.'

'Oh, well . . . And buy yourself something beautiful – a new summer hat.'

Beth smiled at Tory's idea of a good day out.

'But don't come back with string bags full of children's shoes,' Tory went on, 'or I shall be quite cross. When did you say it was to be?'

'To-morrow. I don't believe you are listening to a word I say.'

'My thoughts run on at once to all the important things, you see – what you are going to buy and what you are going to wear.'

'My green suit, I thought.'

'Oh, no! You look all behind in that. I always knew it was a mistake.'

'Well, I *am* all behind. It's because I sit on it so much. I can't disguise it.'

'But of course you can. Everybody else does.'

'What does it matter? I'm middle-aged,' Beth said tactlessly. 'I don't care any longer.'

'Nonsense. You're the same age as me. I will lend you a corset and my new hat.'

'It sounds,' said Beth, 'like one of those indecent slot-machines "The Secrets of an Actress". There is one at the Fun Fair, Prudence told me – a pack of fading postcards flicking over, showing a woman unlacing some black stays . . .'

'Oh, I know! And as soon as she gets them unlaced she skips behind a screen and throws them over the top, and then there is a prim click and that's all. Edward is very fond of it, although he can't possibly appreciate its daring.'

'Where is Edward?' Beth glanced round as if he might possibly have been overlooked.

'He went out early to watch the fishing-fleet come in.'

'Oh . . . well, then!' Beth hesitated and then stood up. 'If you are quite sure about to-morrow . . . I am sorry to have to ask you when I have a grown-up daughter, but Prue is behaving so strangely . . .'

'Prue!' Tory said coldly, alarmed now that she had not escaped after all.

'She is so rude to Robert, as if she had some grudge against him. She sits and stares at him at mealtimes, and yet won't meet his glance. Her manner is – uncomfortable. She is like a thorn-tree encased in ice.' Beth spread the fingers of one hand along the edge of the table and seemed to consider them, while in reality she reconsidered her simile. 'Yes!' She raised her eyes and smiled and Tory saw in them a little flicker of pleasure, of triumph, even, soon filmed over by anxiety.

'I think she ought to go away, you know,' she heard herself telling Beth. She was shocked at herself, had never imagined that she could sink to such treachery or scheming or lack of compassion. The vulgar voice of rationalisation whispered: 'It's true. She ought to go . . .', but she was still too proud to listen to it, and brushed the words aside with shame and impatience.

'Robert won't hear of it,' Beth said in the proud, complacent way some wives describe their husband's obstinacies. 'He says she's much too delicate to go away at present.'

As she was taking leave she suddenly asked with the direct attack dreamy people can often use with good result: 'This … Bertram, is it? … is he fond of you?'

'He appears to be.'

'And what do you think of *him*?'

Tory's instinct was at once to laugh, but that new acuity she despised in herself enforced a sort of coy hesitation, and she shrugged her shoulders in an expressive way, yet without knowing what it signified, only conscious of a desire to fog poor Beth and foist on her imagination notions of romance, of relationships which were welcome and permissible.

Beth, to whom human nature was an open book, which, moreover, she would finish writing herself, could see through her friend's hesitation and drew in her cheeks with a sly smile. This Tory noticed with a confusion of feelings, despising Beth for her lack of perception and herself for misleading her; and, above all, annoyed that a romantic attachment for an old man should be so easily attributed to her.

'So you would consider that a good match?' she asked frostily.

'You couldn't make a good match. You would always be throwing yourself away, my dear, as you threw yourself away upon Teddy.'

'Oh, Beth, you are the sort of person who insists on making gallant speeches at weddings and on the other side of every compliment is an insult for somebody or other. Come in this evening and let me dress you up for to-morrow! We will have some good fun trying clothes on.'

'You shall not dress me up as a girl of seventeen,' Beth insisted.

'It is beyond me how tactless you are!' Tory laughed.

When Beth had gone, Tory leant for a moment against the inside of the front door. 'If I throw away Beth,' she told herself, 'I throw away my best chance of happiness.' And she felt that that must answer the hedonists, since we do not appear to seek what will give us pleasure, nor to feel ourselves satisfied by mere happiness.

Eddie had come walking jauntily in, swinging a fry of fish on a piece of string, wearing his good navy suit over his thick jersey. Maisie was in the shop, wrapping up a pair of broken shoes for a customer, and by her glance he knew that something was wrong. He stood by whistling, until she was alone.

'Mother wants to speak to you,' she then said.

'What about?'

'You'd better go and see.' Maisie hesitated. 'She wants your room. You've got to clear out.'

'She can't do that.'

Maisie could not be bothered to answer such a stupid statement. She turned away.

Eddie opened the door into the back room and went in. Even Mrs Bracey faltered when she saw his expression.

'What's all this?' he thundered.

'Ah, Eddie!' she said. She laid down her book and tried to look pleased to see him. 'I've a favour to ask of you. I know you won't mind giving up that room, but Dr Cazabon says I need the change.'

'Dr Cazabon?'

'That's right.'

'What about me?'

'Well, I made it plain to your auntie at the time that it only

166

held good for so long as I might see my way clear . . .' She had embarked upon one of those formal, meaningless sentences which are heavy with grandeur but difficult to round off.

'I mean, where do I go?'

'Your auntie'll have to put you up on the front-room sofa.'

He saw himself reclining on one elbow upon slippery horse-hair-stuffed leather, the window darkened with curtains which parted only an inch or two to show the plant on what was called the palm-stand, and the room chill and gloomy as a sea-cavern.

'If I go now, I'll never enter this house again,' he said.

Nothing clouded Edward's happiness. Life entranced him. When the sun shone it touched his very bones. Time was un-divided now by bells clanging; so he could drift, beguiled, unchevied, wandering in that maze of alley-ways where the roofs went tipping down so steeply towards the harbour that he could spit down the chimneys from where he stood, he thought. With the sun shining on them, these roofs were the colours of pigeons – the slates of rose and grey and lavender and blue. It was all familiar yet wonderful to him.

He stopped to read the picture postcards at the tobac-conist's – a fat woman bending down to make a sand-castle, red bloomers, 'What would you do, chums?' printed underneath. He laughed aloud at this joke, standing there, squinting with the sun, jingling coins in his pocket.

Then on down the cobbled streets until the sea showed in a little cup at the bottom. Far out, a white-sailed yacht ventured across the smooth stretch of glinting purple. Nearer in, the water was turquoise. In the harbour itself there was the fleet and a great congregation of gulls.

He passed the Waxworks and walked out along the quay. 'For every Pipe Puncheon or Piece of Wine or Spirits,' he read aloud off the wall of the old Customs house, 'and so in proportion in smaller quantities the charge of one florin.'

By the lighthouse an old man with a beard was sketching the harbour. Edward went and stood by him, whistling, clinking his pocketful of coins. Along the waterfront Stevie rode on her tricycle, wearing Beth's torn bridal-veil and a wreath of broken orange-blossom over one ear. The veil streamed out behind her, so furiously she went, and her little legs pedalled at a great rate. Edward laughed to himself.

'Good day,' Bertram said, sketching busily. It was an important moment for both of them, he felt – this first meeting with his future stepson.

'Good day,' Edward said at once, edging a little nearer to the sketch, which was very good, he considered, very like, obviously a harbour.

'I think you must be Edward Foyle,' Bertram said, and he looked down at the boy's slate-blue eyes and the great sweeping lashes on the downy cheeks.

'Yes, I am,' Edward admitted, glancing at the beard with curiosity. He turned his back to the wall and looked out to sea. Bertram turned, too.

'My father had a yacht,' the boy murmured, and he gazed and gazed at that tall, tipping wing of sail, and all his happiness was gone.

'Eddie having gone off in a huff like that, you'll have to fetch someone else in to help me upstairs,' Mrs Bracey informed her daughters. 'I can't be jarred about by a lot of incompetents. Is that bed aired, Maisie?'

'Yes.'

'And pulled up close to the window?'

'Yes.'

'Slip up to the vicarage, there's a good girl, and tell Mr Lidiard I want him urgent.'

'That I will not.'

'He'd come. Though what strength there is in him for a man's job I don't know. Tell him I want him here ready to make my last confession to him in case.' She laughed recklessly.

'That'd be worth hearing,' Iris said.

'Now Mr Hemingway, he's what we used to call a fine man in my young days, before there was all this crooning and moaning and men trying to look girlish. He reminds me of your father.'

Neither of the girls would fetch Mr Lidiard and in the end Bertram brought Ned Pallister in from his afternoon nap.

The short staircase led up from behind a door and was so dark that Maisie went before with a candle. The light wavered over the flushed, set faces of the two men, who a minute earlier had been teasing Mrs Bracey about her weight, and upon Mrs Bracey's own glistening forehead. Maisie went up backwards, the candle held at shoulder-height and great hunched shadows bending, climbing up over the walls and across the narrow ceiling.

They brought her up into the little room and put her on the bed by the window. All colour had now fled from her face and she lay there with her nostrils wide, her lips curved down.

'Thank you,' she breathed at last. 'Many thanks.'

'Perhaps she is going to die,' Maisie thought; for her appearance, her sudden courtesy did suggest this possibility.

She tidied the bedclothes, wiped her mother's face and Iris jerked the curtains wider apart, saying: 'There, now, you can have a nice look out at last.'

But Mrs Bracey would not glance outside until she was alone. Already her throat felt half closed with emotion, her eyes could not accustom themselves to their new limits, these rose-covered walls, or the lightness of the atmosphere.

'Maisie!' she said sharply. 'Run down and fetch that bottle of whisky I won in the Cruelty to Children Raffle. You put it to the back of the dresser cupboard.'

When Maisie had gone she said to Bertram: 'I'd really intended it to be for the bearers when I kick the bucket, but we'll have a nip out of it now and sod the undertakers.'

But as Maisie came back she could not help adding grudgingly: 'Once a bottle's broached it's as good as gone; no hope of keeping any for a special occasion; a sip here and there, a little nip of a cold night or if a neighbour gets a bad turn and you've come to the end before you can feel the benefit of it.'

Bertram sat on the edge of a frail bedroom chair in his shirt-sleeves and sipped from his tumbler. Ned Pallister leant against the wardrobe.

'Here's the best, Mrs Bracey,' he said, holding up his glass. 'Many more years of enjoying the view, I'm sure.'

She bowed in acknowledgment of this toast.

Iris was draped about the bed-post, picking her nail-varnish. Maisie went downstairs and they heard water droning into a kettle. Bertram and Mr Pallister finished their whisky and said good-bye.

'Many thanks,' Mrs Bracey said carelessly.

'A pleasure to do anything for a neighbour,' Ned Pallister replied. 'Any time, you've only to ask.'

'Next time I go down those stairs, I go with the lid screwed on,' she said. 'Show them out, Iris!'

Iris undraped herself. 'As if they don't know the way,' she thought, but did not say so aloud in front of her employer.

Then, when she was quite alone at last, Mrs Bracey heaved forward a little on one elbow and, drawing the curtain on one side, looked out.

'Persevere!' said Tory.

She sat on the fuchsia-coloured sofa in her bedroom window and watched the sea.

'I can't,' Beth gasped, trying to tuck great bunches of flesh into the corset.

'If I can, you can,' Tory said calmly.

Beth stood quite rigid in front of the mirror, not breathing. 'But I'm in agony. Surely it isn't like this for you all the time.'

'You get used to it. Put your skirt on. No, my black skirt.' She turned her head at last. 'You see! Don't breathe in little gasps like that. Put your shoulders back. You've slumped over your writing-table too long.'

'I shall never get out of it again.'

Tory suddenly became enthusiastic and fetched her best white blouse, the barathea jacket. Beth combed her short hair away from her temples and considered the effect rather shyly.

'It's a pity about the spectacles,' Tory said. 'Can't you possibly *not* wear them?'

'I should only get run over, and cut all my dearest friends.'

'There you are! You look like a real writer now,' she said. 'Neat, distinguished.'

'*I* think I look like a Lesbian,' Beth said doubtfully.

'You won't when your hat's on,' Tory encouraged her. 'A silly hat is what's needed. My red-currant hat which shames Edward so.'

'Oh, no!' Beth pleaded.

'I thought you wouldn't. What about this?' Tory twisted round and displayed a wheel of grey and yellow ostrich feathers. 'Or the new white hat. You'll have to go without spectacles. It won't matter for one day, surely?'

Beth put the hat rather nervously on her head at what she considered a daring angle to please Tory; she thought that if she could forget that the image in the mirror was herself, she might approve of it.

'*Not* forward!' Tory corrected her. 'Straight on the top of the head, or slightly back.' She walked round and round Beth. At last, satisfied, she sat on the bed, looking triumphant. 'You do see, don't you? And you won't add any finishing touches, please promise!'

'Suppose it rains?'

'Oh, well, if it rains you must wear your Burberry and just look dull and well-bred and hope for the best. Edward!' she called, going to the door, 'if you are out of the bath, run and fetch the sherry and a couple of glasses, there's a dear boy. I love sherry in the bedroom,' she said, turning back to Beth.

'It makes one feel like – like Becky Sharp,' Beth said, still turning slowly before the mirror as if bemused.

'Watch Edward's face when he comes,' Tory said.

But when he did come, carrying the tray carefully, his dressing gown cord trailing on the floor, his face was expressionless like a good waiter's, although smeared with tooth-paste.

'Do you see nothing different about Beth?' Tory asked him as she poured out the sherry.

'She has your clothes on,' Edward said.

'And does she look nice, do you think?'

Tory handed Beth a glass and they smiled at one another.

'She always looks nice, I think,' Edward said politely.

'Edward, you restore my pride,' Beth laughed. 'I was beginning to feel I was nothing in myself.'

'Good night, darling.' Tory bent and kissed him. 'Don't read too long.'

When he had gone she laughed. 'He is non-committal like his father,' she said, refilling their glasses. 'Sit down, for heaven's sake, Beth.'

'Sit down! I can't go sitting down here, there and everywhere just when the mood takes me. I cannot bend.'

'Then you had better practise. You can scarcely stand up to eat your lunch to-morrow.'

Beth slid uneasily on to a chair, her legs straight before her. They sat laughing and rocking, the sherry a little gone to their heads, the white hat tipping forward again over Beth's forehead.

'I wish I could be there to-morrow to see you,' Tory said weakly. 'That hat will astonish him, especially if it falls forward like that each time you take a bite.'

'*Him!*' Beth said. 'Astonish *whom?*'

'Your publisher, darling. Oh, hell, I can't speak properly now. Hush! the child will think we are intoxicated. I always imagine publishers looking like King Edward the Seventh, but I suppose they don't – no more than anybody else.'

Years fell away from them. They became two silly girls giggling at nothing.

'But my publisher is a woman,' Beth said, looking mystified. 'A woman!'

Tory sobered up at the shock. 'How could a publisher be a woman?'

'She *could* be and she is.'

'Well, I'm damned!' Tory exploded. 'You might have told me. You really are impossible, Beth. What the hell have we been wasting all this time for?'

11

It did rain. In the end Beth went to London in her Burberry and an old felt hat. She carried her night things in a battered hat-box, and took with her some string bags. She did not look at all like Tory's idea of what reviewers sometimes call 'lady novelists', but more like some sensible shopping woman. She also took a new exercise-book, hoping to bring Allegra to her last haven during the train journey. She yearned for the peace and quiet of the railway compartment, as Proust probably yearned for his padded, sound-proof study.

'You will miss that train!' Robert called up the stairs.

'I am just coming, dear.'

It had seemed at that moment as if the sky had suddenly lightened, as if it were going to be a fine, hot day after all, and she was wearing all the wrong clothes; too late to change. She dashed some white powder round her nose and in the middle of her forehead.

'The stew is in the casserole for to-night, Prue,' she called.

'You've told me three times.'

'Don't be rude to your mother,' Robert said sharply.

'This is for you to wear,' Stevie said, holding out a large enamelled butterfly which Beth pinned hastily to her suit.

'It won't show inside your rainingtosh.'

'But when the sun comes out I shall take it off and show everyone the glory.' Beth began to go down the stairs. 'Here I am, Robert. I left the note about the baker on the kitchen dresser. Please ask Mrs Flitcroft to iron Stevie's frock for to-morrow.'

'Beth, you will have to come,' Robert said, very quietly, very distinctly.

'That drawing of Stevie's foot for the new shoes!'

'Where did you put it?'

'Behind the clock.'

Now they were all flying about and shouting: the cats went distracted.

'Here it is!' Robert cried. 'We are now going, Beth.'

Outside the front door Beth stooped to kiss Stevie.

'I don't want you to go,' she wailed, twining her arms tightly round her mother's neck, pushing her hat over her eyes.

'Don't be silly, dear. Have a nice day with Edward and Tory.'

'I don't want to be left.'

'Stevie, go indoors,' Robert commanded.

'I want to go to London.'

Her mouth slowly opened, her face crimsoned, then the tears fell, fluently, easily. 'I haven't ever been to London.'

'You went to see *Peter Pan*, darling.'

'I didn't like it. I didn't enjoy that day.'

'Beth, don't argue with her.'

'But, sweetest, you know how you loved it at the time, and if you are a good girl I will take you to see it again another day.'

'I saw the wires. I saw the wires,' Stevie screamed, becoming slightly hysterical. 'When they flew, I saw the wires.'

'If we are going to stand here in the road discussing *Peter Pan*, I'll say good-bye,' Robert began.

'I can't leave her like this,' Beth said over her shoulder.

'I missed all that on the ship when I had to go out and be excused,' Stevie bawled. 'I missed the best part.'

Robert began slowly to walk away.

'You are always going and leaving me,' Stevie said, and Beth felt the injustice of this so keenly that she could not go without defending herself.

Tory's door opened and she came flying out, wearing the lilac overall in which she so neatly did her housework.

'Darling Beth, please go. She is just enjoying a little scene and she must not be indulged. As soon as you have gone she will lose interest in it.' She led Stevie into her own house.

'She wants a damned good thrashing,' said Robert, that mild man.

Beth's forehead had begun to pulse. 'I don't want to go,' she said unhappily.

'Don't *you* start,' Robert said, holding open the car door.

At the station, having bought Beth's ticket for her, Robert said good-bye and told her to have a nice time, endeavouring not to know that her heart was torn in two.

'Go to the theatre!' he added robustly, handing over the hat-box. 'Enjoy yourself! None of this moping about round the Elgin Marbles that seems to be your idea of a good time. Snap out of yourself a bit.'

Beth looked at him in amazement. He sounded quite unhinged, she thought. As he never kissed her in public, they merely smiled vaguely and drifted apart; she towards her waiting train and he out into the rainy station-yard.

She sat down in the carriage and closed her eyes. Her

forehead hammered dully. 'Prudence. Stevie. Robert. Has Stevie stopped screaming yet?' she wondered. 'I am a bad mother,' she once more told herself and fought back the feelings of shame and oppression which assailed her at this admission. 'When I have finished this book I will never write another word. I'll devote myself to Stevie, get Prue married somehow, turn Robert's shirt-cuffs, have the hall re-papered. I'll get a proper maid' (for the end of authorship would begin the season of miracles, she felt), 'early-morning tea to please Robert, constant hot water, new loose-covers. And I will have a freshly-laundered overall twice a week, like Tory, and flowers in all the rooms. Then, perhaps, when we are all reorganised I shall be able to write a short story here and there. None of that drugged sinking into a different world. No more guilt.'

She sat with her eyes closed and the train seemed to stretch itself and gather its great length forward out of the fish-smelling station to the open sky along the shoulders of cliffs.

'A man,' she thought suddenly, 'would consider this a business outing. But, then, a man would not have to cook the meals for the day overnight, nor consign his child to a friend, nor leave half-done the ironing, nor forget the grocery order as I now discover I have forgotten it. The artfulness of men,' she thought. 'They implant in us, foster in us, instincts which it is to their advantage for us to have, and which, in the end, we feel shame at not possessing.' She opened her eyes and glared with scorn at a middle-aged man reading a newspaper.

'A man like *that*,' she thought, 'a worthless creature, obviously; yet so long has his kind lorded it that I (who, if only I could have been ruthless and single-minded about my work as men are, could have been a good writer) feel slightly guilty at not being back at the kitchen-sink.'

The man began to shift uneasily under her scrutiny, to fold his arms and clear his throat and glance out of the window; so Beth, coming again to her senses, took out her writing things and wrote Chapter Eighteen at the head of a page. But she could not go on. Her spirits were too low to describe Allegra's death. She had looked forward to it so much, but now as she watched fields flying by, wondering where to begin, it was not Allegra's face which interposed, but Stevie's, crimson and tear-furrowed.

'I am sorry to be so rude and inquisitive,' Stevie said, going quickly through Tory's handbag. 'What a dear little silver box!'

'I thought, by-the-bye,' Tory began coldly, 'that you behaved pretty meanly to your mother just now.'

'You see, I wanted to go to London.'

'She never has a day off from you.'

'I never have a day off from her, either.'

'Well, you have got one now.'

'I didn't want it. Look at this photograph of Edward.'

'Don't try to change the subject. What I am trying to say is that you have made your mother set out unhappily on her day's pleasure.'

'She will soon cheer up.'

'I don't think so. Grown-ups don't cheer up as quickly as children do.'

'If she is miserable without me, she could have taken me with her,' Stevie said, exhausted by this absurd argument. 'I wanted to see *Peter Pan* again.'

'*Peter Pan* is not on,' said Tory, taking a false step.

'Yes it is. They go on doing it all the time when I am not

there, and as soon as they finish it they begin it all over again, but they have a cup of tea and go to be excused first. I wish *my* mother was like Mrs Darling.'

'All children wish that. It is very unfair to their mothers, because she wasn't much put to the test. Anyhow,' Tory said quickly, recovering her false move, '*her* children let *her* go out. They didn't make a scene and cry in the street.'

'As soon as she'd gone they weren't safe, though.'

'Do you like the pink junket or just plain white?' Tory inquired, getting up and going to the door.

If Stevie thought that Tory in her turn was changing the subject she was too polite to say so.

'I like the pink,' she replied, 'but it is up to you.'

At eleven the sun came out. At eleven-thirty it was obscured. Later, it rained again. So it went on all day. Mrs Bracey enjoyed the sudden changes. Down below her on the broken pavement the puddles reflected the blue sky or the blown clouds. The baker's van had dripped oil over the wet road and it lay there, a great iridescent splash of colour like a peacock's feather, bronze and pink and green. Now the surface of the sea was dinted like beaten metal by the rain, or pitted, a few minutes later, by glancing sunlight.

At tea-time the fleet put out again towards the fishing-grounds. She watched the trawlers as they were steered towards the mouth of the harbour, one after another until they were all spread out upon the open sea, and in the harbour there were only the coloured rowing-boats rocking to and fro on the littered water, and gulls.

Mrs Flitcroft came out on to the front steps of the Cazabons' house and waved a duster at the first trawler and then, seeing a neighbour from Lower Harbour Street, where the shops were, stood and chatted for half an hour, her hands folded across her stomach, her head nodding up and down. Mrs Bracey watched her grimly.

That afternoon two strangers appeared on the quay. They walked out to the lighthouse, mackintoshes over their shoulders; two school-mistresses, Mrs Bracey decided, watching them. One had a walking-stick with which she pointed out to the other places of interest along the coastline, also the church tower. At four o'clock they entered – rather dubiously – the Mimosa Café for a pot of tea. Lily Wilson, sweeping mice-dirts out of her window, rearranging the show cards, smiled to herself as she watched them. The first visitors.

It had been an exciting day, beginning for Mrs Bracey with Stevie's scene of farewell in the morning and ending now (when Maisie came to draw the blind later in the evening) with a French sailor strolling along outside at the water's edge and entering the Anchor.

But after that it was a dull evening, a long wait for Iris to bring news, no visitors, and Maisie downstairs ironing. 'I wish I'd stayed where I was,' Mrs Bracey thought. She banged on the floor with her stick and when Maisie came she said: 'I meant to tell you, when they was carrying me upstairs, I noticed that hand-rail could do with a dusting.'

'Oh!' said Geoffrey Lloyd, when Prudence opened the door to him after tea. 'Is your mother in?'

'I'm afraid not.'

'She said I might come . . .' He held up a roll of foolscap and then put it behind his back. He looked over Prudence's shoulder to the stairs. Up there, he could hear the sounds of

Stevie being bathed and a woman's voice, and he had the idea that the girl was hiding her mother from him.

'She has gone to London.'

'Then she must have forgotten ...' It did not seem conceivable that she could have done so.

'Prue!' Tory called, coming to the top of the stairs, a damp apron round her. 'Oh, I beg your pardon, dear, but where is Stevie's nightgown? Why ...!' She began to descend the staircase in a gliding, affected way, her hands outstretched in greeting. 'I am sure it is dear Rosamund's boy. I am sure you must be young Godfrey ...'

'Geoffrey,' Prudence said.

'Geoffrey, I meant. How very exciting! Your mother was a most dear friend of mine when we were girls. Come in and tell me all about her.' She stripped off the sopping apron with a flourish and made so decisive a gesture that he was bound to follow her. Indeed, he had nothing else to do with the evening.

In the drawing-room, she still seemed to be entranced to see him. 'But I won't keep you, for I know it is Prudence you have come to talk to, and not I ...' she assured him, 'and if I am making you late for the cinema you must tell me at once ... but first of all, how is dearest Rosamund?'

'She is very well, really, except in the damp weather, when she gets a little rheumatism.'

'She would!' Tory thought secretly. 'And as slim as ever, I expect?' she asked with gay confidence.

'Well, I don't know about *slim* ...'

'I know I should see no difference in her, and yet it's every moment of twenty years since we met. We were in the same form together at school.'

Geoffrey could not believe this, looking at Tory. 'Are we going through all that again?' he wondered.

'Tell her you met Victoria Lawson – my maiden name,' she smiled brilliantly, 'and give her my dear love, and now I won't keep you a second longer, for I know you want to be off to the cinema. Where did you say the nightgown is, Prue?'

'It should be under her pillow,' Prudence began, going towards the door.

'All right, my dear. Don't bother!' Tory went running upstairs as fast as she could.

After a pause, Geoffrey said: 'I had a feeling she was making fun of my mother. I expect it was my imagination.'

Prudence felt a slight warmth towards him.

'I don't think so. She makes fun of *my* mother, too.'

'I am not often ill at ease with women,' Geoffrey lied, 'but with her I felt definitely ...' he shrugged.

'I know.'

'What *is* at the cinema?' he inquired.

'I haven't the least idea.'

'Would you like to take the chance?'

'The chance of what?'

'Of its being a bad film.'

Before she could answer Robert came in.

'Oh, I'm afraid my wife is in London,' he said to Geoffrey.

'I was just asking Prudence if she would care to come to the cinema with me.'

'Oh, fine!' Robert became enormously enthusiastic, Prudence noticed. 'Excellent idea!'

'I don't care for films,' she faltered. 'They give me headaches.'

'Nonsense. Do you good. Make you snap out of yourself. All young girls like films, don't they, Geoffrey?'

But Geoffrey merely waited for her reply, quietly considering her. She stared at her father in a dazed and helpless way. 'Snap out of myself,' she thought. 'What can have happened to make him talk like that?' And then she knew what had happened to her. She had grown up. And she no longer loved him. Nor looked to him for assistance. 'Yes, I'll come,' she said to Geoffrey. 'I'll run and fetch my coat.'

Lily Wilson was the first in. 'Two beers,' she thought, 'and then home before it grows too dark. And beer it must be—' for she was a little frightened of the way her money seemed to melt, leaving no trace.

Iris poured her brown ale carefully.

'And for yourself,' Lily was obliged to say.

Iris filled another glass.

'Here's cheers, then, dear.'

'Quiet to-night,' Ned Pallister said. He stood up on a chair and adjusted the clock to public-house time.

'I always enjoy a drink early on,' Iris said. 'You can take your time over it, then.' It looked as if she might take the whole evening over it, so undisturbed were they.

'How's your mother?' Lily asked.

'She keeps the same, thanks. Well, I never!' Iris lifted the bar-flap and went over to the window. 'Look at that!' she said. 'The doctor's girl out with a boy. Quite nice-looking, too.'

Prudence and Geoffrey walked by, rather apart from one another, and both looking as if they were not on speaking terms. In spite of Ned Pallister urging her to come away from the window, Iris stayed there to watch them go up the steps by the Waxworks into Lower Harbour Street.

'They must be going the cliff way to the New Town,' she said. 'To the pictures, I suppose.'

'What's it to do with you if they are?' Ned asked. 'She's as bad as her mother,' he thought.

'What awful clothes she wears!' Iris sighed. 'That camel-hair coat! You can see it's quite threadbare across the ... where she sits down.' She took her place behind the bar again, not that there was anyone to serve. 'Her mother's dowdy, not like Mrs Foyle. They wear for years, of course,' she went on, rather as if she were talking to herself, 'camel-hair coats, I mean. But that's the very reason I wouldn't want one. You get tired of things. It's no use saying you don't. The only thing I wouldn't tire of would be a nice mink coat ...'

'Mink coat!' Mr Pallister said.

'I wouldn't mind how plain the dress was underneath.'

'That's decent of you, I'm sure.'

'But good material, of course ...'

'Naturally.' He winked at Lily, who smiled uneasily.

'And well-cut. That's one thing that puzzles me about Mrs Foyle. She doesn't have a decent fur coat.'

'Just being cussed, I daresay,' Mr Pallister suggested, with a sarcasm which only Iris ever evoked.

Lily felt too dejected to talk. All the afternoon she had been tidying up for the summer, securing loose spangles upon Queen Mary's bosom and, with a small brush, going over the pink baby-faces of démodé murderers, poking fluff from their eyelids and dust from their nostrils. In a few weeks, the scornful, loutish crowds from the New Town would go guffawing through the exhibition. Or if they did not she had no idea of how she would live.

For the first time, acting on the principle that when one has nothing there can be nothing to lose, Lily asked Iris about Bertram; but she did so casually while sipping her beer, glancing out of the window, as if she could scarcely be expected to listen to the answer. Iris's reply was a matter of delicate insinuation, a tongue in her cheek and a movement of her head in the direction of Tory's house. Then, aloud, briskly, for Mr Pallister's hearing, she said (her voice so forthright): 'I don't know. He's not in the bar so much these light evenings.' And winked.

It was then, in the middle of Lily's great mental anguish, that the door was opened and the French sailor walked in. He looked a little uncertain, rather puzzled, as if he had been bidden to a party and found instead a house of mourning.

Bertram was not with Tory. He was in his little bedroom above the bar, sitting on the edge of the bed in shirt-sleeves, darning a pair of socks. This he did beautifully, with great care, weaving the black wool so finely that it had the texture of linen. Sitting there, unobserved, slack, he looked his age, his head bent with its little bald patch, his beard untidy, and the top button of his trousers undone to ease his belly. He could not send his socks to be washed until they were mended lest some woman should cobble them together.

Out of the swollen, gilded Turneresque sky, a shaft of blood-red sunshine struck the painted jug on the washhand-stand and also a picture of Our Lord carrying a *nouveau*-art lantern and surrounded by a flock of Hampshire Down ewes.

The film was falsely emotional. Prudence sat timidly watching, finding no way of understanding; for her own immaturity had in it the hope of growing up, and that of the people in the film had not. She felt strange, sitting there beside Geoffrey. Other young men in uniform surrounded them, their arms round girls. In the darkness the heads fell together, cheek lay against shoulder, lips whispered into hair.

In colonnaded gardens, the screen-lovers encountered one another in a perpetual moonlight, or stood upon rustic-work bridges looking down at water-lilies; were always on holiday or never worked, created emotional problems to pass the time, kissed often, always unhappily. Eyes flashed and swam with tears, yet behind the grief was always delight and excitement, music surged up, covering banalities of dialogue, to heights which the ears could scarcely endure. Geoffrey blew his nose.

With a little sensation of terror, Prudence felt his foot move against hers, and his thigh came into line with her thigh. His proximity seemed to her too steady, too relentless to be accidental; yet he seemed to be absorbed enough in the film, sitting there bolt upright with his arms crossed on his chest.

When the lights went up he smiled at her in a cool and friendly way. 'Awful tripe. I'm sorry.'

The lads in uniform pushed their young women savagely through the exits, trying to get out before the National Anthem was played. Those who, like Prudence and Geoffrey, were caught, stood stiffly and piously to attention.

'This is a great nuisance,' Geoffrey thought, as they went back along the cliff-path to the Old Town. He felt gloomy, contemplating the walk back on his own.

'You might as well leave me,' Prudence said abruptly. 'There's no sense in coming all this way. I can go home alone, surely?'

'I shouldn't dream of it,' he assured her. 'Besides, I enjoy the walk.'

'But it will be such a long time before you get back to ... to camp.'

'I have a late-pass.' (Though he had not meant to use it in this way.)

They walked on in silence which they could scarcely help doing, for their words would have been lost in the wind and the sound of the sea at high-tide. Waves exploded and crashed one after the other, falling away, sucking and dragging at the loosened shingle. Geoffrey had never lived at the seaside and the great waves fascinated him. He lingered at the railings from time to time to watch just one more break, but then another. Prudence stood by, waiting, her hands in her pockets. The wind lifted her hair in curving wings away from her forehead, 'Like that head of Hypnos,' he thought, turning from the rail and seeing her grave face bent down slightly, her eyelids lowered. He felt moved by this comparison, although he considered an interest in any Greek sculpture other than archaic to be a sign of a bourgeois outlook.

'If she had her mother's intelligence!' he found himself thinking, in spite of Beth having shown little intelligence about his own poetry. He wondered about this as they walked on. Perhaps Beth was not intelligent, after all; indeed, he found it difficult to concede the quality to any woman. 'Intuition,' he thought, and seemed to clasp this word to his bosom, so agreeable did he find it. Having dispensed with the stumbling-block of intellect, he could feel more warmly towards Prudence, especially walking there in silence and in the moonlight.

Prudence enjoyed walking against the wind. As it struck her body she experienced the same sensual delight as she felt when lying in bed with her silken cats warm and heavy in her bare arms.

Even her thick coat assumed the appearance of marble

drapery, Geoffrey thought, and she walked well, meeting the wind with indifference.

They passed one of the little glassed-in shelters which faced the sea, and which were always occupied after dark by whispering and entangled couples.

Prudence walked more quickly, frowning. 'Love,' she thought, impatiently, 'what a scuffling thing it is. How sly and sickening!'

Spray flew suddenly over their heads and they moved back against the side of the cliff for an instant, awaiting the next wave, wondering where the foam would spatter down.

Geoffrey drew her up close to him, half curious to know her reaction, half moved by the look of her in the moonlight. He kissed her cheek, which tasted salty.

Prudence stood quite still, forbearing to scuffle. He had never before embraced a girl who remained completely motionless, and felt a little put out. Then the next lot of foam came down like a canopy. In the silence that followed it, in the backwash of shingle, he said: 'You are very annoyed.'

Prudence said nothing.

'Why?'

'You make me feel like those two back there in the shelter.'

'Well, why not?' His bravado was assumed, for the deep and trembling scorn in her voice disconcerted him.

'Why not?' she asked. 'I expect it is quite the sort of thing you do yourself.'

He was relieved at this, feeling he could deal with mere jealousy.

'No. I can say I have never made love to a girl in a shelter in my life,' he said airily.

They were obliged to stand close to one another to make

189

themselves heard, and he leant against a ledge of sandstone and looked at her. She murmured something, but it was lost in the sound of a wave breaking.

'Is it the shelter you object to or the fact of my kissing you?' he asked.

This time he heard several words – 'furtive' for one, and perhaps even 'loathsome' as well.

'I didn't kiss you furtively,' he pointed out. This was true.

'It wasn't that. But the fact that *they*' – she waved her hand contemptuously the way they had come – 'they put it into your head to do so.'

'Indeed they did not. I don't need other people to give me ideas of that kind. I kissed you because it suddenly came to me that I wanted to; you look so very beautiful to-night. So I did. And I enjoyed it, liked the taste of it.' ('But was it worth all this discussion?' he wondered to himself.) 'I imagine you didn't enjoy it?'

'I didn't mind either way,' she said coldly.

'I *could* kiss you so that you would mind. Shall I try?'

'No.'

'You are deeply upset,' he observed. And he wondered what exactly had been going on in the shelter, and felt like going back to have a look.

'If you so hate things being secret, I will kiss you next time on the Esplanade at noon.'

'You know it is not that I mind. It's nothing to do with you.'

'Then who is it to do with?' he asked more gently.

But she began to walk on, keeping close to the side of the cliff, and he could see her hair and one shoulder wet with spray.

He followed her. As they turned a corner the lighthouse flashed and they saw the little half-hoop of lights along the foreshore. Here the path bent away from the sea, and the wind was suddenly silenced as if it were shut up in a box. In this lull, Geoffrey said: 'I wish you'd listen to me for a moment and not walk so fast.' He wondered what to say next, knowing that she would not answer. 'You are angry with me because I have reminded you of something you would rather forget. Don't walk so quickly. I refuse to skip along beside you as if I were a child. An adult person does not go on and on, trying to pay off old scores. Whatever has happened to you, it doesn't belong to me, or to now.'

'To now!' she thought to herself. 'What is happening now in that house, where both Tory and my father intrigued to be rid of me this evening?'

'People making love in a shelter!' he was saying furiously, his indignation gathering momentum. 'What the hell's that to do with me, or you, or anyone but themselves? Making love is *secret*, not furtive. Secret – like blood.' She started at the word and gave him an astonished, frightened look. 'People who cannot bear the sight of blood have good instincts, for it was meant to be hidden, not seen. The skin keeps it from sight, as convention keeps love from sight. Not shame. It isn't furtive, but meet and proper. You remember what dear Turgenev said: "It is a great sin to bring blood to the light of day."' He knew she would not remember nor ever have known, but he threw in one word after another against her silence. 'And it is the same between men and women.' ('Someone has made love to her who should not have done so,' he decided. 'What else could account for her disgust or that reiterated word?') 'It is my misfortune that I have reminded you of something you are perhaps trying to forget. Let me kiss you again as *myself*. And you think of me as I am. Someone only belonging to *now*.'

She stopped, but he had the wit to know it was not for the kiss but to make some explanation.

'Nothing has happened to me,' she said quite fiercely. 'And I will never tell you.'

'Nothing has happened and you will never tell me!' he repeated drily, for he had overlooked the very words which made the phrase significant.

They came to the flight of steps which went down beside the Waxworks, and Prudence looked quickly along the waterfront and saw light spilling from every window over the cobblestones.

'I don't want you to come in with me,' she said breathlessly. 'I want to go the rest of the way alone.'

Now she seemed agitated. When he took her hands and held them against his chest, she allowed him to, but her eyes implored him to let her go on alone.

'All right. And you won't kiss me good night?'

'Please not.'

'Promise me that one day . . .'

'Yes, one day,' she agreed, nodding hurriedly, not caring what she promised.

He stood at the top of the steps and watched her going along the quay towards her home. As she drew level with the pub, light came from the door like an opening fan. An old man came out and seemed to consider the night air. He closed the door and walked towards Prudence. This little scene, watched from above, had, Geoffrey thought, some meaning which he could not for the moment fathom – the old man's movement towards the girl, and her sudden curvetting avoidance of him, like a cat, or a ballet-dancer. A second later she had entered the house, and the old man was standing on the quayside alone, looking down at the water.

'Someone has made love to her who should not have done so,' Geoffrey repeated to himself. And he had a great deal to occupy his mind as he turned and began the long walk back to camp.

Prudence had not stopped to speak to Bertram, her head ached so. She opened the front door and entered the dim hall. Then she slammed the door behind her with a great crash and went towards the morning-room, where they always sat in the evenings. Robert was writing busily at the table.

He looked up and smiled at her before he spoke.

'Nice hats!' Iris said vaguely, staring at the French sailor.

Lily nodded.

'They don't understand the money, though,' Mr Pallister said. 'Asking for change out of sixpence! Up in London now, you won't get a light ale under tenpence, I'm told.'

'That so?' Lily murmured, her eyes on the sailor-hat with its red pom-pom. As if aware of her scrutiny, he took it off and placed it on his knee. He sat on a high stool by the bar and the light ran over his dark, greased hair when he moved. Each time Lily looked up he was studying her carefully. To prove to herself that this was not coincidence, she looked up more frequently and, yes, his eyes were each time upon her. She felt uncomfortable, and then elated.

He drank very slowly, sipping even. 'They're used to wines,' Lily thought. The idea of wine always appealed to her, of tasting something sweet. The brown ale was so cold, so metallic.

Ned Pallister was pulling beer; Iris had moved away, it was difficult to catch her eye. Lily coughed delicately into her hand once or twice, fidgeting with a half-crown on the counter, not liking to be seen sitting there without a drink.

The sailor suddenly leant forward and spoke to Iris, indicating Lily with a very exact and foreign gesture. 'If he's going to offer me a drink, I'll smile in a friendly way, but refuse,' she decided. But he had merely drawn Iris's attention to her.

'I'll have a small port, please, Iris.'

'Red or white?'

'Red,' she said recklessly. She thought: 'It seems more like wine when it's red.' 'How much?'

'Go on. That's with me.'

Lily protested awkwardly.

'Do you good. Go on.'

'Well,' Lily began, lifting the glass and smiling shyly. 'That's better,' she thought, sipping and glancing at the sailor. He drank very slowly. He picked up the beer and took a small mouthful and their eyes met as they drank, as if they pledged one another.

The wine ran down her throat and then seemed to branch out in all directions, even to her finger-tips. The world was about to burst into blossom as she remembered it doing when she was a girl. The next moment might bring . . . but the wine did not help her to formulate her desires, merely enhanced the mood for indulging them.

Then the sailor drained off his glass, put his hat on and went out.

She felt fooled and baffled: the wine, tasteless now, was wasted. To hide her disappointment, she lit a cigarette, glanced at the clock and fiddled with her brittle, untidy hair.

When Tory spent an evening alone she used it as a successful General might – a pause in the forward movement for consolidation and reinforcement. Clay was spread over her face, her fingers trailed in bowls of warm olive oil, her chin was tightly strapped.

It was obvious that she would not answer the door in this state, and Bertram, who had finished his darning and was lonely, went away again, drawing incorrect conclusions.

Prudence had overlooked the fact that Tory would not leave her son alone in the house, nor could Robert leave his daughter. She had served him with the cheerless stew Beth had prepared, and hurried away to put Edward to bed. At the dining-room door he had held her for a brief moment and kissed her. Then, utterly hollowed, shaken, she had hastened from him.

Just as Lily thought she would leave, the door opened and the strange sailor walked in again. This time he came to her side of the bar, and once more he removed his hat. He felt in his pocket and brought out a handful of coppers, which he laid touchingly, like a child, along the edge of the bar.

'Yes?' Iris asked, showing no surprise; but, as she turned to get his beer, she winked at Lily, who looked down quickly, blowing out a cloud of smoke.

After a while she and the sailor resumed their contemplation of one another, which, as they drank, became more explicit, less veiled.

Another man, she felt, would have sat beside her, bought her a drink, tried his way forward with jocularities, flattery. The steady excitement between them was more subtle, more exquisite. She forgot her terror of going home.

She let her eyes, through the smoke, rest boldly upon his, using her power over him with confidence now. They might have been alone. When at last he had finished his drink he put down the glass, staring at her, and then, without shifting his gaze, stood up and straightened his tunic. He went to the door and, as he turned to go out, his eyes gave her a message she could not misunderstand.

She finished her drink in a panic. 'I'll go,' she thought, 'but I'll walk briskly and turn into home as if that's all I meant. As, of course, it *is* all I mean.'

'Good night, dear,' Iris called after her.

'Good night,' she said huskily. And now she was beyond caring what Iris or anyone might think of her. She opened the door and stepped out on to the pavement. Faint moonlight struck the rounded cobbles, blanched the lighthouse. The dark water slapped at the slime-covered steps. Little chalky boats rose and fell.

He was standing across the pavement, looking into the water. She pulled the door behind her with a bang and he turned and came towards her. To her chagrin, she felt sweat breaking out over her body and drew her coat tightly round her.

He greeted her with some words she could not hear, and when she moved her lips in reply she could not speak, but felt as if she were drowning.

'You are going this way?'

She pointed helplessly along the waterfront, leaning a little towards him to catch his words, so strangely pronounced.

'I am attracted by your face all the evening. I find myself watching you.' He turned his small brown hand in the moonlight, as if the words were not enough.

'Where do you come from?' she asked, hoping that her own voice would steady her.

'From Paris. Unfortunately, they did not yet change my money into English.'

They walked slowly, with bowed heads, beneath the uneven, lowering buildings.

'Do you like scent?' he suddenly asked.

'I ... well ... yes. It depends.'

He looked at her with quick, mournful eyes, as if trying to make something exact out of her hesitation. From his pocket he brought a little square, glinting bottle. Pausing by Mrs Bracey's doorway, he took her bare hand and smeared some scent across the palm and put it to her face.

'Yes, lovely,' she murmured, in a dream. They walked on.

'Perhaps you would like to buy this bottle from me. It is from Paris last week. Only a little money.'

'I'm sorry,' she said quickly, stopping at her doorway. 'This is my home. Good night.' She put the key in the lock, her face turned from him.

He shrugged and slid the bottle carefully back into his pocket and mooched on down the harbour.

She breathed the musty darkness of indoors and closed out the fishy-smelling quayside, shutting the door quickly. 'Oh, Bob!' she thought. 'Why did you leave me?' She blamed the dead, feeling herself exposed to danger and humiliation. As she put her hand up to her eyes her scented skin made her shudder. Her shame seemed to be a real thing, following her upstairs and into her room.

When she drew the curtain and looked out the sailor had disappeared. The place was empty. Only Bertram stood by the water's edge.

Bertram looked down at the water. He felt dejected. Tory had not opened her door. Prudence had avoided him. No one, apparently, needed him. He was tired of the cronies in the bar, tired of the dingy pub bedroom. 'I shall go away,' he told himself. 'In the end I always move on somewhere else, as all selfish people do, who do not let themselves become deeply involved in others, nor bound to one place. For all I feel is curiosity; and curiosity, unlike Mrs Bracey's hunger for life, and Tory's illicit hunger for her next-door neighbour, is quickly satisfied, a fleeting thing, leading nowhere.' Curiosity had tired him, too, but he did not admit that. He would have liked to have settled down now, to marry Tory. To-night, confronted by that silent yet lighted house, he had realised the improbability of such a thing. Standing there, with his hand still upon the brass ring of the knocker, he had felt that Tory's passion was not a thing ever to be put on one side for promises of devotion or for friendship, nor overthrown by conscience or convention. It put her beyond the pale, in every sense, and out of his reach.

But that glimpse of imagined comfort and companionship, of being settled, had fascinated him more than he thought. He no longer cared about what was round the next corner, unless it was Tory and his life running alongside hers.

He walked back towards the lighted windows of the Anchor, his lungs filled with their bedtime breath of fresh air. 'I am a man with a passion for turning stones,' he thought. 'And wherever I went there were always more stones than I could turn.'

When he went in and shut the door there was nobody about. The scene was quite empty.

Twenty miles out at sea the fish fought and slithered in the nets, floundering and entangled.

12

Beth was glad to be back. She came home at tea-time and Tory was waiting for her with Stevie so brushed and tidied that it was almost a reproach. Tory was full of the story of how she had managed to despatch Prudence to the cinema with Geoffrey, and laughed and spoke in a sort of French, above Stevie's head, explaining how she had contrived it.

Prudence was in the kitchen cutting up lights for the cats. From time to time she rushed to the sink and retched, her face drawn, her eyes watering, and then bravely returned to the job. The cats sniffed delicately at the dreadful stench, their nostrils quivering, as at the bouquet of wine. When the dish was put down, Guilbert hunched up over it, chewing, while Yvette sat behind like a squaw, until he was filled. This always annoyed Beth, whose feminism was kindled at the sight.

'It is only their instinct,' Prudence would point out, for nothing would make the queen come forward until her mate had eaten. Beth had for a long time distrusted the nature of all those instincts which work so much for the benefit of the other sex, and she would shut Guilbert outside in the garden and try to make Yvette betray her nature by coaxing her with little scraps of meat.

She would never move. Only her eyes changed, the blue turning slowly to crimson.

Now Guilbert stopped eating, dug his claws into the kitchen rug, stretched, yawned, and walked away. Very humbly, gratefully, Yvette came up to get the leavings.

After tea Beth took the two thousand words she had written in the train and laid them on the top of the pile of papers on her desk. She dared not read them, for it seemed to her now – tired from her journey – that scars, great fissures broke up and marred her work and no genius was there to rivet it together.

She stood for a moment alone in the room. Tory had gone. Stevie pushed her doll's pram along the garden path. Beth watched her from the window, watched how she moved the doll gently on the pillow, murmuring busily to her, adjusted the torn hood, all her interest and emotion centred there in the pram, an absorption Beth had so often noticed in other mothers, never felt in herself. 'But it was through no fault of my own,' she thought, her mind reverting to those cracked and riven chapters of hers; all of her books the same, none sound as a bell, but giving off little jarring reverberations now here, now there, so that she herself could say as she turned the pages (knowing as surely as if the type had slipped and spilt): 'Here I nursed Prudence with bronchitis; here Stevie was ill for a month; here I put down my pen to bottle fruit (which fermented); there Mrs Flitcroft forsook me.'

Round and round the little garden Stevie went, between the old fruit trees which in autumn dropped twisted, pock-marked apples into the grass. Through the ferns, Guilbert wove his way, stealthily, supple, moisture on his whiskers, his eyes diamond-shaped, a great jungle animal now, his lean sides brushed by dense foliage.

Beth rapped with her knuckles at the window. 'Bed, Stevie!' she called. 'It's time for bed.'

After tea, Mrs Bracey felt an aching in her shoulders and Maisie had to leave the washing-up to rub in oil.

'The left side!' her mother said. 'The left side more especially.'

'Well, that's the window side. You must be in a draught. You'd be far better moved away against the other wall.'

'Or downstairs,' her mother suggested, 'leaving this room nice and vacant.'

Maisie shrugged.

Nothing but the threat of death would have persuaded Mrs Bracey to move now. She would not read even, except in the most desultory fashion, nor take her eyes from the window for long. Last night, drowsing, she had been aware suddenly of footsteps stopping outside, of low voices, and she had drawn the curtain along a very little, leaning as close to the pane as she could and, waiting there, shivering, had been delighted to see Lily Wilson emerge from the shadows of the houses walking with a French sailor. Just as they had come to the porch of Lily's home Maisie had brought in the cocoa. Some instinct had made Mrs Bracey drop the curtain and cover her prying; and she sat there sipping, and shivering with frustration.

By the time she was left alone the street was empty, but she did see Lily going to the front window and peeping out between the lace curtains. Lily had not known she was being watched, nor that at that moment her reputation was slipping into that no-man's-land from which one can fall, with so little warning, from respectable widowhood to being the local harlot: and, as it was in Mrs Bracey's imagination that the first move towards that decline was made, the descent, no doubt, would be swift as well as untraceable (for gossip is a fluid, intangible thing). Scandals must have their beginnings somewhere, and the soil of Mrs Bracey's imagination was so fertile that often there seed and flower were one and the same thing.

Peacefully, she let her mind seethe and ferment, relaxed as she did so, and Maisie kneading her oily shoulders.

Beth had put Allegra away in her desk and now tried hard to forget her. She staved her off all the while she was bathing Stevie, and later, when Stevie sat up in bed eating a fruit-salad, Beth told her a story, so determined was she that, beginning with this evening, she would be a good mother. She sat at Stevie's little dressing-table, dreamily reciting, and brushing her own hair as she did so.

'... And as she sewed, the queen pricked her finger and a drop of blood fell on the snow-white cloth ...'

Beth thought of her own mother who had so many times told her this story, and many others besides. Nothing ever spoils the first enchantment, she decided. No overlay of vulgarity from Walt Disney, no sickling o'er from the Children's Hour ever can penetrate to the heart of the first experience of poetry, of cruelty, of beauty. I remember it now with my vivid child's mind, the first heart-catching magic – the golden key lying on the glass table, the castle enclosed by briars; and then words meaning more than they mean in after-life. 'The King sits in Dunfermline town drinking the blude-red wine,' and 'Yestr'een the Queen had four Maries, The night she'll hae but three;

There was Marie Seton and Marie Beaton, And Marie Carmichael and me.'

'Go on,' said Stevie, spooning up juice.

Beth brushed the hair from her temples.

'Eat the fruit, dear.' She watched her through the glass. 'But the huntsman so loved Snow White that he had not the heart to kill her, and led her deeper into the forest . . .'

'I suppose you loved this story when you were a little girl,' said Stevie condescendingly.

'Yes, but darling, don't interrupt . . . That night when the old Queen looked into her mirror . . .'

'You can leave that bit out,' Stevie said. 'I don't like it.'

'Leave it out!' Beth cried. Leave out those sinister reverberations! 'If I am to tell the story I must tell it as it is.'

'All right,' Stevie said quickly. She took a mouthful of chopped apple and began to munch, her eyes turned once more upon her mother.

'Blink your eyes, dear,' Beth said, seeing them unfocused. Blinking and crunching, Stevie waited. A thunderous darkness lay over the forest scene which Beth described, as the story moved on with composed horror. Stevie finished her fruit and laid the dish aside. Sitting up in bed, looking at her mother through the mirror, her eyes were stretched wide, her mouth loosely open.

'But as they carried her down the steep path in her glass coffin they stumbled on a rock and the piece of poisoned apple fell out of her cheek.'

'No more!' Stevie suddenly screamed. 'Stop it! Please stop!'

Beth dropped the hairbrush and turned round.

'Don't go on!' Stevie shrieked, beginning to thrash about in bed.

'What *is* wrong?' Beth asked her, and bunched her up in her arms, trying to soothe her.

'I shall dream about it. I know I shall dream about it.'

'But it all ended happily, if only you would let me finish.'

'I don't want another word even. It isn't a nice story. A sensible mother wouldn't tell her children stories like that.'

'Well, I won't ever again. Now stop crying.'

'I can't. When I start a thing I can't ever stop until I've finished. I never can.'

'What is the matter?' Robert asked, putting his head round the door. 'Stevie, pull yourself together. Let us at least hear ourselves speaking.'

'My mother frightened me. She's been trying to frighten me. She made my heart beat.'

'Well, really . . .!' Beth began.

'All right, Stevie,' Robert said, in his nice, kind, calm, doctor's voice. To Beth he murmured, 'Leave her to me. I'll manage her.'

'Good night, Stevie,' Beth said politely.

Going downstairs she could not see that she had done anything wrong, could only assure herself that children nowadays are too coddled. Everything was round the wrong way. In the days when she had been a little girl, the horrors were in the story-books (*Sister Anne! Sister Anne!*) and the outside world was cosy: now, the horrors were real, and, to compensate, the child's imagination must be soothed and cosseted with innocent bread-and-milk.

She took Allegra out of the desk again and turned the pages, altering a word here, a word there. No good had come out of the last hour except that her hair had had a good brushing.

*

Bertram was brought down to spending the evening with Mrs Bracey. He would not try Tory's door again. Mrs Bracey was in two minds: whether to feel pleased or exasperated. While he was there she could not peek out of the window to see what Lily Wilson might be doing; on the other hand, Bertram's company was invigorating and lively. She relished his great sea-faring lies: how, in the moonlight, he had mistaken sea cows for mermaids; how he and many of his crew had watched the sunset over the Pacific form into a vast crucifixion scene, the oddly contorted violet clouds against the blood-red, and eastwards the sky a clear pistachio with one pale star. A premonition, Bertram insisted, since that night one of the crew fell ill of yellow fever. The world came very close to Mrs Bracey as she listened to his descriptions. Sometimes, he told her, diamonds were set in the living flesh, or ears weighted to the shoulders and the skin slashed and rubbed with dung for beauty. In one place, the cold might be so intense that the horses' breath froze solid as it left their nostrils, falling in strange shapes upon the iron roads and breaking there, while only a day's journey away the moon slowly cooled the burning desert sand. The sheikh, folding back his mosque-embroidered sleeve, touched a scorpion's bite with the agate of his ring, the pain vanishing at once.

'I never went there,' Mrs Bracey thought. 'I never went anywhere. I just stayed here at the harbour all my life, and, just as my eyes first focused on that scene, so they will close upon it.'

Bertram was discussing food with her (how cantaloups were fed with arak until a slice would intoxicate a man, how sucking-pigs were stuffed with truffles and melon-flowers crystallised and filled with burnt cream) when Maisie came in with a jug of cocoa and a plate of Marie biscuits.

As soon as Bertram went Mrs Bracey pulled the curtains aside, but there was nothing to be seen.

'There's a button off this jacket,' Robert said as he undressed.

Beth was in bed already, lying there with her eyes closed.

'Remind me in the morning,' she murmured. She heard him taking money and keys from his pockets.

'I wonder how Prue got on with young Geoffrey?' Beth continued. 'What on earth can they have to talk about? For they have nothing in common. Was the stew all right?'

'Very nice.'

'You managed to warm it up?'

'Tory did.'

'That was thoughtful of her. And did Prue say anything about her evening out?'

'Not a word. She came in in a state of excited hostility, I thought, and then calmed down and drank a cup of tea and went to bed.'

Beth sighed. 'And now Tory says she is thinking of going away.' The relevance of this was that it was the last straw.

'Oh, yes?' Robert said casually, as if trying to summon interest for the sake of courtesy.

'She said at tea-time that she couldn't bear the thought of another winter here. I shall miss her so very much that, even if it is for her good, I hope it won't happen. It seemed so lovely when she came to live here, and, even before that, I looked forward enormously to the summer when she came on holidays. If she goes away now there won't be that, even, for she will sell the house, she says. If she and Edward come to stay with us it won't be at all the same.'

He contemplated the idea of Tory under the same roof.

'Aren't you rather leaping ahead?' he asked. 'I can't seem to find a collar for the morning.'

'Top right-hand drawer.' Beth opened her eyes and closed them again. 'Tory's so impulsive,' she resumed. 'When she was a young girl she used to write letters to actors . . .'

'What has that to do with it?'

'And she was always in trouble at school. I remember when she cut off one of her plaits – and she had such lovely hair. She wanted it bobbed, d'you see, and her mother said not on any account. So she snipped it off herself in the school train and threw the plait into some bushes beside the railway lines and when she arrived at the school she said a strange man had cut it off at the station. The headmistress called in the police and Tory told one lie after another until they wore her out and she confessed. She was nearly expelled, but they had to cut off her other plait to match, so she did have her way. She was always so . . .'

'You speak of her as if she is dead,' Robert suddenly interrupted.

'It's just that I can't bear for her to go away,' Beth said pathetically. She lay there imagining life without Tory.

When Robert got into bed, he lay there and imagined the same, but for much longer.

13

Edward went back to school with a different set of clothes and his first cricket bat, the key to his tuck-box hanging on a tape round his neck. Tory saw him into the school train, watched his face reddening and whitening as he leant from the compartment to wave, knew how the tears were hard as pebbles under his lids and so nearly not kept back. Then she walked up the platform and straight to the ladies' room where she wept. After a while, feeling restored, she made her way to the little restaurant at which she sometimes saw Teddy; but he was not there, and in spite of having been drawn to the place, she was relieved. She ate a large meal and drank a glass – to cheer herself – of most ordinaire vin. It was still light when she arrived home.

It was the summer. Mr Lidiard, taking his short cut through the churchyard, walked under flowering trees, carrying books to Mrs Bracey which she no longer read. For, as the warmer weather came, the harbour lost its closed-up appearance and the scene changed. People loitered at the water's edge, front doors were left open, and life overflowed on to the quayside. What Mrs Bracey could not see was none the less indicated and her imagination was ready to supply the rest. Lily Wilson on one side, Tory on the other, Eddie sulking, his hands in his pockets, slouching along the quay, leaning against the Customs house with the other men, always conscious, or it seemed so by his glances, of Mrs Bracey herself at the window.

Each day she saw a little added to their lives: for none of them remained the same. Even in Maisie, so outwardly cold and unmoved that her mother was deceived, the knot of bitterness tightened up, contorted and involved, so that soon it would be the sort of knot no one could manage to untie.

'*That's* my book!' Mrs Bracey would tell the curate, pointing out of the window. Lily Wilson was hanging up a painted card, 'Waxworks Now Open – Admission 3*d*'. Along the water's edge Stevie Cazabon pushed her doll's pram. Presently Prudence came out and tried to persuade her back to the house. She appeared to refuse, her hands gripping the pram handle stubbornly, her face darkening. At the bottom of the flight of steps children played hopscotch on chalked squares, just as Mrs Bracey herself had done, or skipped, with a rope tied to the lamp-post, chanting the meaningless rhymes which alter so little from one generation to another. But life was less varied now, she thought, less rich, the streets less crowded – gone the lamplighter and those yellow, spreading gas-lights; gone the organ-grinder with his wretched precocious monkey; gone the drunkenness, the church-going, the wife-beating, the wonderful funerals, the social calls to see the corpse (now the bereaved kept their dead private as if it were their own business merely, or as if ashamed). Distinctions were smoothed out, no curtsies were dropped, no coins thrown. Even the sea was smoothed out, for it no longer seemed to wash in wreckage, no longer deposited corpses at the cliff-foot. Mrs Bracey remembered the time of wrecks, when the whole harbour turned out with storm-lanterns to launch the lifeboat and await its return. She had sat up all night with the widows of drowned men, tried to coax warmth into frozen limbs, seen a woman lifted from the sea with her wet hair bound round and round her face and over her mouth, as if the waves themselves had tried to stop her cries.

Now she watched the trawlers coming safely in, or sometimes the white, slanting sail of a yacht. On Saturday nights the men sang for a little while, half-heartedly, outside the pub (the beer was not what it had been, either). Then (and they were scarcely stupefied with liquor) they would drift back home, money still in their pockets, and in the morning would go, more half-heartedly than ever, to church or, more likely than not, stayed at home to mend the children's shoes or read *The News of the World*, tame creatures, enfeebled by weak drink.

She would have missed so much if her imagination had not run before her, preparing the way. Thus, she knew that the very fact of Tory and Robert not smiling at one another when they met was a plain endorsement of their guilt: for friendly smiles between lovers are so laboriously devised that when they imagine themselves to be alone they seldom make the effort. So she watched them curtly greeting one another as they did this evening – Robert driving up in the car just as Tory rounded the corner – watched them exchange a few words, and Robert running his eye over Tory's London clothes as if in disapproval: and she knew, as surely as if she could hear their words, how briefly, how cunningly, they laid their plans, their lives whittled down to those few moments when they could be together, a few words passing swiftly between them or their finger-tips contriving to brush together as if by accident, a glance, a touch, an innuendo in the presence of others – the rest darkness.

Up at her window, and in some discomfort (for her shoulder, her chest ached), Mrs Bracey sat in judgment. Guilt she saw, treachery and deceit and self-indulgence. She did not see, as God might be expected to, their sensations of shame and horror, their compulsion towards one another, for which they dearly paid, nor in what danger they so helplessly stood, now, in middle-age, not in any safe harbour, but thrust out to sea with none of the brave equipment of youth to buoy them up, no romance, no delight.

'Rather stark,' Tory said. 'It is all rather stark.' She went on saying the word until it had become absurd, as most words do become absurd when they are repeated.

'Did you see Teddy?' Robert asked, choosing to ignore her comments on their relationship.

'No.'

'You went to look for him, I suppose.'

'Yes, I went to look, but he was not there.'

'Why? Why did you?'

'Curiosity.'

'No. Tory, I believe that after everything, you still love him.'

'I don't love him. I don't understand, though, how it can be that he doesn't love me.'

'If ever he came back to you . . .'

'He won't!' she said quickly, as if she had told herself this so often.

'If he did, would you go back to him?'

'Of course not.'

'For Edward's sake, perhaps?' he suggested cunningly.

'No, not for Edward's sake, either.'

She picked up some sewing, but he took it from her hands.

'Tory, what have you been saying to Beth about going away?'

'Just that – that I am going. What sort of life is this for me? Nothing to look ahead to, but the one thing that must come – Beth knowing about this, and her great distress and horror when she sees what I truly am, and have been all these months. And how can I continue with this ... this duplicity? Being with her part of each day ... the treachery of being with *you* is nothing to *that*, to the lies I act when I am with her. Ask yourself where this is leading to? Are we to go on until we are old, with just these odd moments here and there and danger always so narrowly evaded? Love draining away our vitality, our hold on life, never adding anything to us. Always ...' and she put her trembling hand into his ... 'always ourselves fanning up the flames which will torment us until we are consumed. It cannot go on for ever. You must know that. The only way of dealing with love is being alone together for a long time, the world shut out, being in bed together all night long, waking together in the morning. What prospect of that? Ever? None at all, as you know full well. Meanwhile, these furtive ...'

'Please don't. Please not that.'

'Well, my God, what else? Stark, then. These stark embraces and the painfulness of it all. For myself, I think I deserve better than that ...'

'Where will you go? When?' he asked, relinquishing her hand, almost as if he relinquished her.

Indeed, that was a different matter. She no longer had a man to make all the arrangements of changing house for her, had not the remotest idea of dealing with that dull world of leases or deeds, of agents and commissions. Between herself and her noble intentions these difficulties stood formidably.

Since she did not answer him, Robert glanced at his watch and said, as he seemed always to be saying to her: 'I shall simply have to go.'

When she was alone she stood at the window looking out to sea and wondered how she had become the sort of person she now was. Deeply as she felt she loved Robert, she thought that the answer must be only in herself and looked for it back through her married life to girlhood; childhood, even; saw herself, at six years, standing between her mother and her governess, head bowed, in some sort of disgrace, so that she remembered of that scene only their long skirts and their shoes, and above her the voice of the governess saying: 'She is a lovable child, but such a butterfly.' Shame and elation, then: for, though 'butterfly' was a delightful image to her, the thin voice suggested another interpretation. Shame, yet elation. Did it all begin there, back in those shadows which were only broken into now by these disquieting and isolated memories? A girl at school, in trouble always – the day when she cut off her hair, the punishments devised to humiliate her, but which she turned into public triumphs in order to hide her secret shame: and all the time, Beth so doggedly loyal, helping her to cheat with her lessons, saving her trouble, shocked as (poor dull soul) she sometimes was, shocked as she continued to be by the letters in violet ink on scalloped paper to Sir John Martin-Harvey, Sir Gerald du Maurier; Beth having to engage authority in conversation while Tory, on the off-side of the crocodile, slipped these notes into the letter-box: Beth, later, safely married, trying to steady Tory into some sort of betrothal with one or other of the young men who seemed all exactly the same – except that Teddy Foyle was not so impoverished as the rest.

'I didn't exactly marry for money,' Tory now explained to herself. 'But neither did I marry for love. It is all very well to say one should wait for it, but the waiting might be for ever, and there's no denying that it is pleasanter not to be on one's own. Far pleasanter. In the end, all I ever asked from life was pleasure. And perhaps those artful people in the Bible are right, and the only way to get happiness is not to think about it, or to think of other people having it instead, and so, fooling it, catch it at last in the nets of one's own indifference. "Father Christmas will not come if you stay awake for him." Indeed, he cannot: so there is truth and commonsense in it, and all that I have netted in (with my disregard for cautionary tales) is this empty house, the frightening future, this stark present, and a cupboard full of hats without an occasion to wear any of them.'

To attract the attention of Bertram, passing by with a large parcel under his arm, she tapped her knuckles on the window-pane. He looked up and smiled, hesitating, and then came back towards the house as she ran to open the door.

'If I were tied to the mast I should bring the mast with me,' he began, wiping his shoes on the mat, '. . . so impossible would it be to resist . . .' he placed the parcel on the hall-table '. . . your spell,' dusting his hands with his beautiful handkerchief and following her into the sitting-room.

'A drink against the long evening,' she said, kneeling before a cupboard full of bottles.

'There need be no long evenings if you would only marry me,' he told her, walking about the room, his hands clasped behind his back.

'Are you a great evening-shortener, then?' she laughed, bringing out a bottle of gin and holding up the vermouth against the light to see how much was left and then, her more generous impulses deserting her, returning it quickly to the cupboard.

'We should go to bed earlier,' he said with tremendous confidence.

'Oh, I see.'

'Late nights never suit me. I like to be up early in the morning.'

'Well, I don't.'

'We shall find a way of agreeing about it, no doubt.'

'I am sorry I have nothing to drink with the gin,' she said blandly, handing him the glass. 'But it doesn't mean we can drink more just because we have nothing to go with it.'

'You make me feel really welcome. Women always stint their friends in these trivial ways. How silly this little drop looks at the bottom of the glass. However, to your beauty!'

'These first evenings after Edward goes away are like the beginning of the war and my husband going back from leave. A curious emptiness. Once, in desperation, I packed up and went with him, but regimental life was intolerable. The wives are thrown so much together and scheme and intrigue without pause, or, at best, endlessly discuss domestic affairs, their children, their furnished flats, shopping.'

'This was the Army?' he asked condescendingly.

'Yes. It was in the Army that Teddy met his downfall – if we may be allowed to call her that. I packed up and went home a little too soon. In a fit of pique at his nagging after I had rebuked his C.O. He simply couldn't see that *I* was not in the Army, too.'

'Wives are a damned nuisance, anyhow,' Bertram said,

feeling sympathy for Teddy. 'What had the C.O. done to deserve your rebuke?'

'Oh, I thought he dealt too harshly with one of the men.'

'It appears that you were the one who forgot you were not in the Army.'

'It isn't pleasant to see a man letting loose all his repressed aggressiveness just because he is temporarily in authority.'

'Repressed aggressiveness!' Bertram repeated scornfully, draining his glass, staring into it, putting it at last sadly upon the table.

'You wouldn't know. At heart you are gentle. The quality I admire above all. You would not willingly hurt anyone.'

'To avoid hurting people needs constant vigilance. As one grows older one is less and less equal to the task. There are so many cruelties of omission.' He thought at once of Lily Wilson, of how in the beginning he had implied perhaps that he would do much for her. And had done nothing. (He did not know that he had done worse than nothing.)

Lily Wilson got through the evening in one way and another, writing a letter to her brother in Canada, doing a little knitting, making herself a cup of cocoa. At nine she went to bed, lying down with a sense of achievement that another day was gone, that there was one day less to be lived through. She lay there a long time without moving; but she could not sleep.

On his way out Bertram took up the parcel from the hall-table and tucked it under his arm. 'Canvas!' he said casually. 'I'm going to begin working in oils.'

Tory thought he was like a little boy, so transparent, and she smiled in the indulgent way her son found so irritating.

When Bertram entered the pub it was quite full. Eddie was leaning over the bar talking to Iris. Bertram, hailed at once by the old cronies, the local characters, made his way through the blue smoke to buy beer for them.

'How's Maisie?' Eddie was asking Iris.

'She's all right. Nothing to stop you finding out for yourself, though.'

'Nothing at all, bar the fact that I said I'd never enter the place again.'

'That's childish. You know what Mother is . . .'

'I do. And I also know what I am not, and that's something on a chessboard your mother or anyone else can move where they like. I manage my own life. Things don't change me, *I* change *them*. Like anyone with any sense, any guts.'

'I'm so glad. What's that got to do with Maisie, though?'

'She's got no guts. I liked her, but I've got my own life to lead. I'm not one of those to go on wanting what's hopeless. What I can't get, I cut out for good and turn my attention to other matters.'

'We're hearing a nice lot this evening about what you do and what you don't do.'

As she spoke, she was drawing beer for Bertram, her breast moving slowly as she bent her arm.

'What about the pictures to-morrow afternoon?' Eddie asked, watching her.

'No, thanks.'

'Why not?'

'Because I'm going to wash my hair. What's on, anyhow?'

'James Mason.' He cast the line and waited. Saw her indecision, but realised that it was over a film actor, not himself.

'No, thanks,' she said finally. 'I shall have to wash my hair.'

She knew he was watching her intently and lifted her glass of beer and took a long, steady drink. Her creamy throat moved beautifully as she drank.

Mrs Bracey was sure that Lily Wilson had escaped her. She had watched the street but no one came or went. The old Librarian took his evening stroll along the front. Just as Eddie had come to symbolise death to her, so this old man symbolised culture, the dusty novels, the little dead worlds of other people's make-believe, the antithesis of life – that real magic which only Bertram seemed to bring to her.

She leant back on her pillows and closed her eyes. Pain froze her chest and shoulders. Her throat ached. Maisie would only say it was the draught from the window and try to move her. For once in her life she decided not to complain. But in a few minutes she was banging with her stick upon the floor for Maisie to come up and tell her what she had been doing downstairs.

Robert followed Beth when she went to the kitchen to make coffee, leaving Prudence and Geoffrey in the midst of an uneasy silence.

'Beth, dear!'

'Yes, Robert?'

He paused awkwardly and she glanced up.

'What is it?'

'I hardly know how to say . . . I am sure you don't realise, but all this conversation about books leaves Prudence out; I think she feels at a loss . . .' Nothing but his love for his daughter could have made him stumble for words in this way.

Beth was not in the least annoyed, only surprised.

'I was just talking to cover up the silence. I had a feeling that they had quarrelled. Prue was glum before we began, and I thought it all seemed so very awkward.'

'You know how it is with young people. We were the same before we were married – at your parents' house and mine.'

This reference to their first true love embarrassed them both. Beth blushed and measured the coffee in silence.

'I believe that cat is pregnant,' Robert said suddenly to change the subject. Yvette gave him a wounded look and turned her head.

'It would be great fun if she were,' Beth said. 'Prudence might begin to make some money after all.'

'How nice to retire – just sit back and let the cats do the work.'

'I have a good idea, Robert. Let us drink our coffee here by ourselves.'

'Don't be so ridiculous, dear. There is no need to lose your head because of what I said.'

'Women are so coarse-fibred, so tough, so lacking in sensibility,' he thought. This was constantly borne in upon him. 'If they talk like this to men, God knows what they say to one another when they really throw back their veils. Even Beth,' he decided, 'shows an astonishing lack of delicacy sometimes ... And as for Tory ...' But he had so much delicacy himself that he did not formulate his feelings about her in his thoughts, even.

'Prudence,' Geoffrey murmured quietly, as soon as they were alone, 'I should very much like to talk to you some time. When can I?'

'Why not now?' she asked.

'I mean – when we are alone.'

'We are alone now,' she pointed out.

He was afraid that someone would interrupt them, and therefore did not waste time trying to break down her hostility. 'To-morrow evening I'll be in the churchyard at nine. Will you meet me there?'

'The churchyard!' she said incredulously.

'Yes, I like it there now the trees are in flower. That pink may by the gate. There's a seat there and I take a book and read sometimes.' He also wrote poetry on the backs of envelopes, but he did not tell her this, feeling, quite correctly, that she would not have been interested.

'Will you come?'

'I don't know. I might.'

With all this so swiftly planned, there was nothing more to say. Her parents were out of the room longer than either had expected. She sat and twisted her handkerchief. There was silence and a sense of anti-climax between them, until they heard cups rocking on a tray and Beth's unnaturally bright voice saying: 'Here we are, then,' or some nonsense of that kind.

'Only the creative artist is ever really happy,' Bertram thought, as he unwrapped his canvas up in his little bedroom. He sat on the edge of the bed and imagined the picture he was going to paint – the harbour buildings seen across the harbour water, the crumbling texture of plastered walls, the roofs of purple, of grey-blue, the grey church on the shoulders of the other buildings, the green weed on steps and the sides of the harbour wall, silk-fine and damp like the hair of the newly-born – all the different surfaces and substances, the true being of it coming luminously through, the essence of such a scene, and he the focal point, painting from the end of the harbour wall, 'or perhaps,' he suddenly thought as light outside thrust across the darkness, 'perhaps they would allow me to make sketches from the light-house, up in the lamp-room itself.'

He smoothed the creased quilt and folded it back neatly and began to undress. Soon he began to think of Tory and his conversation with her in the early part of the evening. Had he begun to discover, as her husband must have discovered, that warmth and wit and loveliness are not enough? Not enough to compensate for the selfishness, the cussedness of her.

This evening, for the first time with him, her desirability admitted doubts. 'Perhaps it is as well,' he decided, thinking also of the passion which was eating her away, conceal it cunningly as she might. 'I, who see to the core of things, of people, as a painter must, see her pinned down by misery, in a way I am incapable of being pinned down myself, with my genius for always making off when I feel another personality throwing its shadow too close to mine.'

He feared the unhappy, the possessive, the single-minded, the intense, and was gallant, rather than tender; flirtatious, but not loving. He was also rather a coward and, because he thought he saw Tory drowning, felt it safer not to notice, lest, forced to go to her rescue, he might be involved in her struggles and dragged down to depths he had no wish to visit.

14

'Are you tearing pieces about yourself out of the newspaper?' Stevie asked reprovingly.

'Pieces about my book,' Beth corrected her; for there was a world of difference between the two, it seemed to her.

'Will you keep that paper?'

'I daresay I shall, dear; for a time, at least. Why not?' Beth leant over the kitchen table, reading.

'It has those little round things all over it, like Tory's party frock.'

'Fish's scales,' Beth said, brushing her hand over the paper; then looking up at her daughter with new interest: 'Sequins, you mean. Yes, they are like sequins.' She folded the paper and went at once to her desk in the morning-room. When she had noted down Stevie's simile, she said to Robert, who sat by the window reading *The Lancet*: 'I found a review of my book wrapped round the cod.'

'That was nice for you, my dear.'

'Robert.' She said his name and waited, as if to imply that she would not go on until she had his attention. Annoyingly, he put his forefinger upon a word and looked up. 'Robert, I shouldn't say my books were gloomy, would you?'

'I shouldn't say they were hell of a gay, either,' he said, waiting, still looking up.

'Listen to this!' Beth's amazement seemed to increase. '"Macabre,"' she read. '"Funereal!" What do they mean?'

'Well, I suppose "funereal" means "to do with funerals", and that's what your books mainly are.'

'How worrying!' Beth went on. 'I only put the funerals in so that they shall not be too frivolous, the novels, I mean.'

Robert's eyes dropped to the printed page again, and then he lifted his head and sniffed. 'What an appalling smell of fish!'

'It's this piece of newspaper.'

'Well, for God's sake! Must we have it in here?'

'No, dear. I will put it on the kitchen fire,' Beth said gently, almost tiptoeing away, as if his irritability were a serious illness.

'Are you famous?' Stevie asked her, waiting for her in the kitchen.

'Famous! Good gracious, no!' Beth said, quite startled.

'Will you ever be?'

She considered this and then said quietly: 'No, I never shall be.'

'How do you know?'

'How *do* I know?' Beth wondered. She watched the flames reaching up and over the crumpled newspaper and shook her head, smiling. But to herself, she said: 'I can never know because all behind me there lies a great darkness and over all that I have written. I can see nothing of it. Only what I am going to write to-morrow is clear.'

'Where is Prudence?' she asked, unwilling to be catechised any further.

223

'She is making herself a dress.'

'A dress?'

'Yes. She told me to go away. She is up in her room sewing hard. She has made the two sleeves already.'

Fearing a crisis, Beth ran up the stairs at once and tapped on her daughter's bedroom door. Prudence sat near the window in her petticoat, one arm covered with a tacked-together sleeve of sage-green. Her lap was full of the material and her golden hair swung forward over her bare shoulders. Light rained down from the ceiling, reflected from the wideness of sea and sky, and there was no need to go to the windows or to listen for the cries of gulls and water lapping to know that it was a seaside room.

'Ah, there you are!' Beth said foolishly. 'What a very clever colour!'

'Clever?' Prudence repeated suspiciously.

'I meant, dear, with your hair and your grey eyes. I didn't know that you could sew.'

How cautiously she trod, as if her daughter were a dangerous lunatic to be smoothed and flattered into tractability. Prudence sewed quickly, with large, slanting stitches, gathering a wide skirt into a narrow bodice – though 'gathering' was scarcely the word to describe the wild bunching-up that was going on. Ends of cotton and pieces of material littered the floor. Beth picked up a few, but without any hope of tidying the room.

'Are you warm enough up here?' she asked, looking vaguely round.

Prudence stood up, scattering pins from her lap, and held the dress against her, turning slowly before the mirror.

'Well, you have tacked that together quickly,' Beth said in a heartening way.

'I don't know what you mean by "tacked". I suppose you are being sarcastic. If I were not so poor, I shouldn't have to be cobbling up my own clothes out of cheap material. I could go out and buy something new.'

'You have your allowance. It is not very kind to talk in that way.'

'My allowance!' The words seemed to scorch themselves up and fade as soon as she said them. Beth felt scorched, too, as Prudence had intended she should. 'The same wretched pittance I had when I left school! Can I help it that I'm not allowed to earn anything of my own? Am I to go on for the rest of my life pinching and scraping on eighty pounds a year? I know just what you're thinking – that it's vulgar to talk like this, but you shouldn't come up here worrying me with your sarcastic remarks. I thought . . .' – and then all desire to hurt, to cut her mother, left her and tears came into her voice. 'I thought it looked very nice.' And she held the frock uncertainly in front of her, staring at her reflection.

'But it does!' Beth said eagerly. 'It shows that you have a real cleverness about clothes that I never guessed at – a cleverness like Tory's, only much *cleverer*, because you have done it all yourself. I only thought that some of the stitches were a little on the large side, but you know how short-sighted I am and how easily I might be mistaken over such a thing. And as for the money, I daresay something can be arranged, but I wish you had mentioned it when it occurred to you, not in a sudden rush now because all this needlework has unnerved you . . . I had no idea of your difficulties.'

Prudence sat down to her sewing again. 'No, I don't think you had,' she said calmly. 'I don't think you have the slightest idea of what goes on under your nose. Not the slightest.'

'I cannot be expected to read your thoughts,' Beth agreed. She went over to the window and looked down at the harbour. Stevie was wandering along the quayside with a bunch of gulls' feathers in her hand. Dreamily she seemed to walk, her brows drawn thoughtfully together, her lips moving. Sometimes she stooped to pick up another feather. 'I know the world she walks in,' Beth thought. 'The lovely world of her own choosing. She has sunk into it, as I sink into my Allegra's world, a world that is small and enclosed like a rock-pool, as safe as the womb, a world where grief is never dull, as it is in real life, nor joy clouded always by feelings of guilt or anxiety, where one does not suffer continually from frustration or from stubbing one's toes against unexpected sharp edges.' (She thought of Prudence's moodiness, and her furious, unaccountable sewing.)

Now Stevie stroked her cheeks with the feathers and smiled to herself. Beth watched her as she came towards the house, her rather moon-like face, her pale, straight hair and her enormous eyes, the sort of little girl who might one day be a beautiful woman, or might not be. The fine features were there, but they awaited some illumination from within or, later, some cleverness from without.

Just as she came to the door, and as if Beth had called out, Stevie lifted her head and looked straight up at her mother, and her face seemed to clear, all her pretending thrown back like a veil. She smiled and held up her bunch of feathers, and Beth waved.

'Who is that?' Prudence asked sharply.

'It was Stevie. What a lovely day it is!' For the sea danced and glittered with little points of light, as if composed of minute strokes of colour.

'I will give you my coral bracelets,' Beth said suddenly, turning round. 'They will look well with that silvery-green, and I shall never wear them again myself. Bracelets are for young wrists.'

Prudence did not feel inclined to mourn her mother's lost youth for her. 'Thank you,' she said, but rather grudgingly, and without looking up.

Little blobs and clots of colour lay isolated over the canvas. This puzzled Bertram. The sea was composed of little strokes of colour, he had decided, and he had told himself that he had only to take things calmly, go slowly at it, and he could translate it to his canvas ... ('a dazzling little marine study by Bertram Hemingway') ... but it was as if there were mocking devils between him and his canvas, and the paint, which should have drenched the scene with light, had the congealed appearance of sealing wax. Each little blob was separate, meaningless. 'It has no prevailing light,' he thought; but would go on. 'For it will have to do,' he decided. 'I promised a picture and they shall have a picture. After all, it's better than that other effort in the bar. Far better. All the same, I won't sign it.' (Though he had scarcely meant to creep away at the end of his stay, meek and anonymous.)

Above the speckled water he was now painting in the scabrous, flaking walls of the Fun Fair, violet shadows, picturesque, if hackneyed, upon the white; shutters mouldy, an acid green like the patina on bronze.

'It does not quite come off,' he thought, painting recklessly, for all his self-admonishing. 'Never mind; it is, after all, a new medium to me. Better luck next time.' The thought occurred to him then, as he painted-in their building, that the Fun Fair people had never come. After hearing so much about them. No visitors either. One or two elderly people, that was all. Like being in a dead world. 'And now!' (he laid a bar of shadow at Mrs Bracey's window, representing Mrs Bracey herself), 'time to knock off for a pipe.'

'It is for you,' Stevie said, coming to lean against Robert's knees as he read. 'It is a shaver.' She laid the bunch of soiled gulls' feathers upon Robert's waistcoat. They were loosely bound with coloured wools.

'Is it indeed?' Robert said, scarcely lowering his paper.

'It is for putting the soap on your face with instead of a shaving brush.'

Then he picked up the feathers and examined them. When he had thanked her he glanced across at Beth, and they smiled gently at the thought of him dipping these grubby feathers into lather and painting his cheeks with them. Amusement and affection linked them together for a moment.

'You see how soft it is!' Stevie said, entranced by her own generosity and the loveliness of the gift.

'It is very soft indeed,' Robert agreed, flinching away. ('What the devil do I do in the morning when I shave?' he wondered.) 'Next you should make a hat for your mother,' he said, his eyes challenging Beth's. 'A nice feather hat for her to wear when she goes to London.'

'Of course not,' Stevie said. 'I am too young to make hats.'

Beth nodded with triumph and malice at her husband.

'Dear Mother,' (Tory read, walking back along the hall from the front door),

'I am sorry this is such a short letter. Please send a 100 what bulb and flex also battery. Please send at once.

Father's wife sent me a book about ghouls that drink blood out of a corpse. It has been taken away. I am sorry this is such a short letter. I am a bit off colour. Please send things urgently. I hope you are quite fit.

Kind regards – EDWARD

P.S. If you send a note saying I have got masstoid I don't have to learn boxing. I don't want to learn boxing you might get hurt. Yours – EDWARD FOYLE.'

Tory wandered into the kitchen. As this letter worried her in almost every possible way, she sat down upon a chair, trying to be calm.

Lily climbed the street to the Library. As she reached the crest of the hill, the landscape seemed to spill and flow away inland like a broken wave, bearing on its crest the stricken trees, their branches streaming before them, the scattered stone cottages, the solitary macrocarpas: below, like a great coral reef, lay the white buildings of the New Town.

The Institute was railinged off and set among bleached coarse barley-grass and convolvulus. The narrow Gothic windows excluded sunshine, the fusty smell was sharp as the slash of a knife as Lily pushed open the door and entered, coldness, darkness falling over her.

The Librarian was counting out coins from an old Oxo tin. He had a habit of running his tongue between his lips so that they were perpetually moist between his moustache and beard. He looked up at Lily and nodded and then went on counting. The room was empty. Lily hesitated. She was always at a loss before these shelves of books, especially standing as she was now, in a strange no-man's-land with fiction behind her ('For real life is far better,' Bertram had said), and non-fiction such an unknown conglomeration, from books on etiquette to Buddhism or Backyard Poultry-keeping.

'Clinical Survey of the Manic-Depressive,' she read at the heading of a page and she slipped the book back into its place and chose another: *The History of Newby* by some old-time vicar. She turned the book sideways, looking at the engraved plates – the pictures of boats on the open sea, sails bellying out, gravid as the clouds above, which were like thumb-bruises on the sky: a little shawled woman came out of the Cazabons' house, her mittened hand steadying her bonnet; Mrs Bracey's shop looked like a warehouse, with a front of clap-boarding: Lily's own house was a pub, leering, tottering like a palsied thing, a lamp stuck out over the flight of steps at the side, and the name – The Pilot Boat Inn – painted between two upstairs windows: the lighthouse, the Cazabons' house, the Anchor, were the same; bare-footed children played along the foreshore; a woman with a fish-basket on her head lifted her skirts crossing a great stretch of puddles at the foot of the steps leading down to Lower Harbour Street.

'Bad times, evil tunes,' the Librarian said over Lily's shoulder. She started, even dropped the book, which he picked up and opened again, glancing through the pages. 'Every fifth house a public house and gin a penny a measure. Your nerves are in a state, Mrs Wilson. I apologise for making you start. Yes ...' he glanced back at the little picture ... 'children without shoes, filth and squalor everywhere. And vice ...' he said this word lingeringly ... 'vice indescribable. It goes with poverty, hand-in-hand, the pawn-shop and the brothel.'

Lily blushed at this. She had been brought up so rigidly that only since the war had she known that the word did not mean a soup-kitchen, and still in the midst of her confusion saw the picture of a painted harlot in a swansdown-bordered negligee ladling soup from a large tureen and handing it to the poor.

'And now if you have selected your book I am afraid I must lock up. It's past closing-time,' the old man was saying, and she noticed then a large key dangling from a piece of string on his fingers.

'Yes, I will take this,' she said, receiving the book from his warm hands, in a panic at the thought of being shut in alone with him, with his talk of vice and brothels.

He followed her to the door, lifted his hat from a peg, and they went out together.

'Perhaps I might accompany you down the hill,' he suggested. 'Such a beautiful evening.'

It was like emerging from a cave to come out into the sunlight. Down below them the sea was encrusted with silver.

'That little yacht!' he said, and pointed with his walking-stick. 'A picturesque sight. I've noticed it several times of late.'

'Yes,' said Lily, wondering how she could be rid of him. His manner of speaking was so lofty, yet the words themselves were rooted in ... She paused to wonder what. 'In filth and squalor,' she decided, going down the hill beside him. 'In filth and squalor.'

The sunlight filled the room as if it were wine in a glass, flashed on the knives and forks, showed up the smeary windows. The meat was tough, so conversation was spasmodic. Red-currant jelly gradually subsided into hot gravy and was lost, the cauliflower was stifled beneath a heavy sauce with a hard skin on it.

'Such a lovely evening!' Beth said.

No one answered. Robert chewed and chewed, and Prudence, reaching forward for bread, split her new frock under the arm.

'What was the trouble with Stevie?' Robert asked presently. 'I heard her screaming long before I turned the corner.'

'She wanted me to read another chapter, but I had said only one as she was in disgrace.'

'For what?'

'For rudeness. I told her to get out of the bath and she refused. And then she looked at me and said: "You can put that in your pipe and smoke it." She gets those stupid little sayings from school . . .'

'It would be nice,' Robert said, 'to find a mother whose child originated some of these rude words and phrases. I have never met one yet. And what did you do when she screamed? Gave in, I suppose.'

'Not exactly. I said I would read a little more on the strict understanding that she would be very good to-morrow.'

'Oh, my God! Prudence, when you have finished tying up your frock with bits of cotton, would you pass the cauliflower? You really spoil Stevie, Beth. Of course she screams. It pays her to. She's no fool and obviously everyone does what is to their advantage. Next time she'll try it on still more.'

'Surely her promise is worth something?' Beth protested.

'Not a thing. No, she's quite pampered. When I was a boy, if I'd behaved as she behaves, I'd have been thrashed. I was never read to at bedtime or any other time . . .'

'Well, I was,' Beth said. '*And* I was spoilt, and had my own way. And look at me now. Every bit as nice a person as you are, Robert. So it seems as if all your misery was wasted.'

'I didn't say it was misery.'

'Well, it certainly didn't sound much fun.'

'Fun or not, I wasn't allowed to be rude.'

'Then perhaps you exhausted your politeness when you were young, for you're very often rude now.'

Both Robert and Prudence looked up in amazement, but Beth went on calmly trying to cut her meat and at last put some of it into her mouth and began to chew. Since she apparently had no intention of saying any more, Robert asked in a voice that was like the snapping-off of icicles: 'Perhaps you will tell me in what way I am rude.'

'Of course,' Beth replied, in the tone of one who does not bear malice. 'Firstly, you often speak very roughly and inconsiderately to me ...'

'Firstly? Is there to be "secondly" as well?' he cried.

'And secondly, it seems to me that although I don't care in the least for etiquette or meaningless gestures such as your standing up when I enter the room, or walking on one side of the pavement rather than the other, sometimes I *do* carry very heavy trays and you never move to help me, and I run to and fro fetching things, and rather wait on you, like a ... servant.' She smiled calmly and pleasantly as if she had been praising him. 'And thirdly,' she continued, 'your patronising airs, as if only men's work is important, and my writing an irritating and rather shameful habit ... "If we ignore it, she will grow out of it," you seem to imply.' She laid her knife and fork neatly together and looked up.

'I see,' Robert said and tried to weight with meaning these meaningless words – a grim sarcasm, perhaps, or the implication that he said merely that because he could not trust himself to say more. But it was obvious to the three of them that he said no more because he was too confounded to think of anything.

'There *is* nothing else to eat,' Beth said, and stood up with an air of triumph. 'The junket has not set and there is no cheese.'

She left them and went out to make the coffee. 'People who are outspoken all the time,' she was thinking, 'must grow dulled to the excitement of seeing people shocked, the jaws dropping, the incredulous eyes. So stimulating.' Very light-heartedly she stirred the coffee.

'Well, I'm damned!' Robert said when she had gone and still at a loss for words. He was very much put out, for it seemed to him that he had jogged along for years, unobserved, uncriticised. Now it appeared that Beth had been observing him all the time with meticulous concentration, and criticising him, too – dispassionately. The thought connected with others and left him profoundly disturbed. 'I must go and tell Tory,' he told himself, wondering how he could slip away.

Prudence had now split her frock under the other arm and ran frantically upstairs to mend it.

'Coffee's ready!' Beth called gaily.

The sun was slowly drained from the room as wine is drained from a glass, leaving a faint flush only to show that it was ever there.

'My Dear Edward' (wrote Tory),

'I am afraid I am unable to say that you have mastoid, as this clearly is not so. I cannot think of any way out of it and I am sure your father would say that it would be good for you to learn boxing . . .'

('He is so in my power,' she thought, her chin resting on her wrist, her mouth drooping.)

'Dear Mr Bancroft,' she began again, drawing another sheet of paper towards her, 'I should be grateful if Edward might be excused boxing lessons for the time being, as he has occasionally been troubled by slight . . .'

('And that, of course, is bringing the child up to be a liar . . .!')

Just as she was tearing the paper across Robert came to the door.

'You must help me,' she said, leading him back into the room. 'I am torn in two.'

'What is it?'

'It is Edward's boxing lessons . . .'

He was surprised and annoyed to find that he himself was not the cause of the trouble.

'He so terribly doesn't want to do it.'

'Why not?'

'He is afraid of being hurt.'

'Good God!' He seemed scandalised.

'Is that so unnatural?'

'Unnatural. It seems a very morbid attitude in a little boy. You must have been putting cowardly ideas into his head . . .'

'Not at all. You obviously think he must be made to do it.'

'Obviously.'

'That sinus trouble he had, do you remember . . .?'

'It wasn't sinus. I told you at the time. It was simply a catarrhal condition . . .'

'He was always sniffing.'

'That was habit.'

'Oh, doctors infuriate me. Habit indeed!'

'What is wrong with the boy?'

'Nothing is wrong.'

'But you are trying to hit on something to get him out of his boxing. What the devil would Teddy say to all this?'

'I expect he would agree with you. You already have so much in common.'

'We quarrel before we know where we are,' he said. He stood with his elbow on the mantelshelf, examining a scratch on the back of his hand, as we are inclined to concentrate on the smallest detail in a time of crisis, the same despairing effort with which, Tory conjectured, a victim might stare at a mole on the chin of his torturer. 'And as I stared at the clergyman's boots when I was married,' she thought.

'Why are you smiling?' he asked, raising his eyes.

'I was remembering my wedding.'

He lowered his eyes quickly.

'You look very lovely this evening,' he murmured in a cross voice and without glancing at her.

She thanked him with the automatic graciousness of one practised in acknowledging compliments. And then, to bring the conversation back to himself, Robert said: 'I am worried about Beth.'

'Is she ill?' Tory asked quickly, prepared to believe only the best.

'No, she's not ill: but, either she has guessed about our feelings for one another, has put two and two together as any other woman would have done months ago – either that or she has gone mad.'

'Which do *you* think?'

'Quite honestly, I think she has become a little peculiar. But I've no doubt I shall soon find out.'

'What has she done or said?'

'This evening she quarrelled with me. She was tart and

argumentative, almost abusive. Women often are, I know' – he gave Tory a brief look – 'but not Beth. Not ever before in all the years I have known her. And done so coldly, as if she no longer cared for me, rather as if she were enjoying herself. I can't explain how uncanny it was.'

'Don't pick at that scratch! You see, you are making it bleed.'

He put his hand in his pocket and looked up wearily.

'What do you want me to do?' Tory asked.

'I am very worried,' he repeated.

'Then I had better make one of those grand renunciations,' she said haughtily. 'I will go miles away and hide myself in a little bed-sitting-room and live on my memories. Where I can harm you no more.' She saw herself lying on a chaise-longue, coughing a little, her hands full of camellias.

'It was too hackneyed a role for you,' he said, when she had described this to him. 'And you would want to get up every evening and go for a drink.'

'The trouble with renunciation is the giving-up part. All women fancy themselves doing it, but do they *enjoy* it, I wonder? It is too negative to be really uplifting, except in literature. The gesture is more beautiful than the thing itself, which does so go on and on – the next day and the next, and for ever. In books one just dies.'

She talked, giving him a chance to trample on all her avowals and intentions, but he did not do so. He seemed to wait gravely, looking at her.

'I harm everyone with whom I come in contact,' she said recklessly.

'You don't harm me, my dear.' He put out his hand and clasped hers. 'You throw everything else into shadow, but that is not the fault of your beauty. It is the drabness of the world and the monotony of my life in this place day after day, so, until I die. You lit up every hour for me, made one day different from another, brought me back to life. Each night I have taken you to bed with me. I closed my eyes and folded my arms round you, imagining that you belonged to me, disposing of all the obstacles in one moment, and so fell asleep. You could not harm me ...'

Tory moved her hand restlessly in his. 'You speak of me in the past tense,' she laughed awkwardly.

'Don't make fun of me!'

'All right. But I am not much good at love scenes, especially when they are so sad. I am much more inclined to the lusts of the flesh. And now you are crushing my hand.'

He thought he would waste no more time on words and began to kiss her, seeming to imply that if it were the lusts of the flesh she contemplated, he did not himself disdain them. Shutting his eyes he felt at first hollowed, and then as if he were filled with music, the smooth, warm sound sweeping through the corridors of his mind, until he stood quite alone with Tory, the rest of the world obliterated.

But the rest of the world is not so easily effaced, and the further we escape the more ruthless our dragging back and the greater the vehemence which will splinter upon us, like the smashing of vast sheets of ice upon our loosened will. So it was no ordinary bell ringing which made their eyes fly open, their mouths whiten.

'What was that?' Robert cried.

Tory was the first to recover. 'I expect it is Prudence to fetch you away,' she said coldly, glancing in the mirror. 'Perhaps Mrs Bracey wishes to come downstairs again.'

It was in fact Prudence.

'Well!' Tory exclaimed. 'What a pretty frock!'

She appeared very smooth and controlled, with all her wits about her once again.

'Come in, my dear.'

In the hall she snapped off some odd bits of cotton from the hem and moved Prudence slowly round, turning her by the shoulders, enraging the girl.

'I want my father in a hurry.'

'Your father? Yes, of course, dear. Robert! Robert! Here is Prudence!' And still, as if absorbed, she pulled and tweaked at the new frock. It was as if she would not let Prudence go into that room, as if the passion which they had suffered there had been so tangible that it might hang still in the air.

Robert came into the hall.

'Mrs Bracey has sent for you,' Prudence began at once.

Tory's eyes seemed to dance as she looked at Robert.

'What the hell for? Does she think I am for ever at her beck and call?' he asked.

'Her daughter came and she said it was urgent and that her mother cannot breathe.'

'Then she must be dead by now,' Tory said with a satisfied air.

'Did your mother send you?'

'No. I was just going out and I met the girl on the steps.' Prudence looked very levelly at her father, as if to say: 'It was as well for you that I did.'

'Excuse me, Tory,' he began; and then as he reached the door, had not the courage merely to go, but turned and made matters worse by saying: 'I will think it over about Edward's catarrh and let you know.'

'Edward's catarrh!' Prudence said lightly as soon as he had gone.

Tory did not make the same kind of mistakes as Robert, and she said nothing.

'There's one thing I've made up my mind about,' Prudence went on. 'If ever I get married I won't live next door to my dearest friend.'

'Yes, it is a good idea not to,' Tory said in a careless tone.

'You see, I know all about you and Father.'

'Do you?'

'And I think you're hateful. I had always heard of people doing vile and dreadful things, but not people I knew, not my own father.'

Her emotion came up shakily and broke like waves upon the rock of Tory's assumed indifference.

'Then that makes your readiness to conjecture all the more odd,' Tory said, and added: 'Especially, as you say, about your own father.'

'Nothing *you* say is any use.'

'No, I don't think it is.'

Tory's pretty little clock struck nine, the notes floating towards them down the hall.

'Oh, damn you!' Prudence suddenly said, dashing tears away with the back of her hand and groping for the doorknob.

Tory took a folded handkerchief from her cuff and held it out.

'I don't think it would do for you to rush out into the street weeping,' she said, playing for time because she felt that Prudence, propelled on a surge of self-pity, might fly to her mother, or make a scene elsewhere. But Prudence, having smeared her tears across her cheeks, threw the handkerchief down upon the hall-table and seemed not to be able to go quickly enough.

When at last she had managed to open the door, Tory said: 'The frock, by the way, is quite a success, but those dingy little coral bracelets ruin the effect.'

Then she closed the door very quietly and went directly to the windows overlooking the front. She was just in time to see Prudence before she disappeared. She was running, almost, in the direction of Mrs Bracey's house. When she was quite out of sight Tory still stood there, conscious of a dreadful foreboding of disaster.

'I am sorry I am late,' Prudence said breathlessly.

In the churchyard the air was warm and steady and scented with the lime trees in flower. Geoffrey put his book in his pocket, but he could scarcely have been reading, for the light was slowly retreating and had already taken the green from Prudence's frock, and the blossom on the trees was a shape, not a colour, against the sky.

'Will you be warm enough if we sit here and talk?' he asked.

'Yes, thank you,' Prudence said, shivering.

She sat down beside him, fidgeting with the coral bracelets on her white wrists. 'How peaceful it is!'

The gravestones were sunk in the deep turf, a marble angel implored them to hush, holding up its hand warningly, as if it were a fitful sleep only down there below the bed of granite chippings. The sea was hushed, too, so that only Geoffrey could hear it, not Prudence.

'I have been reading Donne as I sat here waiting,' said Geoffrey.

'Oh, have you?' Prudence murmured warily. A dreadful fear that he was going to read some poetry aloud beset her, confused her, and she could think of nothing to stave him off. 'But it is

241

too dark,' she decided. 'Unless he has a torch. Or' (and this was so much worse) 'knows it by heart.' 'I don't like poetry,' she said roughly.

Geoffrey chuckled appreciatively, as if she had made a little joke.

'But I don't!' she insisted.

'Don't you, darling? I love you in your grey frock, but I am sure you are cold.'

'It isn't grey. It's green.'

'It is grey at the moment, so therefore it is grey. Colour can only be what it appears to be.'

'I think it can be what it is.'

'Put my jacket round you!'

'No. It doesn't matter.'

'Let us share it, then.'

'Oh, no, thank you.'

'I like the bracelets, too, and the way they fall over the back of your hands and make your wrists seem thin. "A bracelet of bright hair about the bone,"' he added. He felt at home among the graves with her beauty close to him and made more moving when it lay side by side in his mind with the grim and the corrupt and the melancholy.

'My mother gave them to me,' Prudence said, ignoring his last remark which scanned too much for her liking and was, she feared, the beginning of some poetry.

'I love your mother very dearly,' Geoffrey said quietly.

Prudence drew herself up, very taut and shivering, her face – but it was nearly dark now – puzzled, and her lips parted.

'Yes, I love her very dearly, and revere her,' Geoffrey went on.

Prudence relaxed. 'Oh, I see,' she said easily. 'I am so glad.'

'There is an innocence about her I delight in,' he went on condescendingly. 'And she has passed it on to you.'

As Prudence did not answer he said: 'Oh, it is no use you telling me otherwise, implying this and that, as you did the other night. I still believe you are as clear as crystal, but like all innocent people you rather veer towards ideas of romantic guilt: as if to be good is not to be interesting. You are shivering, Prudence. I shall have to take you home. Why didn't you wear a coat?'

'I had no time ... There was a fuss, an upset as I set out. In the end I just ran away – without thinking.'

'Ran away from what?'

Prudence thought for a moment and then she said: 'From Tory Foyle.'

'What was she doing?'

'I couldn't tell you, I'm afraid.'

'You quarrelled with her? Why? Please don't be stubborn with me!' He took her hands and held them, shaking them gently. 'I am glad you quarrelled with her,' he went on. 'There is something unkind about the woman. Insolent, and even cruel.'

His hands slid up her cold arms and into her sleeves.

'Come into my coat, there's a dear girl.'

He bunched her up to him and kissed her. 'Please don't move your head away. I love you very dearly, Prudence.'

'Do you revere me, too?' she asked with sarcasm.

'No. I can't say I do. I wish you loved me the very slightest ...'

'Oh, love!' she said impatiently. Then, looking down at her bracelets, remembering her mother, she put up her hands and covered her face.

'What is it, Prudence, my angel?'

243

'I don't like it here. All these graves. I want to go home. I'm cold.'

He wrapped his jacket over her shoulders. She felt the warm lining of it on her arms and was comforted. After a while she said with a stagey sort of bitterness: 'I daresay I expected too much.'

'Of what?' he asked gently.

'Of love. I always imagined it would be a sort of increasing excitement ...'

'And it is so dull?'

She thought hard. 'Yes, I think it is dull as well,' she said.

'As well as what?'

'As well as frightening.'

'I wouldn't frighten you for the world.'

'You?' Then she laughed. 'Oh, I wasn't thinking of you.'

'Then of whom?'

'Of Tory Foyle and my father.'

Her teeth were chattering and he drew her closer to him. She began to cough. 'Oh, I see,' he said thoughtfully. It was as if a strange landscape were suddenly unrolled before him and he looked at it through her eyes.

When she had stopped coughing she said in a husky voice: 'I thought of love being like a flower, a rose ...' She cupped her hands together in her lap and her fingers spread slowly apart ... 'and I thought of it opening, unfolding, one petal after another, something new each day ... but now I shall always know that this horrible thing may come crawling out of its heart ... an excuse for every sort of treachery, and grubby deceit, and meanness ...'

'If they love one another ...'

'But he is supposed to love my mother!'

'Supposed!' Geoffrey echoed, and laughed in a worldly-wise fashion; but he was a little shaken all the same. Through their young eyes they surveyed Tory's and Robert's guilt and felt, in contrast, a quality of superiority about themselves, uplifted, triumphant, in the dark graveyard.

Tory went to bed early and had a good cry. Into the middle of the weeping came the sound of tapping on the street door. She put a wrap over her shoulders and went to the window. Down below stood Robert and he lifted his face and called to her in a low voice: 'I do wish you'd come down, Tory. I must speak to you.'

Filled with dread, unconscious for once of her appearance, she ran downstairs and opened the door. Coldness hung about his clothes as he entered the hall.

'What happened to Prudence after I left?' he began at once.

'She went, too ... I thought she must be going after you ... it was in that direction.'

'She didn't say?'

'No.'

'Did she say anything?'

Tory sat down on the only chair. 'Yes, she did. She knows, and told me so and was rather hysterical ...'

'Oh, my God! You see, she's gone. I can't find her.'

'What time is it?'

'About eleven ...'

'Well ...'

'But where would she go?'

'I don't know.' ('I shouldn't have taunted her about the bracelets,' Tory thought. 'It was wicked of me.') 'She'll come back,' she said, unconvincingly.

'I don't know where to look now. I've walked all along under the cliff straining my eyes into the darkness. Why have you been crying?'

'Yes, I must look a pretty sight – oh, I've been crying because of going away from here, from you, and … but don't worry. I shall go. Very quickly, I promise.'

'If it isn't too late,' he said cruelly. 'Suppose she doesn't come back?'

'She will. She's just trying to punish us, to frighten us.'

'And she's succeeding.'

'What about – Beth?'

'She is sitting there writing and saying how naughty of Prudence to stay out without letting us know.'

'Where does she think you have been?'

'Mrs Bracey has pleurisy. She thinks I have been there all the time … or rather, as far as she has any ideas about what's been going on, those are the ideas she has.'

'What was that noise?'

'I thought it sounded like our front door.'

'Perhaps it is Prudence.'

'Yes, I must go at once.'

'If it is not, come back and I will go out with you to search.'

'Yes. Good night, Tory.'

'Good night, Robert, dear. And I am – so sorry.'

'If only it is all right,' he began.

'It will be all right,' she promised.

When he had gone, she went to the bathroom and bathed her eyes. 'It will be all right,' she promised herself, but with a sinking heart.

Prudence was at the foot of the stairs, coughing, her head bent, her hand grasping the newel of the staircase. Her forehead reddened and whitened and a great twisting vein divided it.

Robert went to her and steadied her with his arm.

'Come into the surgery and have a draught,' he told her.

She followed him obediently and sat on the slippery couch waiting.

'Where have you been?' he asked, busy mixing her dose.

'Where have *you* been?' she replied.

'I have been to Mrs Bracey's, and to Tory's,' he said carefully.

'And *I* have been for a walk.'

'Tory tells me you have imagined a lot of nonsense about – about Tory and me.'

'I don't want to talk about it.'

'Neither do I. I only want to say that almost nothing you imagine is true, and the rest – won't be true any longer.'

'I don't want to discuss it, I said.'

She felt sickened by him, as the young are by the love affairs of their elders.

'Drink this up!' He handed her the glass and she drank, making a wry face. 'And don't go out in the damp night again,' he added, trying to regain normality.

'I shall do as I please. I am not a child.'

'I am talking to you as a doctor, not as a father. Good night, Prue.'

Without answering him she walked out of the room and up the stairs.

'Good night, dear!' Beth called out from the morning-room, but in the muffled voice which meant she had not raised her head from her desk.

'Good night, Mother, dear!' Prudence called loudly and warmly.

'She has come back safely,' Robert thought. 'But not to me. Not ever to me again.'

*

247

Prudence lay in bed with her cats in her arms. She was in no hurry to go to sleep. 'To-morrow!' she thought. 'And to-morrow. And so on, perhaps, for always.'

For the rose, in spite of Tory, was beginning to unfurl.

15

The day comes in slowly to those who are ill. The night has separated them from the sleepers, who return to them like strangers from a distant land, full of clumsy preparations for living, the earth itself creaking towards the light.

Now, a great hand seemed to hold Mrs Bracey back to her pillows; the hand of God, she thought. She had always been aware of the concentration of God upon her, an omnipotent God, vaguely, and yet, over small matters, still at her beck and call. When she wished Him to give her His attention she opened a little shutter in her soul: in this way she could be sure of His presence at her prayers; He would receive her orders and listen to her explanations (taking them at their face value), but at the same time could be excluded from any shameful thoughts or family quarrels, nor need He soil His ears listening to any obscenities or what Mrs Bracey herself euphemistically called 'suggestive stories'.

When she shut God away she did not imagine Him turning His thoughts to any others of His flock. It was rather like giving a maid the afternoon off, except that she imagined Him mooning about, idle, restless, waiting to return.

Always He had revolved round her, as the moon about the earth – until the afternoon of the previous day, when the world had come at last to a standstill and the pain in her chest and shoulders a great weight pinning her back, so that all her energy must be expended on the business of filling and emptying the lungs so cramped beneath that burden.

Children know, too, those long periods of watching light as it fans out across ceilings, descends the walls. The ghost against the door returns to dressing-gown, the chest-of-drawers stands forward at last, so prosaically, a piece of furniture merely. Then, somewhere in the house, a bed moves, a grating, a creaking, prelude to the day.

So Maisie stirred and stretched. The door standing open reminded her at once of her mother's illness, and she groped for her slippers, sitting on the edge of the bed, her bosom grey in the early light, her body criss-crossed from the wrinkled cotton nightgown, her hair netted up close to her head. Iris lay curled among the draping bedclothes, an arm crooked round her profile and her lips parted, smiling almost.

'How do you feel this morning?' Maisie asked her mother, rattling the curtains back along their rod. But her mother only turned her head wearily on her pillow, unable any more to play her own rôle. It had all been effected by words, by the quick lash of her tongue, and now she had not the breath for talking.

'I'll bring you up a cup of tea,' Maisie said, looking at her. 'I'll change the poultices.'

Mrs Bracey turned her head towards the window. 'Anyone about?' she whispered.

Maisie went over to see. Her mother watched her breath come and go upon the pane.

'No, there's no one.'

The buildings were so sharply outlined. There were no shadows and there was no colour. 'An exquisite little ink drawing,' Bertram might have called it. (But he was finishing his last half-hour of sleep, peaceful, rosy, and wearing striped pyjamas, like a schoolboy's.)

Then, suddenly, Maisie saw the doctor come hurrying out of his house. He put up the collar of his coat and shut the door carefully. Setting off with that familiar jog-trot of his, he soon rounded the corner and was out of sight. In the silence of the morning she could even hear him starting up his car in the garage behind his house.

'The doctor,' she said aloud. 'It's all hours for him; when we call him out late at night we forget that; we don't think how early he may have to get up, or not go to bed at all.'

She admired Robert. He was a quiet, sensible man, she thought, without eccentricity, flamboyance, like, for instance, Bertram Hemingway's. He was a man you could trust, rely upon, she decided, and she placed this reliability far above any other of his qualities. She sighed as she turned from the window, partly for him and a little for herself, feeling a sympathy with him, the two of them up so early and each leaving another undisturbed in bed.

Mrs Bracey moved her head quickly from side to side on the pillow, denoting impatience, and indeed Maisie had been standing there a long time staring out at the harbour.

'I'll go,' she said. She stayed a moment longer pulling at her hair-net until presently the hair flopped down over her shoulders, unrolling into corkscrews. She yawned until her eyes watered and then groped her way down the dark stairs to the kitchen.

Mrs Bracey lay still, trying to think about the doctor, endeavouring to keep her thoughts along their old road of seeing evil where she could and sensing guilt before it was committed. But she could not do so. The doctor retreated and faded a dozen times and instead vague memories of childhood, her own childhood, ranged across the landscape of her mind. Dr Cazabon no longer mattered. She did not care if Tory Foyle eloped with him. 'Yet I want to live,' she thought. 'I still want to live. Perhaps if I could but look out of the window all the old interests would come back to me!'

The light lay full over the room now and a gull rose on its wings, gliding close by the window and crying. The fleet was out in the fishing-grounds, all the men withdrawn from the place like a tide that has fallen back. 'There's a whiteness over the ceiling when the harbour's empty,' she thought. 'Almost as white as if there was a fall of snow outside.'

Robert could not say that every time he went into his garage he remembered having kissed Tory there; but sometimes he did, and this morning, perhaps because he was sleepy, he felt her presence there very palpably. As he drove up the hill towards the nursing-home he thought of the evening when he met her at the station, when they had for the first time acknowledged their secret. 'It's no use,' he now told himself (his patient, almost ready to be delivered of her child, imagined him speeding towards her, all his thoughts on her and on this important hour of her life), 'it is of no avail to excuse ourselves by saying that facts cannot be hidden, for of course they can be and should have been, and nothing but wretchedness would ever result from bringing them to the light of day.'

He drove in between shining laurels, lawns sopping wet

with dew, geraniums. Small bleatings now arose from rows of cradles, where mauve, mottled fists were crammed against hungry mouths, furiously strong lips fastened upon and rejected knuckles and fingers. A young nurse lifted the babies and carried them, two at a time, to their mothers' bosoms.

'Good morning,' Robert said, leaving his hat on the hall-table. 'Good morning,' he repeated to his old enemy advancing down the corridor, her skirts and veil snapping and crackling as she came. 'If I had not succumbed that evening,' he thought, going up the stairs, 'if I had been five minutes earlier or later passing the station, Prudence might have been spared. I should not have lost her love and her confidence in me, and my own peace of mind.'

The Matron preceded him through a door and stood aside as if in triumph. 'Brought to this by a man,' she seemed to announce, directing Robert's attention to the woman on the bed who turned restlessly from side to side, seeking to evade pain.

'Vomiting,' Matron said, 'since five.'

The woman put up her hands and took Robert's, gripping them tightly.

'So very cold,' she whispered apologetically, and smiled.

At that moment Robert was dearer to her than her own husband. She put her life in his hands with love and confidence. While he gave his orders to the nurse he stood there close to her, chafing her wrists with the utmost tenderness. She no longer thrashed about in the bed, but lay very still, and when the pain overwhelmed her she merely closed her eyes.

'Perfect weather!' customers said, turning away from it into the dark coolness of the public-house. 'A really lovely spell.'

Ned Pallister, that indoor creature, was glad, he implied, for their sakes.

Bertram wore a cream alpaca jacket and Tory a large floppy hat to shade her face. When she encountered Bertram on the quay he remarked on this.

'It would not suit me to be sunburnt,' she explained, and, with one of those impulsive gestures she thought out so well beforehand, she tucked her hand under his elbow and strolled with him along the waterside towards the cliff-walk.

'You are good at knowing what is right for you,' he agreed. 'Your face is like painted china.'

'I hope it is carefully painted.'

'All the same, I can also admire the Californian type of beauty.'

'Those sun-baked women?' she asked coldly.

'I like the little white bits that get left.'

'Oh, I see,' she said. 'I imagined them so bold that there'd be none of those.'

They sat down upon a blistering hot seat among plants with rubbery leaves, dismal blossoms puce in colour. The sea quivered with light and was purple above the rocks, green elsewhere. A yacht was passing out of sight round the Point.

'I never would go sailing with Teddy,' Tory continued. 'It roughens the skin, tangles the hair. It is no use trying to be what you are not. Now, he has married a very sporty girl called Dorothy, who romps about and tousles his hair and is a real pal to him, a real comrade and helpmeet. And I expect goes sailing with him, wearing trousers, and hoisting the jib whenever she's told ... or whatever else it is wives are supposed to do on boats ...' She spoke disdainfully, looking out at the distant yacht.

'What is that noise?' Bertram asked.

'Oh, I think it is the band on the promenade at the New Town.'

'Surely we could never hear it from so far?'

'Oh yes,' she answered carelessly. 'It sounds better like this.' And then she suddenly said: 'Bertram!'

'Yes, my dear?'

'You may remember that you have often asked me to marry you . . . I daresay you spoke in jest . . .?'

A sense of great danger came over him. 'In jest?' he repeated, to gain time in which to digest, make use of this warning.

'Yes, in jest!' She laughed, bowing her head.

'How could I jest about such a thing?' he asked with automatic gallantry.

'Then if you meant it before and mean it still . . . well, it will give me great pleasure to accept, that is all.'

He said nothing for the reason that he could think of nothing to say. As if his feelings were too deep for words, he took her hand and kissed it. ('It is just that I have not had time to think,' he comforted himself. 'I am really transported with joy.')

'It is high time I settled down,' he said aloud. 'But no other woman has made me wish to marry.'

'Of course, there is Edward,' Tory said.

('Yes, of course, there is Edward as well,' Bertram thought.)

'He is just the sort of boy I should like to have for a son,' he said. 'But let us talk about ourselves. What has made you change your mind? For I think I now have the right to ask you that, my sweetheart.'

Tory thought, too, that he certainly had a right, but that that could not be a guarantee of receiving the truth.

'Oh, I am lonely,' she said.

He held her hands and from time to time lifted them and put little kisses into the palms.

'I am lonely, too.'

They looked at one another and laughed.

'One thing merely,' he began, 'any prospective employer would wish to know the same – before I take you in marriage, I feel I am entitled to know why your former husband left you.'

'Oh, you feel that?'

'You see, you might fail me in the same ways.'

'I didn't fail him. I irritated him.'

'In what ways?'

'Oh ...' She looked out to sea. The yacht had gone and there was nothing to concentrate upon. 'For instance, by unwinding balls of string from the outside, squeezing my toothpaste from the top – those sort of things.'

'Those are not reasons for divorce.'

'I also thought they were not.' Suddenly she said: 'I forgot to tell you that I want to be married at once. I hate making plans and waiting for things. And I want to get away from here and find somewhere else to live. I am so tired of the seaside and all the squalor of this dreadful little place ...'

As her agitation grew – and he could feel it in her hands as she spoke – his pity for her grew, too, and his uneasiness about the future.

'Look at me!' he said, when she had finished speaking.

She raised her eyes and smiled at him, the warmth gathering and breaking over him.

'I am not a passionate man ...'

'You reassure me,' she said lightly. ('Why, it is quite a lark

256

after all,' she thought. 'It is quite easy – so long as it is quickly done.')

'Let us go for a drink!' she suggested. 'Let us break the news a great deal, and celebrate.'

16

There really were a few visitors at last, but only day-trippers from the New Town. They hired boats and were rowed out of the harbour into the open sea. After half an hour, perhaps, they turned and came back, for there was nothing to see, they said, only the view: they did not often marvel at or even notice the transformation of the harbour buildings, dulled and diminished, becoming picturesque. Ashore once more, they ate crab-teas at the Mimosa Café or were shown over the lighthouse, exclaiming at the steps, commiserating with the lighthouse-keeper, so that he began to boast, telling them how sometimes (because they were directly in the line of migration) he was obliged to sweep up the dead birds from the outer balcony with broom and shovel, the poor creatures dazed by the light and dashed to pieces. As he told this story he believed it, but it was not true; he had merely read something of the kind in a book. 'How terrible!' the visitors exclaimed, and felt that something was added to them, something they could take home after their holidays. They did not feel this over the threepence they paid to see over the Waxworks, and grumbled openly, so that Lily Wilson, sitting in the little pay-box at the entrance, heard them and was frightened.

Their voices floated up to Mrs Bracey through the open window. Her bed was moved away from the draught now, but there must be an abundance of fresh air, the doctor said. Mr Lidiard sat beside her, but she did not want him, and was glad when Bertram came. She did not want to talk, but to listen, and Mr Lidiard seemed incapable of holding a one-sided conversation, which Bertram, fresh from the silent service, did admirably. He rarely had such an opportunity and was inclined to forget Mrs Bracey and pretend to himself that he was giving a talk on the wireless – one of the things he had always wanted to do.

But this afternoon, the minute Mr Lidiard crept away, he leant over the bed and whispered dramatically: 'I am going to be married.'

'Who to?' she asked, looking up at him grotesquely out of the corners of her eyes because it hurt her to move her head in his direction.

'To Mrs Foyle, of course.'

She closed her eyes. 'Then God help you,' she murmured. 'God help you.'

'I thought you would like to hear of my intention to settle down.'

'Not to her. She's a bad woman.'

'I like bad women,' Bertram assured her, for there was no need, he thought, to defend his future wife against the slander of the dying.

'So you may,' she whispered. 'Not to live with, though.'

Then the commotion of coughing smothered her and she snatched frantically at his hands as if she were drowning. When it was over he wiped her face with his own linen handkerchief and laid her back on her smoothed pillows.

Presently she asked: 'They didn't come next door, after all, did they?'

'Next door?'

'The Fun Fair.'

'No,' he said thoughtfully. 'No, they haven't come.'

In the middle of her packing Tory suddenly thought she had enough courage to go to tell Beth her news. The packing was something definitely done against changing her mind, and she was rolling up her glasses in dusters and burying them in saw-dust.

'You are lucky to be betrothed to a woman who has all these lovely things,' she had told Bertram, as she laid her china shep-herdess in a bed of cotton-wool.

'I like this little walnut writing-table, certainly,' he had agreed.

'That was Teddy's. We brought all our treasures here for safety in the war-time. Teddy is left with all the London rubbish we thought would be bombed.'

'This is worth a pretty penny. But suppose he demands it back?'

'Can you imagine a man doing so when he's been divorced all this time?'

'I have read in the newspapers of such things happening.'

'Oh, newspapers!' She laughed merrily. 'Only freaks get into newspapers. Don't worry about that. Teddy is not the sort of person who would let himself get into print.'

'I'm not at all sure where we are going with all these costly pieces,' he began.

'We shall find a little flat in London, I am quite confident,' she assured him. 'It will do for the time being.' And she had taken up the telephone-receiver and put a call through at once to another acquaintance she had suddenly remembered.

'Well, that wasn't any good, either,' he said gloomily when she had finished.

'She said she would look about and ask people. It is another iron in the fire.'

'The fire will soon be so full of irons that it will go out,' he remarked.

Now she laid a half-wrapped goblet down upon the table and decided to go at once to see Beth before she could change her mind. She had delayed and delayed, from one hour to another, wishing to tell Robert first: but Robert had been busy with Mrs Bracey and with a tiresome confinement and she had not seen him. 'So Beth shall tell him,' she decided, letting herself out of her own door. 'He spared me nothing over Prudence. And I will spare him nothing over this.'

Beth had nearly finished her novel. She had reached the stage where she felt that it would be a great pity, a waste, if she were killed suddenly in a street accident (but she was not very likely to be in a street). She took great care not to fall asleep in her bath or to run into any kind of danger.

Yet when Tory came she was pleased to see her and gave her at once all of her attention, even peering into the little bowls and vases along the mantelpiece for cigarettes; but there were none.

'When you are sitting down,' Tory began, as if she had come merely to give good advice, 'it is a good idea to twist your skirt round, so that you don't always sit it out in the same place. When you are alone, I mean, of course.'

'I should only forget to twist it back again.'

'What is this horrid smell in the house?'

'Oh, Prudence is stewing some cow's udder for the cats. I expect it is that.'

'I expect it is. Well, if you don't mind, I will shut this door and sit over here by the window. Beth, dear, I am going to be married.'

'Again?' Beth asked foolishly, her eyes welling up with tears of confusion and sentiment.

'Of course "again". The next time will have to be that, won't it?'

'I know who to,' Beth said, shocked to find herself ending up with a preposition. But she was much thrown out by the surprise of it all.

'Yes, it is Bertram Hemingway,' Tory said, looking over her shoulder out of the window. Then, turning back to Beth, who did not know what to say, she cried: 'There is no need to look smug and knowing – like the Mona Lisa – or – or a lavatory-attendant.'

Beth's laugh was shaky, tear-laden.

'Now perhaps you won't go away?' she asked. 'Perhaps you will go on staying here?'

'No.' Tory moved her shoulders impatiently. 'I want to live in London. As soon as I get a flat I'll go. The very, very minute.'

'Oh, Tory!'

'I shall often come back.' ('I shall never come back,' she thought, turning away again to the window. 'I shall never, never come back, once I am gone.') 'And you will be coming to London about your books and we can go shopping together.'

Beth thought: 'It won't be the same.' But she said nothing.

'You are more self-sufficient than me,' Tory told her. 'You couldn't be lonely as I have been. All these years it is I who have come to you ...'

'I am only lazy ...'

'You dismiss the possibility of my being passionately in love with Bertram,' Tory said coldly.

'Yes, I am afraid I do dismiss that,' Beth replied with all her courage. 'I know you better than you imagine, and I realise that you love one man and will always love him, and no one else will ever take his place.'

Tory got up and now she, too, began to peer along the mantelpiece for a cigarette. She looked helplessly round and then sat down again.

'Teddy, you mean?' she said in a small voice.

'Of course.'

'Yes, it was a pity I got so high-handed with him and didn't realise until too late, for in many ways our marriage went on being good fun. The thing I liked best was sitting up in bed playing cards with him. We used to play this special kind of whist we invented every night and gamble and cheat one another until the early hours. Often I lost the whole month's housekeeping allowance in one night. Then I used to lie down with my back to him and not be on speaking terms ...' She laughed at the memory, but Beth looked puzzled at this picture of wedded bliss. 'I wonder,' Tory went on, 'if he plays that game with Dorothy. It's strange, but if he does, I mind it more than the other things. Much more.'

Prudence opened the door. She was looking for her cats, for the feast was ready. She picked them up from their basket and went out without a word.

'I'm sorry,' Beth apologised. 'I simply can't imagine ...'

'Oh, don't worry. We were much the same at her age. Surely you remember?'

'No, I certainly can't. *I* was a married woman and expecting a baby.'

'She has let in that awful smell again,' Tory complained, waving her hand in the air. 'Well, at twenty I was just as foolish as could be. Standing outside stage-doors after matinées . . .'

'Still writing to actors?' Beth asked drily.

'"Dear Madam, Sir John Martin-Harvey begs me to convey to you . . ." and so on.'

'You've always been a worry to me.'

Prudence opened the door again. 'I think I can hear the telephone ringing in your house,' she said icily to Tory.

'Oh, thank you. Beth, dear, I'll be back in a minute, but I think this may be one of the irons I have in the fire.'

When she had gone Beth went back to her writing, for she could always do that, she told herself.

Bertram was giving a little talk on mangroves at Mrs Bracey's bedside. He sat on an uncomfortable chair, his hands spread on his knees, and the talk drifted slowly, winding like a river, like, in fact, the Amazon which he described. Mrs Bracey appeared to be asleep, but if he stopped speaking she moved her hand and said: 'Please, go on.' Maisie sometimes came in, pausing anxiously at the door; but her anxiety was for Bertram, who sacrificed himself so gallantly, she thought; a stranger, too, who had no ties, no kinship. Standing there with the empty medicine glass in her hand, she would watch her mother and listen to her breathing, thinking how for weeks it might go on in this way.

Bertram talked to a vaster audience than Mrs Bracey. 'I've

heard worse than this on the wireless,' he marvelled to himself. 'The snag is having to write it all down beforehand.' He knew that as soon as he took up pen and paper it would fade entirely.

In reality he had no audience at all, for Mrs Bracey merely used the drifting sound of his voice as an accompaniment to her own thoughts, the fleeting thoughts of her childhood. Against Bertram's voice going gently on, she remembered one scene after another – the house in Lower Harbour Street where she was born; then the shrieking and rushing on the asphalted school playground, the outbursts of wildness in children too rigidly confined; going errands on Saturday mornings, going errands for Father (a pint and a half of porter in a quart jug, hopeful of good measure), 'Rose goes with Bert' chalked on the wall behind the Library; Sunday School, to be out of the way while Father snored in his chair, flushed with beer, bad-tempered from over-eating; on Monday evenings helping to fold the newly-washed sheets, sprinkling water over the coarse nightshirts, the frilled pinafores, and her mother turning the iron up to her hot face or spitting on it and the little silvery blobs slanting off. At the end of this series of memories was a picture of Christmas Eve, of herself as a little girl standing in a dimly-lit shop waiting to buy an incandescent mantle for the gas and the shop smelling of paraffin, of tarred firewood and candles; suddenly, turning the milled coin round in her fingers, a sense of complete happiness came over her, a happiness so pure that Christmas Day itself could only diminish it, could never hope to enhance what was perfect bliss. 'It lasted a life-time,' she thought, 'when I think of being a child I think of being myself in that shop that late afternoon, with dusk coming on fast and a jet of gas like a fish's tail, or a flower – an iris – flickering, warbling overhead. It has lasted a lifetime, but that is as long as it can last. When I die it dies also, and then it might never have been.'

A great desire to communicate to Bertram something of that moment, which seemed to her now the very essence of her life, made her open her eyes and turn her head painfully towards him.

He stopped in the middle of a sentence and was at once solicitous, taking her hand, bending towards her.

'Christmas,' she began, 'that's a wonderful time for children . . .'

He half-glanced at the hot day outside, but quickly said: 'It's part of the magic we lose as we grow older. I remember it as if it were yesterday, the excitement of it all . . . undoing the presents, pudding ablaze, Christmas carols . . . nuts,' he added lamely.

But Mrs Bracey closed her eyes. His recollections were of such banality that she could not lay hers alongside them. She did not know what she had experienced, could not describe it, nor impart its magic to another, and: 'in the things that really matter to us,' she thought, 'we are entirely alone. Especially alone dying!'

Then it seemed as if she were going to cough. Terrified, she waited, and the pain came tearing up through her lungs and throat and there were no more memories, only the struggle to breathe, to keep head above water. She fought furiously, alone.

At last she was quiet and a great peace invaded her, the lulled peace which follows pain . . . She lay for a long time, taking rapid, shallow breaths. When she opened her eyes Bertram had gone and Dr Cazabon stood beside her, his fingers on her wrist.

*

'Where *have* you been?' asked Tory.

Not waiting for an answer, she held out a little piece of paper and Bertram took it and read it, but without appearing to understand.

'A flat,' Tory said impatiently. 'One of the irons in the fire has come up to scratch. I am going to take you to see it to-morrow.'

'To-morrow?'

His way of walking up and down the room with his hands clasped behind him was becoming familiar to her now. At the window he stopped and contemplated the harbour.

'Where *have* you been?' she asked again.

'Sitting with Mrs Bracey. She is dying.'

'Well, I know,' Tory said crossly, for the idea of death affronted her. 'But why should you? A stranger almost. Surely her own family ... those two girls ...'

'I take my turn with them.'

'But why *should* you?'

'She likes me to talk to her about places I've been to. She could have been a great explorer if she had been a man – if class and sex and health had not all been against her ... the intelligence is there, the curiosity, the desire to see round the next corner ...'

'Oh, nonsense. She's a prying old gossip with a very spiteful tongue.'

'No human being is ever quite so simple as that. There is always something else as well ... her curiosity was dammed up by circumstance and ran into unworthy channels ...'

'Well, I wish you wouldn't go in there. You might catch something.'

'Pneumonia is not catching.'

He turned to look at her and she suddenly felt ashamed, as he intended that she should.

'Tory, understand me in this,' he began. 'It is the first important thing between us ...'

'How could Mrs Bracey be that to either of us?' she said incredulously.

('For once I am going to see someone through to the end,' he thought, beginning to walk up and down again. 'For once I am not going to slip away. Then I shall be able to look back and say: "I saw her through to the end, and for as long as she needed me I was there."')

Perhaps Teddy had taught Tory a lesson in worldly wisdom, for she suddenly said in a rather meek voice: 'Very well, Bertram. If you feel that you cannot come to-morrow, I will go alone.' And she smiled, and to hide her sense of self-abasement suggested a drink. But as she poured it out she suddenly brightened and undid all her meekness, saying: 'But perhaps she will die before to-morrow morning. The train is not till nine-thirteen.'

In winter the dusk settles down over the earth like a fine powder, solidifying, making the air opaque, until houses are buried in it, mounded over as if with snow, and all the pastel colours deepen into darkness.

But now, in summer, the twilight was fluid, luminous, sharpening the outlines of things standing against it, the silhouettes of buildings, of the telegraph poles along the railway cutting, emphasising stillness, and as it grew later and lamps were lit, the light fell as if through the petals of a dark flower.

Seen from afar, the lighthouse merely struck deft blows at the darkness, but to anyone standing under the shelter of its white-washed walls a deeper sense of mystery was invoked: the light remained longer, it seemed, and spread wider, indicating greater ranges of darkness and deeper wonders hidden in that darkness.

17

But when Bertram called early in the morning Mrs Bracey had rallied, as Maisie said; her voice had gained strength, she had tried to stage a little death-bed scene (a sure sign of recovery, Iris felt); had accused them of drinking the whisky she had reserved for the bearers at her funeral; had called for the bottle to be shown to her; said this was proof indeed; and, finally, would not be convinced that the girls were not hiding Eddie Flitcroft downstairs in the kitchen.

So Tory went to London alone.

The day wore on and the fishing-fleet came in. Prudence knelt at her bedroom window, her elbows on the warm stone sill, and she watched the harbour slowly filling with the rusty and dirty trawlers, while overhead the gulls circled deliriously. As time went on day-trippers from the New Town arrived and straggled along the waterfront, trying the empty slot-machines, glancing with regret at the shuttered façade of the Fun Fair and, when they emerged from the Waxworks, blinking crossly at the sudden brilliance of sunshine. Then Prudence saw Mrs Flitcroft come out on to the step below. She dealt the wall a blow with the doormat and a fountain of golden dust-motes rose and fell about her as she paused and looked out at the boats in the harbour, her elbow crooked on her brow to shade her eyes.

At lunch it seemed that Robert would rather discuss his patients than have Tory's name mentioned, and when Beth inquired after Mrs Bracey he seemed relieved to have the subject introduced and said that she would surely die.

'I didn't know she was seriously ill,' Beth said slyly.

'But I *told* you she had pneumonia.'

'You also told me not so very long ago that no one need die of pneumonia nowadays,' Beth reminded him, and she looked blissfully content as if she had wondered if this moment would ever come, and now it had.

Mrs Bracey's sudden improvement did not mislead Robert as it had misled her daughters, and he failed to be impressed by Maisie's report. 'She is very ill,' he said at the end, and began to go upstairs.

Maisie followed, rolling her hands in her apron, feeling suddenly overwrought and agitated.

As Robert climbed the stairs he was aware of a continuous droning sound, and, opening the bedroom door, saw Bertram sitting at the bedside, his hands on his widespread knees, light striking the bald patch on his bent head, and his voice continued placidly as if he were oblivious of everything that surrounded him.

Robert stood at the door and waited. When at last Bertram glanced up, Maisie began to throw their names at one another across the general awkwardness, in order to cover up the silence and because this was her notion of an introduction.

Bertram, feeling creased and dishevelled, at least said how-do-you-do; but Robert only glanced out of the window.

'Come back!' Mrs Bracey murmured pettishly in a slurred voice as if she were drunk. Her teeth had been taken away and her cheeks and lips fell in weakly.

'I will wait downstairs,' Bertram assured her. 'I shall always be about when you want me.' He straightened his shoulders, adjusted the handkerchief in his breast-pocket and, with an air of great nobility, walked past Robert and down the stairs.

'What is *he* doing here?' Robert asked Maisie, as he opened his case.

'He has been such a good friend ...' Maisie began, her eyes brimming with tears, she was so tired.

'He must have a genius for insinuating himself,' Robert said. He went across the room to Maisie and looked at her kindly, drawing down her lower eyelid, tilting her face to the light. Before he moved back to the bed, he patted her shoulder, and she thought that he seemed to say to her that it would not be much longer. She had no defence against his sympathy, and put her apron to her eyes, turning briefly away.

'Where's he gone?' Mrs Bracey asked thickly. 'We was just having a nice chat. I tell him he'll rue the day he marries that bitch, but he's so wilful ...'

'All right, Mother,' Maisie said. 'Lay still, I should.' She had not the heart to reprove her on her death-bed, for such, from Robert's seriousness, she now took it to be. Robert stood very still, checking her pulse, seeming remote from her, interested, in a dispassionate way, in the roses on the wallpaper, not interested at all in what his patient had to say. Between them they let her ramble on until Robert calmly laid her arm back across the sheet and said: 'I will look in again, this evening perhaps,'

272

and then he too, like Bertram, put back his shoulders and straightened himself.

The afternoon did indeed seem to wear on: only to Beth did it pass quickly, her hand flying over the paper, pain in the muscle above the elbow, but she could not feel it: to Beth – and to the lighthouse-keeper, for whom an hour was a short space merely between the long climb up the stairs to wind the clock in the lamp-room.

During the afternoon Lily Wilson sent over a cup of veal broth for Mrs Bracey; but it would only stand in the larder until tufts of mould dotted its surface, for Mrs Bracey could no longer take even a sip of milk from a spoon. Utterly alone, she lay and awaited death, cut off, discarded, like a man in a condemned cell. Pain had merged into sensation and there were no longer any definite feelings, nothing firm or decisive or with boundary. She could not be sure even of the bed beneath her, or of Maisie's two hands clasping her own.

No one could reach her, she knew, and in that knowledge lay all her helplessness and terror. She was slipping out of their reach into total darkness, as once her husband had slipped away from her. Fold his hands tightly in hers as she might, none the less the ties had loosened and he had gone swimming away from her out of her life. 'To meet Our Lord,' she had thought then; but her religion had always been a matter of words, of catchy phrases, and now she had not the strength to form a word or put together a phrase for her own consolation. There was only this strange feeling of floating left to her, her hand something people took up and touched to try to give comfort. But no matter what they did they could not penetrate to the small clot of fear which was the only reality now. All else had gone: her childhood, her married life, the triumphs of birth, the sorrows of death, good, evil, ambition, love; nothing remained but the little centre of fear in her amorphous body, floating on its bed, without weight, without pain, without anchorage.

She began to breathe through her mouth sharply, and Bertram, seeing this, shook his head slowly at Maisie and got up and began to walk about the room. Iris sat on the edge of a chair, her hand over her mouth, her eyes wide.

Outside, the trippers passed along the pavement and when some of them began to sing Maisie went to the window and closed it, feeling that it was no longer necessary to do as Dr Cazabon had said. Then there was only the sound of Mrs Bracey's coarse, irregular breathing and the floorboards creaking softly as Bertram paced up and down.

At tea-time there was a letter for Prudence from Geoffrey making an assignation in the churchyard and concluding with a short quotation from John Donne.

Tory, coming home in the train that evening, flew from one extreme to the other in her mind: first, she was elated at the idea of leaving the rather colourless and windswept landscape which hinted already at the proximity of the sea; and then a root here and there tugged unexpectedly at her, making the tearing-up unbearable.

Being shown over the flat earlier in the day – lacking in response to the present tenant, lukewarm, rather off-hand and non-committal as she went from room to room – she had suffered the same fluctuating emotions. The various rooms only reflected the changing state of her heart as she followed round, peered into cupboards, asked questions. In the kitchen, for some reason, Bertram triumphed; for she could manage to be happy, she thought, with a new life, the married status restored to her and bolstered up by all the dozens of acquaintances who awaited her in London: but in the large living-room, which looked down into the leaves of a lime tree, the thought of Robert struck at her heart: 'I cannot allow myself to be so hurt,' she thought; and she stood for a moment watching sparrows in the dust under the tree, and had a prevision of herself standing thus for the rest of her life, time after time coming to look out of this window at the pillar-box at the street corner, the dusty trees in the square, the sparrows. She felt extraordinarily depressed.

'. . . and the curtains at valuation,' the other woman had been saying, carelessly, as if money could not matter to her. And, quite absent-minded and because of her wretchedness, Tory put out her hand and fingered the woman's curtains, just as if she were at a market-stall, and then blushed. They both blushed. The woman turned awkwardly aside. 'When her husband comes home this evening,' Tory thought, 'he will bear the brunt of it all. She will pour out stories of my effrontery and insolence.'

She moved from the window and faced in to the room, which was lofty, its ceiling wreathed with plaster flowers.

'A nice room for parties,' she said, with her warm, rare smile, which did not enchant this woman, who never gave parties, she explained, her husband being recently dead, and before that for years an invalid.

When they continued their little tour Tory would not permit herself a glance even at photographs or personal possessions spread on dressing-tables, but quickly surveyed the walls as if taking in space, proportions, lighting, nothing more interesting.

'No,' her heart said in the bathroom: 'yes,' it replied at the landing window. When it was all seen, she suddenly said 'yes' to the woman, and saying 'yes' was not merely the matter of the flat, but of saying 'no' to so much more at the same time.

No trumpets, however, came thrusting out of the clouds to acclaim this triumph of virtue. On the contrary, the enthusiasm was taken from the moment by the woman saying coldly: 'I have left everything with the agents. You must communicate with them,' and she felt that thus she punished Tory for humiliating her over her best chintz curtains. 'And, of course,' she added, indulging herself a little more, 'they may already have made arrangements elsewhere.'

'Yes,' Tory said, frowning as she smoothed her fingers in her gloves.

Outside, at the edge of the square, she paused. But so little does the rest of the world seem to care if we act nobly or otherwise that no help came to her, no taxi appeared, nor any encouragement. She was obliged to walk all the way to the estate agents, losing herself several times in the rather crumbling Regency environs of her prospective home.

Now, in the train going home, her mind reflected the chaos and indecision of the day, and she felt that she was acting extravagantly and absurdly in contemplating such a future.

'It is false and melodramatic to run away because of Robert, still more ridiculous to marry Bertram,' she told herself, 'a man I hardly know.'

The train had run into the cutting, and she began to look for her ticket. 'Although, curiously,' she thought, 'I *do* seem to know him and seem to have known him for so many years that now it would be indecent almost to marry him, to change the relationship.'

Rather tense, her ticket in her fingers, she sat on the edge of the seat and waited for the train to slow down into the station. Bertram would be waiting for her, she supposed, and she would be glad of that, for she was tired and it was almost dark. The station was empty and through the smeared and broken glass roof clouds could be seen moving cumbrously over the sky. Dull yellow light filled the refreshment-room, shone on a sandwich inside a glass dome and into the large, cracked cups.

Robert, not Bertram, came forward to meet Tory. As she paused to hand in her ticket, he walked ahead to the car, his carriage suggesting offence taken. 'In fact,' Tory thought, 'I should call it "stalking".' His legs moved stiffly, as if by clockwork.

'What are you laughing at?' he asked, opening the car door for her.

'Once I saw the ghost in *Hamlet* walking just like that. I knew I had come across it before. You looked as if you were on the battlements.'

He sat beside her and slammed the door. Then – rather cleverly she thought – he said, as he pulled at the self-starter: 'Perhaps it is a walk peculiar to those who have been betrayed.'

At that the car should have swung forward but did not. He had meant to gather her up from the train and sweep her masterfully away and keep her away until she would see reason, but the car shuddered a little and was silent.

'Oh, damn this battery,' he said peevishly, and climbed out with the starting-handle in his hand. She watched his reddened face beyond the car bonnet. The car heaved as if it would vomit, but in the end sank back again into a sullen stillness.

'Look!' he began in a different voice, coming to the door, 'would you mind pulling this choke out when I tell you?'

'Certainly,' Tory said kindly, feeling that she had the whip hand.

This time the car maintained its shuddering, lapsed at last into a steady pulsing, and Robert could get in and drive off.

'I am furiously angry with you,' he began, in order to set the conversation on its feet again.

'It was certainly all over your face for all the world to see.'

'What the devil do you think you are doing?'

'I appear to be going in quite the opposite direction from my home.'

He ignored this.

'You think it was pleasant for me, I daresay,' he sneered, 'to have such a fantastic piece of news broken to me by Beth.'

'Why "fantastic"?'

'You can't ruin your life in this way.'

'It won't be ruined because I marry an agreeable and gallant person with whom I feel always perfectly at ease, who will always consider me and spoil me, and never quarrel with me or say a harsh word.'

'Whom you don't love and never could, an old man, and a silly old humbug into the bargain.'

'We shall get on well together,' Tory said placidly.

'Marriage is more than that.'

'Oh, is it? It is often less. What about your own marriage?'

'I don't care to discuss it.'

'You seem most intent on discussing mine, though.'

The car ran up over the cliff, and between the trees they could see the lights of the New Town strung out along the bay in hoops and clusters and the pier dropping ribbons of light down into the water. Robert stopped the car at the side of the road and took his hands from the steering-wheel. ('Everyone knows this car,' he reflected bitterly.)

'Shall we get out and walk?' he suggested.

'Good God, no. I've been on my feet all day. And walk where to?'

'I have to talk to you and make you see reason. You've avoided me, so I was obliged to do this.'

'It was lucky Bertram was not there to meet me,' she pointed out, and she felt piqued that he had not been, and tried to hide it.

'He is with Mrs Bracey, I expect. I saw him earlier on. I rather wondered why he was there.'

'He knows them and likes them . . . They do his washing for him.'

'Oh, well, then, of course he must be there. That makes it entirely necessary.'

After this the discussion obviously withered and died. Both could hear their own hearts and the other's thundering, but could find nothing more to say.

'No, please!' Tory gasped, edging away. 'Please don't touch me, Robert. I am very tired indeed and should like to go home.'

'Not until you promise me to send that old fool away for ever.'

'I won't talk about it to you. You are rude and abusive. I only want to be at peace.'

'Surely you can go away without feeling obliged to marry the first doting old man you come across?'

'You want me out of the way, but you want me to be miserable as well. You are intolerably selfish.'

'I don't want you out of the way. I can't bear you out of the way.'

'The other night you made no effort to stop me. What about Prudence?'

He was silent.

'Prudence is an unsurmountable obstacle,' Tory suggested.

'I suppose so.'

'But not Beth! We could probably rely on deceiving her for years.'

'You are very – hard,' he said distastefully.

'Oh, that is what the sloppy always say when they cannot bear the truth.'

'Are you posing as a truthful woman now?'

'At least I can always *see* the truth, even if I don't tell it or act upon it. I don't deceive myself, as men always hope to do.'

'You ought to write some of those articles about "Are women more honest than men?"' he suggested.

'Yes, I think I will.'

'And while we are discussing hard facts ... what about money, if you marry this man ... Has he any?'

'Half-pay, or whatever they call it.'

'That won't buy you many hats.'

'The two of us can live more cheaply together than separately and we both manage well enough now.'

'That about living more cheaply together is only the wool young people pull over their eyes when they are much in love. Besides that, what money will you have if you marry again?'

'What I have now,' Tory said slowly.

'So Teddy is to finance your second marriage as well?'

'Don't laugh in that affected, reckless way. Do you mean he will stop paying me?'

'My dear Tory!'

'Well, whether I marry Bertram or not, I am still being

inconvenienced by not being married to Teddy. It is very unfair if he is to evade his responsibilities just because I have the courage to make the best of a bad job.'

'Are you still seeing the truth – steadily and whole?' he inquired.

'Well, I shall have the money for this house. Teddy had that transferred to me.'

'It won't be much, you'll discover. A rather odd locality, ours.'

'An artist might like it.'

'Artists have no money, and they are difficult to find.'

'I think one is always coming up against them. Anyhow, however you seek to depress me, I shall go. I am almost packed up. I shall live with people in London until I am married. I can save a little money in that way, by being a guest.'

'*Don't* go!'

'Oh, Robert!'

'My dearest love!'

He slid one shoulder out of her frock. It was a straight and polished shoulder, like a young girl's, and when he bent to kiss her he breathed warmth and sweetness from her disturbed clothes.

'Never leave me!' he murmured, his lips moving against her throat.

When she made no answer he lifted his head and drew her mouth down to his.

'Say you'll never go.'

Instead she kissed him.

'You never will,' he insisted.

'No, Robert, I never will,' she said.

*

Mrs Bracey took little sips of air, her mouth jagging open as she did so. Iris did not go to work that evening, but knelt at her mother's side, her suspenders loosened to ease the strain on her stockings. She stroked her mother's hand with its lizard-like folds of skin, its heavy gold wedding-ring, and sometimes tears fell on to the quilt.

'I thought doctor was coming,' she said, lifting her tear-furrowed face to Bertram.

He put his lips into a thin line and shrugged his shoulders as if to say a doctor could make no difference now. Maisie had the air of one who has not taken off her clothes for nights. She sat on a hard chair, her hands in her lap, and her head jerking down from time to time with fatigue. They listened to the breathing with a nervous concentration, for it seemed that each painful rising of the breast would be the last.

In the end her death was quite simple. She just did not take the next breath. Her mouth was scarcely parted, and her head turned sideways on the pillow. Iris was frightened and drew away, but Bertram held up the little bedroom lamp over Mrs Bracey's face, which showed no signs of struggle or anguish, and seemed so ordinary that they felt she could not be dead. Maisie looked very closely and laid her hand over her mother's heart, but it was certain there was no movement.

As she took her mother's hands and folded them the light from the lamp shone through her own fingers, outlining them with a rosy transparency, but Mrs Bracey's showed only dark and opaque, not living fingers any longer. Only Bertram noticed, for Iris had covered her face and was sobbing.

'Iris!' Maisie said rather sharply. 'I want you to put your coat on and go and fetch Mrs Flitcroft.'

'Mrs Flitcroft, whatever for?'

'Just tell her Mother's gone, and she'll come back with you.'

'Why?' Iris uncovered her swollen face and stared.

'She'll lay her out,' Maisie said, and began to go downstairs. Iris was more frightened than ever and cried louder, but Bertram persuaded her into her coat and promised a cup of tea when she returned, for he would not leave Maisie, he said; he thought she looked faint: otherwise he would have gone himself.

It was quite dark when Iris opened the front door. Boats creaked uneasily in the harbour. The air was warm and full. She walked quickly along close to the walls of the houses, climbed the flight of steps into Harbour Street and, almost running, passed the caverns of shop doorways and rows of cottages each a couple of paces wide. People were in bed. Only here and there light shone from downstairs rooms, printing upon blinds a pot of geraniums or a birdcage.

Mr Flitcroft's was in darkness. On the outside window-sill a row of great curled and spiked sea-shells gleamed in the curdy moonlight.

Iris rapped against the door with her knuckles and stood waiting, feeling set-apart, singled-out, by having been so lately in the presence of death, unable yet to grasp the enormity of this experience.

Above her a window rattled and was drawn up and, stepping back into the street, she saw Mrs Flitcroft peering out.

'Who's that?' she called. 'What's the trouble?'

'It's Iris Bracey,' she answered. 'Mother ...' she began, but her voice faded at the word, as if grief snatched the very sound of it away. This, Mrs Flitcroft thought, did her credit, and she nodded kindly and shut the window.

Then Iris heard her calling down the stairs to Eddie, and

soon a light shone in the front room, falling across the row of shells on to the pavement of the street. Iris could imagine Eddie blundering from his uncomfortable couch, searching clumsily for clothes to put on, the taste of sleep still in his mouth.

When he opened the door he looked alarmed. 'What's up, Iris? What's wrong?' he began, standing back against the wall to let her into the narrow passage.

'It's Mother,' she said, putting her hands up over her face.

'Is she worse?'

'No. It's . . .' She began to cry in a rather strung-up conventional way.

'Dead?' he asked, using the forbidden word, at which she shrank back against the wall as if he had physically hurt her.

Upstairs Mrs Flitcroft padded to and fro: they could even hear her suspenders tinkling as she took up her corsets. Eddie put his arm round Iris to comfort her; although it was beyond his understanding that she should need this.

'I don't want to go back home,' Iris cried, looking desperately round the dingy little passage as if it were heaven itself to her.

'I will come with you,' Eddie assured her.

Mrs Flitcroft came creaking downstairs now, accompanied by a ring of light from a small hand-lamp which she placed on a bracket in the passage. She had assembled herself, clothes, teeth, mother-o'-pearl brooch, and was all ready. Eddie pulled his navy jersey over his head and opened the front door.

'No call for you to come!' his aunt said sharply.

'I'll walk along with you, all the same,' he said, taking Iris's arm. They closed the door and set out, the three of them walking along in the middle of the road, their footsteps echoing between the buildings, Mrs Flitcroft a little in front, going eagerly on, her door-key grasped in her hand. Eddie and Iris followed more slowly, close together, her soft bosom pressed against his arm. Moonlight shone on the roofs, on the water, on the flight of steps: water slapped the sides of the boats in the harbour, made chuckling noises between them; and the lighthouse gave first its fleeting gesture, then its glow, beyond all human interruption, as it seemed.

Mrs Flitcroft went on ahead, but at the foot of the steps she stopped and looked back towards them, beckoning. As they descended after her, Iris's bosom moved heavily against Eddie's arm at each step. He drew her tighter, lacing his fingers in and out of hers.

'That's funny!' Mrs Flitcroft whispered as they drew near. 'I could have sworn I saw Mrs Wilson's door open and someone go in.'

'What of it?' Eddie asked, for the gossip of one generation does not always interest the next.

'What of it! I mean it was a man.'

She stood and marvelled at the look of the place, but the blank façade did not blossom into light.

'Well, we must get on,' she said crossly, as if they had delayed her.

At the Braceys' it was all light. Maisie unfastened the door to them, and at once Mrs Flitcroft hastened through the shop, taking the long steel pins out of her hat as she went.

Eddie loosened his arm from Iris's and looked at Maisie. She was tired and untidy and her face was grey in the moonlight.

'Hello, Maisie,' he said awkwardly.

'Hello, Eddie.'

Then Iris, shivering a little, seemed to grasp her courage, and walked between them into the shop.

18

'Dear Mother,' (Tory read):

'Congrats on you are going to be married. Don't write to Sir about masstoid. I like boxing now. My lip blead I fell out of a tree. I have a pain in my back because I fell out of a tree. I toled Matron she said get along with you but I still have the pain where I fell out of a tree on to my back. The fur trees are out of bounds the branches break. I hope you will like being married I remain

> Your loving son,
> EDWARD G. FOYLE ESQ.'

Before she could think this over Bertram had arrived. He kissed her and sat down among the breakfast things with her.

'Here are the first felicitations,' Tory said, passing the letter. As she sipped her coffee she watched him reading.

'What a delightful letter!' Bertram said. 'I do hope the boy has not injured his back.'

Tory put her cup down. 'I think Matron sounds a little off-hand. He might easily have jarred his spine.'

'Perhaps we should telephone her,' he suggested.

That 'we' took a great burden from her. For so long she had been alone in her anxieties, now here was Bertram entering into her difficulties and the relief was so immediate that she felt completely reassured.

'I really don't think we need. You know what little boys are. He has probably quite forgotten it by now. But I am so very glad that you don't tell me not to fuss.'

Bertram, who felt that he was being compared favourably with Teddy, was pleased.

'What about Mrs B.?' Tory asked, suddenly remembering.

'She died last night,' Bertram said solemnly. 'That was why I couldn't meet your train. I felt I could be sure of your understanding.'

Tory recoiled a little from him, as if death might still hang about his clothes and person. She resented people dying and made this quite plain to the bereaved. It is the peasant types who draw attention to death, make ritual out of it, she felt. The more civilised one is, the more one returns to the first and natural dignity, the dignity of animals, the concealing of death, the dying creeping into dark corners, decently, ignored discreetly by the living. She rated elegance too highly: when it was overthrown she turned her head.

Now Bertram further affronted her by asking if she believed in God.

'As if I trouble my head with questions I can't answer!' she cried.

'It is curious being beside the dying,' he continued 'One moment they are there, the next moment they are not. There's no summing-up, but a sense of incompleteness. After years of building up each unique personality, in the end there is no

287

moment of putting lines beneath the sum and adding up to see what it all amounts to.'

'Who should do the adding up, but those of us who knew the dead when they were living? It is *here*,' Tory said, touching her blouse in the place where she supposed her heart to be. She felt herself perfectly willing to add up Mrs Bracey's personality and make it come out to some very unpleasant result indeed.

'But we all see our friends and enemies differently. No two answers would be the same,' he objected.

'Exactly,' Tory agreed, as if this were a very good reason for not bothering herself.

'It is where God would come in so handy,' Bertram said, spreading marmalade on an odd piece of toast.

Watching him, Tory began: 'The flat is not so bad, Bertram, I think it will do . . .'

'I was just going to ask you about it . . .'

'You were not. You are so full of vague thoughts about death and God that you had completely forgotten the important things.'

She gave him a malicious and exaggerated account of going over the flat, of her interview with the estate agent. Then, getting up from the table, she suddenly said: 'I have, in fact, decided to go at once.'

'What do you call "at once"?'

'In a few days. I am nearly packed up.' She glanced round at the empty shelves.

'But how can you move in so quickly?' he asked in great alarm.

'The woman wants to go. Death again. Her husband has died and she is going home to Mother. Oh, I hope he didn't die there,' she said suddenly. 'But I expect he was in a nursing-home. There were certainly no traces . . .'

'What traces could there be? Bloodstains? Or a shroud hanging on the hall-stand?'

'Please, Bertram! I thought I would go up to stay with friends and take my time making the flat pleasant. Then we can get married, and soon Edward will be home for the holidays. It will be a nuisance if we have to have him at the wedding. He is so critical of all I do that he makes me quite self-conscious and ill at ease.'

'We can easily be married before the end of term,' he said soothingly, and once more she felt a sense of relief at his words.

'I am going to do a great deal of telephoning, so I mustn't waste any more of my time,' she said.

'And I will put the finishing touches to my picture,' Bertram said.

'We will have good fun, Bertram, won't we?'

'If you are quite sure of me.'

'Quite sure.'

'And will never regret ...'

'Oh, never!' she said with emphasis.

'Then we shall have a wonderful time,' he assured her. But he did not see it thus. He imagined himself settled, a home of his own for the first time in his life, pottering about – a hinge to be oiled here, a rawl-plug to be fitted there – contented, finding a new circle of cronies at the local – and in London there is always a local – doing a little painting.

They both contemplated their different pictures of married life, but neither with any overwhelming excitement. He would have liked to have taken her in his arms and said: 'I will make you forget him. I will help you to escape.' He felt tenderness and admiration for Tory, but felt, too, that it was better that she did not love him to distraction. He was more jealous of her old, easy, undemanding relationship with her erstwhile husband than of the ungovernable passion she felt for Robert. He rather relied on this passion keeping their marriage on more placid and companionable lines.

Maisie pinned a little card to the shop-door blind: 'Owing to the recent decease of the Proprieteress this establishment will remain closed until further notice.'

The shop was dark with the blinds drawn, a submarine light filtered through the hanging clothes, shadows passed across continually.

Maisie gathered up all the half-empty medicine bottles with their dusty shoulders and stained labels and threw them into the dustbin, feeling free and uncluttered when she had done so. She worked feverishly, scrubbing and scouring and turning-out. Iris did not go to work but sat about in the kitchen, afraid to go upstairs, afraid to go to bed at night. The time passed very slowly.

Bertram glanced at the little notice on the door as he went by on his way to an old shop in Lower Harbour Street where he hoped to buy a frame to fit his picture.

Mrs Flitcroft carried the news of death up and down the alley-ways, the courtyards of the harbour. The Guvnor at the Mimosa Café, whitewashing 'To-day's Menu' on his window, noticed the blinds drawn at the Braceys' and took the news out to the kitchen. Lily Wilson, peeping from behind her lace curtains for the expected signal, felt suddenly chilled.

Tory telephoned a woman in London and extracted from her an invitation to stay. They were 'darling' to one another a great deal and seemed amazed and entranced at the very sound of one another's voices. The idea of having her friend to stay apparently threw Christabel into a state of ecstasy; yet they had managed to live for some years without meeting or communicating with one another; not a letter had been written and even the Christmas cards had long since ceased to pass between them.

When these arrangements had been made, Tory unwrapped her china shepherdess from its nest of cotton-wool and took it in to Beth, who was secretly appalled at the sight of it, calling it an 'ornament' in her mind and thinking it would mean more work.

'A little keepsake,' Tory was saying, standing the china figure on the sideboard in front of the display of tarnished silver, where it looked at once incongruous and lost. Stevie was delighted.

'Why are you not at school?' Tory asked her.

'I have the quarantine,' Stevie said, on tiptoe before the sideboard. 'I love the golden ribbons and the strawberries all over her dress.'

'Yes, she is exquisite,' Beth said.

'I think she is exquisite,' Stevie echoed.

'It is very sweet of you, Tory.'

'It will remind you of me in years to come,' Tory said, laughing carelessly to show that she did not mean this.

'Nothing could remind me better, if I needed reminding,' Beth began; but tears rushed to her eyes and she could not continue. To bring the conversation to another level she said: 'I hear Mrs Bracey has died. It is probably what is called a merciful release.'

'Will she be burnt or buried?' asked Stevie.

'We do not know,' Beth said, with a look at Tory across the child's head.

'If she is burnt I am sure she will find it too hot,' Stevie said.

'She will not find it anything of the kind,' Tory contradicted, 'because she is not there to feel warm or cold any more.'

'She is in heaven,' Stevie said casually.

'It is a depressing morning,' Beth sighed. 'Mrs Flitcroft hasn't turned up either.'

'I am going at the end of the week,' Tory said, as if she were determined to make matters much worse.

Beth paled, but had no answer to this.

'I know you don't agree with me over marrying Bertram,' Tory continued, 'but as my mind is quite made up, there is no point in delay.'

'On the contrary, if your mind were really quite made up there would be no point in all this haste,' Beth argued. 'You are only afraid that you will change your mind, and I can't understand why you should so much fear to do that.'

As the conversation promised well, Stevie sat quietly down on a stool, as much out of sight as possible.

'I am tired of living alone,' Tory said restlessly.

'But why . . . for God's sake, why Bertram Hemingway?'

'Perhaps because, like all oldish men who have managed to evade and escape women, his gallantry is still intact.'

'So, I'm afraid, are other qualities less desirable than gallantry.'

'Such as . . .?'

'Irresponsibility, a dreadful sort of boyishness . . .'

Tory flushed.

'I am only anxious for your future,' Beth apologised. 'Stevie, don't do that!' she said sharply. 'Use your handkerchief!'

Tory walked over to the window. 'Where is Robert?' she asked casually – a thing she had never done before.

'Robert?' Beth said in surprise. 'Why, I think he is at the hospital. Your handkerchief, I said, Stevie. Did you want him?'

'Only to ask his advice about something to do with the house.'

'I'll tell him when he comes. I'll ask him to look in.'

'Any time will do. Here comes Mrs Flitcroft.'

'Then I can get some writing done,' Beth said contentedly.

'How is your book going?'

'I have nearly finished,' she said. But she did not expect this to mean anything very special to Tory; nor, indeed, to anybody but herself.

Bertram found his picture-frame and went round to do a little carpentry in Tory's kitchen. When he had propped his canvas up on the kitchen-dresser he stood back, awaiting her praise.

'Yes,' she said at last. 'It is very good. Very like. There is only one thing . . . it is quite obvious where it is, but not what time of day . . .'

Bertram said sadly: 'In fact, the very thing I most hoped to do I have failed over.'

'But it is a lovely picture, none the less. I am sure everyone would think so. I should like to take it with us . . . to remind us of here.'

'No,' Bertram said. 'I painted it to be left behind. I promised it to old Pallister and he shall have it . . . after all the false starts I made and this is all I have finished! It will be a souvenir we shall leave here . . .'

'In the bar-parlour,' Tory laughed.

'In the bar-parlour. I can always paint another one, especially for you.'

In the evening Robert came.

'Beth said you wanted me.'

'Yes, I wanted to say good-bye.'

'Your mind is absolutely made up.'

'Absolutely.'

'Well ... there isn't anything I can do, or say, is there? It means that last night is quite discounted.'

'Not discounted.'

'You promised ...'

'Well, then, I am breaking my word. It was only a word, and spoken at a time when words mean nothing. All the while, I knew I was going and you knew it, too. Now, I feel that even days count. I can still hope to rush away with some of my self-esteem, but not if I leave it much longer.'

'Why must you?'

'Prudence comes into the room and walks out without speaking to me. Beth notices. She disappears at night and Beth worries ... no, I know not much, but still, a little ... then I have begun to talk about you and she is surprised.'

'Begun to talk about me?'

'I know it sounds incredible, but I cannot help myself. To say your name to her suddenly has a terrifying attraction. "Where is Robert?" I ask casually, having ignored you for years. So it is just about time I went.'

'You have never really loved me. Of course I know that. When you've gone away I shall manage to forget, perhaps, that it was always Teddy you loved, could not help loving, I shall forget that you scarcely even *liked* me, but had only a pathetic need of me. I daresay I'll concoct a tremendous romance out of all this, something to look back upon when I'm old, secret, *couleur de rose*, poetic. I'll forget the quarrels, the pain, the harshness – and your reason for needing me.'

Tory stood very still. 'At the very beginning you spoke to me in this way. Then I could bear it. But now, at the end, I find I can't.'

'I am sorry for this man you are going to marry.'

'Robert, I want you to say good-bye to me and then keep out of my way until I am gone. I have to put on what is called a brave front for Bertram's benefit and also for Beth's, and I cannot do that with painful farewells confronting me.'

'Every day, I shall get up and go to the hospital, sit through surgery, eat meals with Beth, and go to bed, and it will be like that for all the rest of my life, a thousand times duller and sadder than ever before, other people perhaps going in and out of this house, and for me nothing but work and thoughts of you married to someone else. We only have one life. Surely we mustn't throw it away? Surely I shall see you again?'

Tory looked uneasy.

'You mean we might?' he asked slowly.

'I don't know.'

('Ask me again in a year,' her heart cried. 'Surely I cannot be so wicked that I would marry Bertram, deliberately intending to be unfaithful to him?')

'A sort of sordid reunion in London once a year?' he continued, and his lip curled, so that she was thankful she had held her tongue.

She put her arms round him and her head down on his shoulder and her throat ached intolerably so that she could not speak.

'My sweet Tory, forget the things I said ...'

'None of them was true.'

'I know. It has been the only really wonderful and miraculous thing in my life, the way you lifted me out of the dullness of my everyday existence. It will be painful to sink back again and know there will never be anything like it for the rest of my life.'

'Please go quickly.'

'Shall I write to you?'

'Yes, write. Always write.'

'Good-bye.'

'Good-bye, Robert. And, Robert!'

'Yes?'

'Don't see me again.'

'I promise.'

When he had gone Tory ran upstairs and flung herself across her bed.

While the sun was setting Prudence and Geoffrey sat under the may-tree in the churchyard. Prudence wore her sage-green dress, her coral bracelets. Geoffrey read poetry out of a little suede-covered book. Prudence passed her hand across her jaw and put a little yawn into it as she did so.

'Good night!' Robert said briefly, lifting his hat to Tory and Bertram as they passed at the street corner much later in the evening.

19

When the furniture-vans arrived Beth felt as sickened as if they were tumbrils bound for the guillotine. Stevie, however, was pleased with all the excitement and went out and stood at the kerb to watch. Strange men carried out, as if unaware of their importance, sacred and heartbreaking objects such as Edward's high chair, Tory's bedroom furniture stripped of its petticoats, Teddy's walnut writing-desk. All the morning it went on and Beth tried to work, but could not. 'So it has really happened,' she thought, drawing little faces down the edge of the page.

Bertram worked hard, feeling himself in command, quite indispensable. The removers, taking a cup of tea at ten, decided that 'he was the sort who knows everybody else's job better than what they know it theirselves.' And all his care for Tory's glass and china they considered unmanly.

Meanwhile, Tory conducted the estate agent round the echoing rooms, standing against patches of damp, and bewildering him with her appeal to his manhood, concealing cracked plaster, damaged woodwork, with smiles and arch remarks, until he thought her the most accessible woman he had ever met.

'And now,' she said, sweeping him past Edward's bedroom door on which was scribbled 'Private Mr E. Foyle Esq. Kindly knock', 'now I will show you the little garden.'

He followed, with yardstick and notebook. The men sitting round a box in the kitchen eating sandwiches, watched in silence as they passed through. Significant glances were exchanged.

'Oh, delightful!' the young man said, as Tory led him out to the paved courtyard. 'Quite Continental, isn't it?'

'I hate leaving it,' Tory said simply. She did not explain that she was leaving only the paving-stones, and that as soon as the young man was out of sight, iron chairs, bay-trees in tubs, Alpine garden in old stone sink, hydrangeas, were all to be snatched up and taken away.

'Creeper-clad walls,' the man wrote in his notebook.

'Hardly "clad",' Tory laughed, glancing at the thin growth of virginia-creeper straggling up one wall, and seeking to imply that she could only be frank with him about her property. When he had gone she took up a bottle of milk that was left and went to say good-bye to Beth.

'This is left over,' she said, putting it down on the hall-table and glancing nervously round. 'And Bertram is bringing you a loaf of bread and some butter and three rashers later.'

'What time are you going?'

'The taxi is coming in about half an hour. Bertram will see the vans off and then he is coming to London in a day or two.'

'I see.'

'I am no use at saying good-bye. I always howl.'

'And I.'

'Once in London when a maid left, Teddy came in and found us in one another's arms weeping. Yet the next day I had forgotten her. But this isn't really a good-bye at all for us. We have said so many in all the years we've known one another, this is just another, like the end of term, or the day we left school, or our little booze-up the night before you were married. I thought then you were going out of my life for ever.'

Stevie came in from the sunshine to have a good look at them.

'I'll always remember your telling me,' Beth said, 'that one day something would happen that I'd never be able to bear writing about . . . and I feel this is it . . .'

A wild flash of thankfulness seemed to strike Tory's heart at these words, a sense of relief at unimaginable danger safely escaped. The appalling disaster she had so nearly not spared Beth she saw in all its enormity for the first time.

'You haven't said good-bye to Robert and he is out,' Beth was saying.

Tory looked down steadily, for great tears came up so solidly in her eyes that if her lids moved they would surely fall.

'I will say good-bye to him for you,' Beth suggested.

'No . . . I – no, don't do that. I did say good-bye to him. I met him outside . . .'

To hide her face from Beth, she stooped and drew Stevie to her. 'Good-bye, darling! You shall come to me in London and I will take you to the theatre.'

Stevie remained calm, feeling this to be the kind of promise that is never fulfilled.

At last, for a second, Tory managed to raise her eyes to meet Beth's.

'Good-bye, then.'

'Good-bye, Tory dear. I hope you'll be so very . . .'

As they did not ever kiss one another there was nothing left for Tory to do but to go quickly out of the house into the blinding sunshine.

'Steady, steady!' Bertram said, as she collided with him. Stevie followed and watched her disappear into the house. When the taxi arrived Tory came out with Bertram, looking quite restored, but Beth did not appear at the windows. Only Stevie waved, standing at the kerb, wearing on her head a battered aluminium jelly-mould which Tory had thrown away. Bertram put a suitcase into the car and then got in himself. They both waved to Stevie as they drove away.

Upstairs, at her bedroom window, Prudence knelt in the sunshine, watching, her cats in her arms.

All along the waterfront blinds were drawn down. Maisie, wearing black, opened the shop door from time to time to receive wreaths and crosses with black-edged cards tucked among the lilies, carnations, or mauve and white everlastings.

At lunch Robert asked Beth to lower the blinds as soon as the meal was finished.

'But, Robert!' she protested. 'What good can it do? Such a ridiculous custom! And the house seems quite sad enough as it is to-day.'

'You only need to do it at the front. The point is, it means a lot to others and does not inconvenience us greatly.'

'How long must they stay down?'

'Oh, I think until the cars have gone to the church. In fact,' he added, 'I had thought that it would be much appreciated if you yourself went to the funeral.'

'I?' Beth cried in alarm 'But, Robert, I couldn't! I have never been to a funeral in my life. I shouldn't know what to do. I should hate it. Oh, *hate* it!'

'All right, my dear. There is no need to wring your hands. I didn't mean to upset you. On the contrary, I thought it would be quite your cup of tea. But it doesn't matter in the least. It is true you hardly ever saw the woman. You are eating nothing.'

'I know.' She sighed.

'Prudence! I've asked you a thousand times if I've asked you once to leave those cats outside at mealtimes.'

Beth pushed her plate away with a gesture of finality. 'And, Stevie! will you please use your handkerchief,' she said sharply.

No one mentioned Tory.

When she and Prudence had cleared the table Beth went to the window to draw down the blinds.

Outside, Bertram was standing in the road and the removal men were just closing the door of the remaining van with a great rattling of chains. Bertram stood watching it as it moved off, his hand sheltering his eyes from the glare of the sun. Then he turned in at the Anchor and Beth drew down the blind, so that a thick, syrupy light lay over the room.

'There we are, then!' said Bertram, hanging his picture in the bar-parlour. As the curtains were drawn the painting looked quite subdued.

'Capital!' Ned Pallister exclaimed, struggling into his funeral jacket. 'Yes, well that makes a nice pair along with Mr Walker's picture.' He went from one to the other. 'Interesting,' he observed, 'what two people can make of the same view. We all see places a bit different to what the next man does. That stands to reason.'

'We see with our souls,' Bertram said sententiously. 'And what we reveal in our paintings is the soul of man, not a mere row of buildings.' Standing in front of Mr Walker's picture, he felt complacently that Mr Walker's soul did not come off too well, looked dingily out from behind the gravy-like paint.

'You coming along?' Mr Pallister inquired.

'No,' said Bertram. 'I am going for a stroll. I did what I could for the woman while she was alive, but I feel it would be imposing myself to go to the funeral.'

'I shall be glad to have Iris back to-morrow,' Mr Pallister said, glancing round the dusty bar.

Just as Bertram set out, a hearse and two cars pulled up outside the Braceys'. Children began to congregate. He saw Stevie emerge from the Cazabons' house, wearing her jelly-mould, but she was immediately drawn back inside by an arm probably belonging to her mother, since Mrs Flitcroft was at the Braceys'. At all harbour funerals she was the provider of teas; she was the one who stayed behind to put the kettle on, to slice beetroot into glass dishes and cut currant bread.

The Waxworks was shut, the lace-curtains drawn together.

'Well, I compromised myself there,' Bertram smiled as he passed by. 'If all I hear of that girl is true. I should never have believed it, scarcely *can* believe it, either. It is amazing how one can be so mistaken about people.'

He walked on down the side of the harbour. The fleet was out, and the trawlers still visible, smudging the skyline with tufts of smoke. Bertram thought of Tory, wondered how near to London she might be, and contemplated, without any more uneasiness than would be natural in so established a bachelor, his coming marriage.

The lighthouse-keeper went up into the lamp-room to wind the clock. Glass flashed in the sun, with rose, with violet. Just at that moment the door opened at the Braceys' and the wreath-covered coffin was borne out rather unsteadily to the hearse – a moment Mrs Bracey herself had often touched upon in conversation. Bertram thought of this, pausing in his walk, standing for a moment and looking back. Then Maisie and Iris came out, followed by an assortment of relatives who had never been seen at the harbour before but who had been gathered up from the length and breadth of England almost for this occasion.

The sun steadily drenched the scene and a cracked bell dropped a note or two down the narrow streets, over the rooftops, even out across the water. The pause between each note was so long that there was no rhythm or regularity, it seemed; only one sound idly following another and floating out over the harbour.

Up at the church Mr Lidiard, with many strange thoughts locked in his heart, awaited the funeral cortège.

Doors were closed, and very reverently the cars moved forward. The children dispersed and Bertram continued his walk.

The lighthouse-keeper, looking out to sea, saw the trawlers wide across the horizon, and noticed, too, the white sails of a yacht approaching across the purple, the turquoise water.

And now, one by one, discreet hands released blinds along the harbour-front, and Mrs Flitcroft, with a flourish, as if to a burst of music, parted Mrs Bracey's bedroom curtains, threw up the sash, letting death out of the window and sunlight in.

Prudence and Stevie had been peeping at the funeral from between their curtains.

'Did Tory come to say good-bye?' Prudence asked casually.

'Yes. And Mother cried. Her face went red and she put her hands over her mouth.'

'Did Tory cry?'

303

'No. She was the one who was going away. Prudence, will they bring Mrs Bracey out and sit her up in the taxi?'

'Mrs Bracey will be in a coffin,' Prudence said.

'Yes, I know. She is a corpse now,' Stevie agreed.

'Don't tell Mother I let you look.'

'No, I won't. But why do those children watch so close up?'

'Because they don't consider other people's feelings,' Prudence explained, wiping the breath-steamed pane with her handkerchief.

In the morning-room, at the back of the house, Beth finished her novel, her arm cramped, her wrist throbbing. She wrote the last sentence, dwelt on the full stop with her pen, and then drew a little line.

'This is it,' she thought. 'This is the only moment and the whole reward. The ends of the circle are brought together and tied, and in the tying of the knot is perfect bliss, a second only, before all the doubts and anxieties begin again and other people step in.'

She felt empty, clean, deserted, as if a whole world had been swept away out of her bosom, leaving her clear as crystal. And her heart turned over painfully as she laid down her pen.

As the yacht came into harbour, the view unclenched itself, the houses sank down tier after tier, the church tower lowered itself behind the roofs, the lettering on the shop-fronts grew clear.

'Nothing has changed,' Teddy Foyle thought. He climbed the iron ladder and stood for a moment on the quay, the breeze combing his hair. Then, with sensations in his heart of both dread and delight, he set off along the curving arm of the harbour wall towards the waterfront.

1978—2018

40 YEARS OF
VIRAGO MODERN CLASSICS

The first Virago Modern Classic, *Frost in May* by Antonia White, was published in 1978. It launched a list dedicated to the celebration of women writers and to the rediscovery and reprinting of their works. Its aim was, and is, to demonstrate the existence of a female tradition in literature, and to broaden the sometimes narrow definition of a 'classic'. Published with new introductions by some of today's best writers, the books are chosen for many reasons: they may be great works of literature; they may be wonderful period pieces; they may reveal particular aspects of women's lives; they may be classics of comedy, storytelling, letter-writing or autobiography.

'The Virago Modern Classics list contains some of the greatest fiction and non-fiction of the modern age, by authors whose lives were frequently as significant as their writing. Still captivating, still memorable, still utterly essential reading' **SARAH WATERS**

'The Virago Modern Classics list is wonderful. It's quite simply one of the best and most essential things that has happened in publishing in our time. I hate to think where we'd be without it' **ALI SMITH**

'The Virago Modern Classics have reshaped literary history and enriched the reading of us all. No library is complete without them' **MARGARET DRABBLE**

'The writers are formidable, the production handsome. The whole enterprise is thoroughly grand' **LOUISE ERDRICH**

'Good news for everyone writing and reading today'
HILARY MANTEL

VIRAGO MODERN CLASSICS

AUTHORS INCLUDE:

Elizabeth von Arnim, Beryl Bainbridge,
Pat Barker, Nina Bawden, Vera Brittain, Angela Carter,
Willa Cather, Barbara Comyns, E. M. Delafield, Polly Devlin,
Monica Dickens, Elaine Dundy, Nell Dunn, Nora Ephron,
Janet Flanner, Janet Frame, Miles Franklin, Marilyn French,
Stella Gibbons, Charlotte Perkins Gilman, Rumer Godden,
Radclyffe Hall, Helene Hanff, Josephine Hart, Shirley Hazzard,
Bessie Head, Patricia Highsmith, Winifred Holtby, Zora Neale
Hurston, Elizabeth Jenkins, Molly Keane, Rosamond Lehmann,
Anne Lister, Rose Macaulay, Shena Mackay, Beryl Markham,
Daphne du Maurier, Mary McCarthy, Kate O'Brien, Grace
Paley, Barbara Pym, Mary Renault, Stevie Smith, Muriel Spark,
Elizabeth Taylor, Angela Thirkell, Sylvia Townsend Warner,
Mary Webb, Eudora Welty, Rebecca West,
Edith Wharton, Antonia White

CHILDREN'S CLASSICS INCLUDE:

Joan Aiken, Nina Bawden, Frances Hodgson Burnett,
Susan Coolidge, Rumer Godden, L. M. Montgomery,
Edith Nesbit, Noel Streatfeild, P. L. Travers

To buy any of our books and to find out more
about Virago Press and Virago Modern Classics,
our authors and titles, visit our websites

www.virago.co.uk
www.littlebrown.co.uk

and follow us on Twitter

@ViragoBooks

To order any Virago titles p & p free in the UK,
please contact our mail order supplier on:

+ 44 (0)1832 737525

Customers not based in the UK should contact
the same number for appropriate postage
and packing costs.